THE BEGGAR

THE BEGGAR

A. H. SCHULZ

THOMAS Y. CROWELL COMPANY

NEW YORK, ESTABLISHED 1834

DESIGNED BY ABIGAIL MOSELEY

Manufactured in the United States of America

ISBN 0-690-12917-3

1 2 3 4 5 6 7 8 9 10

Library of Congress Cataloging in Publication Data

Schulz, A H
    The beggar.

    I. Title.
PZ4.S39Be [PS3569.C554]   813'.5'4   73–84
ISBN 0-690-12917-3

CHAPTER ONE

Au Ka-kau sat on the inside ledge of the window, hung his elbow over the burglar bar, and stared dreamily into the darkened street below. The shops, part of Canton's medicine row, had herbs and twigs, leaves and animal horns, barks and roots, all the ingredients to cure man's physical ills. But their inability to salve wasted years or to draw from the years a promising future was sad.

The year was 4660, the Year of the Tiger, an auspicious year for sternness; it was the year 1962 on the Western man's calendar. And it was a year in which China's ancient curse returned, mocking, exposing its victims to hunger that was real and a fear of famine that was historically ingrained. Books, teachers, folklore, songs, movies, opera, every medium repeated tales of famine until all felt they had known a famine themselves. The fear was so deep only fools spoke openly of it. It was so vivid that nepotism, feudalism, corruption, begging, anything offering immunity was justified. When the city buzzed with rumors of starvation the stories were believed because belief matched the pattern etched by the country's history.

The year was also one in which China's white comrades to the north and northwest suffered shortages of their own and were unable to help. But, ironically, the Russians had enough money to buy food from the common enemy—the imperialistic capitalists. Au studied the darkness below while searching for history's deceit. The white comrades were saying what China knew all along. Anything that perpetuated life was either acceptable or forgivable. Life continued, beyond the existence of those living this day. Life was family. Life was great-grandfathers and grandfathers and fathers and sons and grandsons. Life was the family name surviving the generations.

China was now unified for the first time in centuries. The last time was so long ago it was remembered only in historical records. Yet what good was unification? The scourge of famine was as indifferent to unified governments as farmers were indifferent to soldiers. After having spent years soldiering for his government, Au was now planning to run away. To run from the ideals he had spent his youth creating. What good was war and victory, the painful confessions of lost pride, and allegiance to new ideologies if, after all, the nation still suffered the hunger that pockmarked its history?

When the greatest war was won and the newest ideology successfully installed, it still remained true, though hidden, that man lives for his family. While droughts, plagues, medicines, sages, wars, and governments come and go, families live on. Fathers, sons, brothers, uncles and cousins are tied by blood regardless of the distance between them and in spite of what the world might do to them. Death to a man without a family is the work of the devil. Death to a man with a large family is elevation to godhood, an immortality that feeds and grows upon ancestral worship.

This was Au's pain, the pain for which the street below had no cure. After sacrificing years of his past to the revolution, he discovered he had sacrificed also all contact with his parents, his family. And, in fear of criticism, he had not searched his village or its records for his parents. Travel required official sanction, and sanction required acceptable reasons. The practice of ancestor worship was forbidden. Au's past was dead, bartered for a gamble on the future. It was too late for him to rescind the trade.

With a sigh Au turned from the window to peer into the shadows of the room. Chung-kin, his wife, stared back, waiting. She rested on her bedroll, no longer feigning sleep. He had married her during the revolution, at a time when the heat inside a man and the accident of proximity substituted for family arrangements and marriage brokers. The harshness of those days had robbed him of the family consolation he needed today. The hardships endured during the revolution had killed his first two children before they were born, before he had time to care if they were sons who might someday stand by him. The single son who came after the war now lay huddled on the floor. This one, the lone survivor, was more of a handicap than a promise of future security.

Aware of her husband's dilemma, Chung-kin used her eyes to plead her side of the discussion which had ended the previous night. Au was forty-three. She knew men his age enjoyed edging into retirement by bleeding in annual drops their responsibilities to their sons. Only slightly younger, she knew also a woman her age had few years left for childbearing, and fewer years still to justify her life by bouncing grandchildren on her lap. She reached over to touch gently her son.

"All right," Au agreed, yielding to what Chung-kin's eyes requested, "the boy goes with us." He took two steps to reach down and jostle his son awake. "Get up," he ordered quietly. Feeling bone too near the surface of the skin he added, "You'll have to help him," as a clause to the agreement made with his wife.

Although Po was his son, Au felt he knew the children of the neighbors better than he knew Po. And what he knew about the neighbors' children he did not like. The government was tempting the children into betraying their parents. No longer trained, as he had been, to kneel in reverence in front of their ancestors' graves, the children of the revolution yielded all too often to the prizes offered. Au had no way of knowing how his son felt.

Po got off the floor slowly, his pride demanding he show no signs of joy or excitement. The secrets, supposedly hidden from him in the few words exchanged by his parents, were not secrets at all. If there was a true secret, he was the one who owned it. He was a kitten to be stroked and loved by his mother, but a pet that had trained itself to be indifferent by living too long with the fear of being expendable. He shuffled across the floor, absentmindedly bumping into a wicker chair, and began collecting methodically the few parcels of food he felt arranged on the table. Unable to think of anything more to do, he stood silent at the door, waiting for a hand to lead him farther. So much time had been spent waiting. Au and Chung-kin were doing something, most likely gathering remnants; their movements were audible. The pressure of doing something wrong was absent when Po waited. Waiting could be enjoyable if only it could be done unaccompanied by thoughts. Thinking itself was not bad—if done in moderation. Trouble arose from thinking what others might be thinking. Po concentrated on maintaining an indecipherable expression.

The street was foreboding in the predawn darkness. China's streets never surrendered to anyone the luxury of feeling alone. Even at night there were hundreds of eyes peering through slits and spying on movement. The sudden burst of a baby's cry jerked nervous heads and drew the attention of the curious who were anxious to learn of anything that might be exchanged for favors.

Au walked in front of Chung-kin and Po, feeling as uncomfortable as an actor portraying someone else's part on a stage. He led his family down the lonely street, out of the suspicious city, and into the country. Here the skeleton shadows of commune watchtowers warned him his sin would be better hidden at night. In the sandy soil of the southern hills the rice crop was sparse, off-color, its green weak and faded rather than lush with promise. In the normally fertile valley of the Pearl River the rice seedlings had been damaged by spring floods. His decision in need of support, Au let his imagination explain that food rationing would be worse this year than last, and then used the conclusion to repress his qualms about leaving Canton.

5

By the end of the second night of walking Au had strengthened himself through dreams. In the future he would have more children and grandchildren, who would praise him for braving the hazards of this escape. They would know he left the great land so that they might be born. He would not have to apologize for leaving. His family would know that Hong Kong belonged to China, that it was an area rented only temporarily to foreigners.

Au's visions flourished under the beating, sleepless heat of the days and the dull walking of the nights. Chung-kin had encouraged the escape attempt so that they might salvage Po's future. It was possible Po's handicap was, as Chung-kin preferred to believe, a blessing. Children told government officials what their parents had said in the sanctity of their homes with the hope that the officials would be more lenient than the strict parents. Hunger had drawn tight around the individual the circle of self-preservation that had once surrounded the country. Deceptions and lies that might be acceptable among strangers had invaded families. But Po, who would be eleven years old on New Year's, had remained loyal.

Chung-kin smiled proudly at seeing Po's strength increase as the walk went on. The exodus was challenging Po's right to membership in the family, and she drew courage from seeing how he accepted the challenge. Chung-kin laughed each time Po childishly bid for Au's respect by attempting to continue whenever he sensed Au had to stop for a rest.

During the last two days of the march other refugees filtered out of the hills to join the Au family. Each found courage in the sight of the others and grouped silently for the final daylight effort. The funnel was

6

narrowing. It would end at the bridge leading over the Shum Chum River into Hong Kong. Early one afternoon word that the border was visible around the curve of the next hill passed along the rows in whispers. After Au dutifully relayed the report to those walking behind, he watched the forward line stagger in wavering curves as those ahead veered for a better view of what still could not be seen.

Confucianism insists good be balanced by evil and success be tempered with an equal supply of failure. And so it was. All the good of Au's bringing his family so near the Hong Kong bridge without being stopped or hindered was offset by a closed gate on the Hong Kong side of the river. At the entrance to the bridge, and forming a semicircle as in an amphitheater, were hundreds of hopeful refugees squatting on their heels, facing their destination, waiting as though a miracle must of necessity come to open the gate for them.

Au, like those around him, stared in disbelief. Hong Kong was a city open to any Chinese wishing to enter. Treaty demanded it stay open.

By twilight the puzzle of the closed gate clarified itself. There were as many refugees inside the fence on the opposite side of the river as there were outside waiting to get in. The opening of the bamboo curtain had come to Canton by rumor. News of the closing of the Hong Kong gate apparently had not yet reached the city. The river had flooded Hong Kong with people, forcing the British to alter their policy just as the mainland government had altered its own. Hong Kong, for having food, was being inundated. China, its pride wounded, sought revenge by allowing refugees to flood the colony.

Silently Au cursed both governments for using

him and his family in their political maneuvers. He had neither the connections to get on a border-running junk nor the money to influence a corrupt Hong Kong official. He waited until well after dark and then, leading Chung-kin and Po, joined a small flow of people leaving the area of the bridge. They walked parallel to the fence along the river, stalling or increasing their pace in search of seclusion. When he was alone at what appeared to be an appropriate site, Au raised the barbed wire and shoved both Chung-kin and Po under.

Together they slowly waded the river, Au and Chung-kin carrying Po tightly between them. A predatory thrill surged through Au's tired body when at last he stepped on the bank of the southern shore. Although controlled by foreign devils, this soil belonged to China. It had been taken in an unjust war, one which only the white man thought was concluded. To Au, touching the soil and moving his family over it was sweet revenge. It was, in a way, like collecting for his country a small part of a long overdue debt.

Chinese farmers on the Hong Kong side quickly led them from the water's edge, away from the area where soldiers used dogs to search for refugees.

Hurrying to keep up with the farmers Po slipped from the narrow dirt ridge dividing the paddies. Quickly, he shoved a hand to the soil to push himself up. But the other hand touched a crisp, growing cabbage head. "Ay-yah!" he shouted recklessly, announcing what he had felt.

Chung-kin jerked Po's arm high, forcing him to half hang in his struggle for footing.

"Be quiet!" Au demanded in a strong whisper.

"A cabbage!" Po dared to whisper, gambling that

Au wanted to eat as much as he did. The sting of Au's reprimand and the pain from being hung by his arm was overcome by Hong Kong's promise of food. "I felt food," he growled obstinately.

Po's determined voice surprised Au. "Be quiet," he nevertheless warned again and clapped an open palm over Po's small mouth.

"Don't talk," the farmer whispered. "The best way to avoid suspicion and attention is to be calm and quiet." The narrow track opened onto a farm entrance where a truck was silhouetted by the brightening morning sky. "Each day," he explained as they approached the vehicle, "we send cabbages to the market in the city. The trip is hard," he added with a helpless shrug, "but it should get you safely away from the border. It's much easier to hide in the city."

Workers walking in a continuous circle emptied basket after basket of cabbages onto the truck with a nonchalant rhythm that belied the unusual circumstances. As they passed, they stole glances at the family to see if coincidence had brought some forgotten relative across the border. Then at a signalled moment two of the workers picked up in turn the three refugees, and, with the efficiency developed from enjoying wicked deeds, tossed them onto the truck's flat bed. The rest of the men laughed appreciatively at this opportunity to deceive a thing as large and as inaccessible as the white foreigners' government. Their enjoyment of evil was justified because this chance had come without their going to find it.

Two men stacking produce on the truck quickly folded the three bodies into embryoid curls and covered each with an empty wicker basket. While working they bantered curses, happy curses, believing their pretense of anger would minimize the seriousness of their mischief.

Au watched through the small rectangular openings until the cabbages surrounded him and kept him from seeing anything more than the food. As he poked his fingers through his cage for a loose leaf, he heard Chung-kin encourage Po to eat. His mind reviewed, one by one, the faces of those he remembered seeing pass the truck. None came back as being familiar. Once he got away from the farm there would be no obligation, his debt belonged to his people and not to any individual. They had helped because he too was Chinese. There was no way of knowing how many refugees had been smuggled to safety by these simple farmers, and no way of knowing how many other farmers working the border region were doing the same. Their method, however, was so smooth and well organized that Au decided thousands must have traveled the same way.

The journey, after beginning with a sharp jerk, settled into a bumpy ride, the cabbages snuggling ever tighter against the protective baskets. The ride was hard. Little air seeped through the compressed load. There was little room for anything other than thought.

Well over two hours later the truck's engine slowed and coughed tiredly into the public market of the city. As it inched through the preoccupied and unruly morning crowd, the voices, bargaining, begging, demanding, and eventually laughing, filtered through the truck's load to Au's alert ears. When the engine shut off, the sound of cabbages thumping and rolling told him he was about to be unloaded. Just as the tops of the illegal baskets became exposed to daylight Au saw strong fingers curl through the webbing and jerk the cage up. The violent action caused cabbages to spill and roll, taking Au with them until he landed on the cement of the street.

"Are there any more?" an excited, strange shout asked over the din.

Au's head reeled. "Two," he answered weakly, holding up two fingers to keep the confusion from misquoting him.

At the sight of Au's signal, bare-legged men popped out of the crowd and jumped onto the truck. Their hurrying sent more cabbages rolling. Curious heads turned toward the unusual search, but to see and to stare was to become implicated, and implication was dangerous. Through the glances the market's business missed barely a heartbeat. Even the two Chinese policemen turned their backs to keep the small plot against the government from disrupting their quiet day.

When Chung-kin and Po at last stood beside him, an authoritative voice demanded of Au, "Get into a taxi!" and a hand signalled toward a small red diesel lingering nearby.

"We have no money!"

"Do you have someplace to go?"

"Yes."

"Pay at the other end."

The taxi jumped into position and had not fully stopped before its doors were opened and the three bodies shoved in. Fast forward tugs kept the passengers liquid, scrambling for an upright position.

The driver, stealing sharp glances at his rear-view mirror, forced his machine like a blunt hammer through the restless market. He caught sight of one head after another come up from the seat behind.

"Refugees," he moaned. "They keep coming." He shook his head sadly at the wide eyes staring out at the excitement of Hong Kong. Refugees. Low paying, perhaps non-paying. A man could waste his life and savings driving refugees who were too poor to pay, passengers who teased him into believing he might be paid, even tipped. He cursed himself for having lingered so foolishly at the market. "This is dangerous," he exaggerated. "I could lose my license for hauling you!" He gave the damaging remark a moment to hit its target. "I should get something extra for this," he insisted as he stared at Au's face in the mirror.

Au leaned forward, centering himself so the driver might keep his mind more on his driving than on his troubles. He folded his arms over the front seat cushion. "My cousin will pay," he recited calmly, trying to sound positive. Then he recited just as surely the address he had memorized in Canton for use at this time.

The driver maintained his pout. Peace was not to be purchased with promises.

"Who are the men we saw standing around the market?" Au asked, trying to channel the driver's mind to safer subjects. "What do they do for work?"

"It's difficult to find work here," the driver answered, misinterpreting Au's motive. "When we do find work we end up having to do dangerous things," he added, taking advantage of the opportunity to get back to his grievances. "The people in the market are buyers," he went on, pressing himself deep in the cushion to get closer to Au. "Some buy for the hotels and shops, and others for their families."

"Those in the back, Au prodded. "Those leaning against the buildings. Who are they? What do they do? Why do they wait?"

"Coolies," the driver answered contemptuously after looking where Au was pointing. "They wait for a call to unload the lorries. Some of them helped unload you!" he added, pleased once again to steer the conversation to where he wanted it. "They have to be paid for their work," he lied. "Did you pay them? Did you keep enough money for me?"

The small taxi leaned away from the sharp corner. "These too?" Au asked when the new street exposed the quay with more men lining its curb. The men, dressed in cheap black cloth wrapped to their bodies by strings, rested against bamboo carrying poles.

"Coolies," the driver repeated. "They're waiting to be called by some junk master. Did you give the money meant for me to the coolies at the truck?"

Au noted the waiting coolies had enough money to buy cigarettes, and that the quay was lined with junks bulging with cargoes of food. The junks rubbed sides as they bobbed in the waves splashing against the cement retaining wall. Small crafts, they appeared to be rocking to the rhythm of the coolies parading in circles, on and off, unloading the cargo in bundles hanging suspended from their poles. "My cousin will pay," he mumbled. There were more coolies than jobs. Still, those waiting were better dressed and in better condition than the coolies employed by the government to work the shipyards of Whampoa in Canton. The way the men smoked and laughed and gambled in fours around the ships they had to have money. The whole city had money. Plenty of it. But there was also unemployment.

"All this food," Au sighed, begging righteously for the driver's sympathy, yet believing it was not necessary. A taxi driver would get little support from his fellow men in a fight with a penniless refugee. There was a chance a fight would develop, for Cousin Liu was the husband of Chung-kin's cousin. Not truly a relative. Cousin Liu would be within his rights to deny help to Au. "I can't believe it!" Au said, laughing, carefree for the driver's benefit. "Our trip is finished! We're in Hong Kong!" He punched playfully at Po.

And Po wiggled in delight. The stabbing elbow was a sign of union.

Full of happiness, Po allowed his young hands to run over the imitation leather upholstery, around the door's edge, touch and pull back cautiously from the peculiar form of the door's handle, the window's crank, the flatness of the window's glass.

"We're here!" Au barked, encouraging Po's happiness to remain a while longer.

Then, deciding Po's shyness was ugly and wouldn't be seen if the conversation excluded him, Au turned his attention back to the driver who was waiting to be appeased. "What kind of work is there around taxis?" he asked.

"Driving," the man answered tersely. He frowned appropriately the dissatisfaction one is expected to feel toward his own work. "We live off the tips," he proclaimed, punctuating the statement with a disgusted shrug. "There's work in the petrol station, the repair shops . . . " He stopped in mid-sentence, forcing himself to fake disinterest. Giving away too many secrets could lose a man his job. "Most of the work demands skill," he insisted belatedly. "It isn't easy work and it doesn't pay a living."

Au tried to keep the driver's answer from worrying him. Getting safely into Hong Kong was just the first step. Work came second. It might be harder.

Long bamboo poles, bent into gentle arches by the

weight of damp laundry, stretched from upper level porches on both sides of the street, their density blocking out the sky. People popped in and out of the many doorways to wander listlessly, their hands hooked safely behind their backs, or to move hurriedly, impatiently, yet gracefully on some mission. Children pranced irregularly, playing their games both on and off the road, untamed except by nature, which urged them to pause and stoop at the curb for their morning toilet. Old people sat quietly watching, indifferent, family baby-sitters.

What Au saw were the normal trademarks of an overpopulated but living city. Canton had once been the same. There was hope in Hong Kong just as there was hope in the security of active congestion, whether of family or strangers. He saw hope in the faces of those who cared to hope. But there was no way of knowing how many were refugees, or how many of those sliding past the cab's windows cared that the city had to contend with three more refugees. The uncountable small shops had barrels of rice and baskets of food to display. The rest of what Au saw mattered little.

The taxi honked caution into the disobedient children as it tried to steal a path through them. The human curb moved unpredictably. Wisely slowing to avoid an incident that might draw police attention to his passengers—and perhaps send the passengers scurrying away without paying—the driver inched his machine forward until it stopped in front of the address he had been given. "That's the door you want," he said, pointing at an opening of steps. "Will your cousin pay?"

The engine shut off as proof of the driver's patience. "He'll pay," Au promised. He pushed his family out the door to keep them from being held as hostages. When he closed the door he saw the driver fake figuring the charge for the unmetered ride.

The rattling knob aroused Cousin Liu and drew him toward the door. Opening it just a slit he tilted his head to align his eyes. The position cheated him from recognizing his visitors. When the sight at last had time to register, he allowed his glee to overwhelm his wisdom. Babbling incoherently, he fanned open the door and dragged in the family, ignoring all but his own happy surprise.

Au shook him to attention. "Someone must pay for the taxi or the driver will go to the authorities!"

When Liu started down the steps and no longer blocked the two women from seeing each other they came together quickly, remembering their endearment and speaking as though their distant relationship had to be revived in a matter of minutes. Au went to the window to look down while Liu confronted the taxi driver. The driver was straining himself across the front seat to argue out the side window. The unnatural position seemed to put him at a disadvantage. The driver demanded more money in exchange for silence while Liu bargained for more silence and less money. They battled with skills developed from survival instincts, skills a man had to learn and use to keep himself above begging.

Although instinctively wary of the new arrivals and of what changes their presence might bring, Cousin Liu's wife was genuinely pleased. She began showing it by pouring tea. Then surmising their tiredness she took Po to the still warm cot before surveying a shelf of food. She talked constantly as she moved.

"Why didn't you come sooner?" she prodded Au. "Two weeks ago the north border was open and the Hong Kong soldiers turned their heads when the refugees came in!" She lowered her fleshy hulk on a chair beside him. She was bigger than Au. Not taller, but heavier in frame and flesh. The size Chung-kin might have been had she had enough to eat. "Things were good here," she confided, jabbing a fat elbow into Au's bones, "until we got too many refugees." Air whistled as it rushed between her teeth, blasting at pieces of nestling rice. The rice, stubborn, liked the crannies, She enlisted the aid of a toothpick. "The north tried to destroy us by flooding us with people," she scowled, then gave a coarse laugh meant to say the north's plan wasn't working.

Liu came back in time to admonish his wife. "That's not true. The people up north had nothing to eat. They came here on their own." He looked at Au, hoping to see a partner. "Isn't that right?" he prodded when Au failed to take a side.

"Hah!" Liu's wife laughed. "Then let them give their food to their own people instead of sending it to Hong Kong for us to buy. They want too much money for it!"

"Hong Kong closed the border," Liu explained quietly, willing to slow the argument yet persisting in his efforts to protect his native land against his wife. "Hong Kong shouldn't have closed the border."

"The Hong Kong border has always been open," his wife sneered back. "It was the north who broke the rules first." The debate soon made the heavy woman pant. She scoffed defiantly at her obstinate husband a moment, then took the sting out of the look by turning to see if Chung-kin had noticed. The play was enacted to acquaint Chung-kin with the fact that Hong Kong women had no fear of their husbands.

"It took us almost two weeks to make the walk," Au cut in calmly, a peacemaker plagued by conscience. His appearance had been instrumental in renewing what appeared to be an old fight. "We left as soon as the rumors about the border being open reached Canton. We didn't know if we should believe them. We had to try," he explained, excusing his presence and the friction it brought.

Liu's wife took Au's statement as proof that she had won and attempted to seal the victory by closing the subject. "You must be hungry," she decided belatedly. "Your food is being sold on our markets. I'll give you some." She tossed a flippant glance at her husband and retreated to the stove. "How did you get into the city?"

"Farmers helped us."

The water in the pot on the small burner bubbled and hissed its readiness. Liu's wife was a symphony of wasted motion as she rinsed dishes dirtied at dinner the previous night. She stopped to watch Chung-kin walk over to Po. "I have a job for you," she told Chung-kin, but hoisted herself to male status by directing the statement at Au. "Jobs are hard to find," she added, twisting her head to one side to emphasize the truth. "Our sons work in a plastics factory but only four people work there. They don't need anyone else. It's on the other side. Near Kai Tak. Do you have any other relatives in Hong Kong? Any friends? Classmates?" she ranted, saying whatever came to her mind. "How is Po?" she asked, stopping her work to look across at Po on the cot. "What can you do about him?"

"Leave them alone!" Liu shouted, guessing the family was not ready for such personal questions and using the opportunity to get even with his wife. Nevertheless, he gave Au time for silence, proof that no answer was coming. "Can't you see they're tired and hungry?" he growled. "A baby could starve to death before you got your blouse open!" He stared sternly at his wife, gratified that she pouted at the insult. She was a good woman. True, she had the fault of intruding into the affairs of others, but she supported the intrusions with good intentions.

Po lay on the cot with his eyes closed. The question asked about him by Liu's wife pleased him. It said he belonged. It said he was part of their troubles. Facial expressions could be read, so he kept the muscles from moving. If he lay absolutely still they might not be able to see him. He tried to keep his chest from rising as he breathed.

The pout Liu's wife wore soon tired. It was replaced by a beaming reflection of the pride she felt in having a stern husband to obey. While the others ate their breakfasts she caught up with the morning by combing her hair. The mirror showed she might not be as attractive as some of the streetwalkers, but it also showed the smile of a woman with a good husband. Chung-kin was bent and ill kept, dull as a farmer's wife. Chung-kin was lucky to have found a husband. New clothes would help her appearance, but she was still lucky.

Au's guilt increased in the silence of eating. He finished and went to dream at the window. The morning had only begun and he already owed Liu for a taxi fare, had already reopened an old argument over border conditions, and was now faced with begging permission to stay in the flat until better things came. The city looked like a riot heading in all directions. It was confusing. People moved, freely, busily. Somewhere out there a job waited for Chung-kin.

"Is there work for me?" he asked Liu.

"Jobs are hard to find," Liu confessed, his face reflecting the embarrassment he knew Au must feel. "My wife and I work in the poultry shop on the corner. She prepares the chickens and I sell them to the customers. The owner sympathizes with the refugees," he shrugged, "but he also likes the cheap labor. He doesn't pay much. In fact, very little. But it's money. When we got word you might be coming we told him Chung-kin was a Hakka and would work hard," he admitted, glancing quickly at Au to see if the lie had been damaging. It seemed not to be. Au's expression had not changed. "He believed us," he ventured warily. "He's been holding the job open for her. He stopped talking, his chopsticks nervously picking up the few single pieces of rice that had scattered over the table in the rush of eating. "Chung-kin's very fortunate," he concluded, "to have work."

Au used tired silence to ask from Liu what he had to have, and Liu, a good relative, understood. "You stay here," he insisted amiably, looking at his watch, "until you can afford a place of your own." He signaled his wife. It was time for them to leave.

Alone with his family, Au smiled at the way Liu had extended the invitation. Liu had had time to let Hong Kong change him if he had wished to be changed. Contented, Au pushed the leftover food to the center of the table, and then lay down on the empty cot. Daylight streaming through the open window and street noises kept him awake longer than he had expected.

20

There were those he knew in Canton who had tried to escape from China several times—always without success and always with punishment for trying. But he had succeeded the first time. Had the gods favored him? Or had they favored those who failed? With the decision that Hong Kong was the good owed him for the curse of Po's handicap, Au rolled on his side to sleep.

During their first year in Hong Kong the Au family suffered many trials and made many adjustments. The Liu flat consisted of just one room large enough to hold double-decked cots and a small table surrounded by stools. It lacked the space to absorb the friction of personalities. The friendship stored during the years of separation between the distant-cousin wives wore thin from the one year of close association. At times the relationship became so weak it existed more in regret then in reality. In silent concession to their helpless condition the two families lived in shifts, slept in shifts, ate in shifts, and took turns standing in line for water at the corner on water day. The women grew closer to their husbands in their need for allegiance, and soon began suspecting each other of stealing items that were lost only for the moment. For the men, cousinship through marriage was a water paste that held but a couple of weeks. After that it was replaced by a thin disguise of man-to-man friendship only because both knew, to be tolerable, the conditions demanded something.

Although Chung-kin was not a Hakka woman, she worked at her job as though she were. The shop's owner was more than pleased with her services, yet he managed to hide his feelings for fear of her finding this out. If she knew, she might slow down or use his satisfaction as an excuse to ask for more money. Most of the time she kept her mind on her own affairs and only occasionally chatted with the other workers.

The shop's owner kept the two women cousins apart, thinking time would be wasted in talking if they were together. Thus, Chung-kin worked a different shift from that of Liu's wife and Liu. This separation, luckily, tended to reduce the friction. Part of Chung-kin's earnings paid half the flat's expenses. The amount was too small to warm blood, but large enough to overcome minor grievances. The balance of her pay was saved in the bottom of a tea tin to hurry the day when the Au family could start life over again on its own. Once the initial clothing and kitchen needs were met, the amount she set aside began increasing noticeably.

The year for Au was one of frustration. He found himself handicapped in trying to cope with those whose lives were adjusted to competition. During the year he frequently recalled the doctrine of equality between the sexes, but it did nothing to ease the shame he felt in having to depend on his wife for his livelihood. After several months he had exhausted all the possibilities he could imagine for finding work and was resolved to accept whatever part-time offers wandered his way. He joined the line of coolies remembered so vividly from his first day in the city.

Each morning he rose early and walked to the wharf to linger with the waterfront coolies and to fight with them for the few jobs that came their way. He answered several calls to unload refugees from cabbage trucks and did so without asking anything for it. Yet, in spite of his own journey, he could not help resenting the new arrivals, for it only meant more unemployment. He joined all the Mah-Jongg games he could, with the hope of finding some new friend who might one day become the key to the door of work. The majority of jobs went to those who were either relatives, classmates, or close friends of someone already employed where the vacancy existed. Au looked for friends. It was too late for relatives and classmates.

After such an auspicious beginning, the year for Po was disappointing. He reverted to the waiting he had learned in Canton. With both Au and Chung-kin gone half the time and sleeping the other half, his solitude returned. He had nothing, thus could offer nothing, and struggled against the thought that it might have been better for his parents had they abandoned him in Canton. The room was one of adults coming and going, eating and sleeping. Initially, he was both afraid to go outdoors and warned against doing so by Au who worried over what might happen to him. Po's place in the combined household was unique in that he lived in forced solitude while the others went to extremes to avoid each other.

There were times, however, when Po had to leave the one-room flat. And he learned to sense their arrival. When the Lius were home and their cot moaned from shifting weight and the air became loaded with foolish giggles and grunts over something not explained to him, he accepted his exclusion and left. He would go to sit on the steps that led to the sidewalk and shyly listened away the hours until Chung-kin came to rescue him. The longer he sat outside the more he enjoyed the experience. The outside was exciting, mystifying.

Po's vigils on the steps continued until time fed his courage and he began to go outdoors without being forced. Repetition made the street's sounds less strange and less awesome. To renew his pride in his life's sole achievement, the long walk from Canton, he ventured into the neighborhood streets. When his mother bought him a cane for protection, he understood it to mean encouragement. He allowed the length of his trips to increase, and familiarized himself with the local odors, quirks, and sounds, and used them to mark a trail. Eventually the neighbors accepted his peculiar presence and stopped commenting on him.

On particular days, days when nothing else of interest was offered to prick his curious mind, he walked the two blocks to the theater where he could listen to the crowds as they exited. A picture of any kind was mysterious, but these people talked of pictures that had the power to move. As he leaned against the wall of the building, safely out of the path of the moving, preoccupied masses, an occasional hand would touch his shirt. And, since he was already pinned as far from them as he could get, there was nothing more he could do to avoid the touching fingers. They touched. He waited.

Strangers dropped small coins in his shirt pocket.

The visit of a year was not predetermined. It was by chance that at the end of the year the Au family had saved enough money from Chung-kin's wages and Au's part-time work to entertain the idea of making the desired break from their cousins. Once the tea tin held enough money, Au was quick to find the proper place to spend it. Each day he watched the corners of buildings for pasted advertisements of rooms to let. In a short time he found what he wanted, a new sign telling of a one-room flat close to the poultry shop where Chung-kin worked. He ripped the notice from the wall. Following instructions he located the land-lord who allowed him to visit the room. It was a small room on the first floor, above a street-level stationery shop, and its only window looked out over the street instead of down into the hot and smelly air shaft where tenants often dumped their refuse. The rent was high.

"Rent is going up," the landlord explained, "with the increase in refugees." Thus he told Au it was Au's arrival in the colony that had made living more expensive.

"The landlord wants seventy dollars a month," Au explained to Chung-kin that night, "but I think he would take sixty from us. He looked surprised when I told him there were only three of us. I don't think he believed me," he laughed, "but it was what he wanted to hear. The rooms in that building must have at least two families in each."

Po listened silently through the debate. Au and Chung-kin had discussed their reasons for and against the room, but did not include him. His reasons for wanting the room were strong and also selfish. With only one family in the flat he would not be jostled back and forth, the shared problem of all.

The pressure of existing in the fractured relation-ship with the cousins and the shortage of rooms at any price made Au's decision inevitable. "We have enough money to pay two month's rent in advance," he summarized, "and still buy a couple of cots. The rest of what we need can wait. I think we should take it."

Since it had been his father who had made the suggestion, Po accepted it as final. The outcome delighted him. He would no longer be a minor individual caught between two major fighting factions—and he searched for a way to strengthen his position. Most of the conversation he had overheard involved money. Money was salve made of cement. The absence of money started as many arguments as its presence ended. Money had power. Its absence lifted voices to shrieking and its presence turned the same voices to soft cooing. Even the Lius sounded different on the days Chung-kin paid half the rent.

A sense of the accuracy of his reasoning stimulated Po to a decision. "I have a dollar and forty cents we can use for food," he told his father, and pulled the change from his pocket. He slapped down the coins, rattling them across the hard table, then withdrew to test the offering's effect.

Stunned by the presentation, both parents jumped mechanically to stop the coins from rolling to the floor. Au looked at Chung-kin only to see her eyes asking him the question his eyes were asking her. The Lius complained Po ate too much, that he upset the financial balance between them, so surely they hadn't given him the money.

When all ideas were exhausted, Au asked, "Where did you get it?" He sharpened his voice, signaling a reprimand if Po's answer was unacceptable.

"At night," Po began, stammering fearfully since the money had not produced the expected reaction. "I stand by the theater. The people talk when they leave. I like to listen. Once . . . once in a while . . . someone drops a coin in my pocket." He waited. His answer, given so carefully, had not brought a hint of acceptance. The silence pushed him into childish defense. "I didn't ask them to do it," he pouted. "I only stood still!"

"What fools would reach out to drop money . . .

in . . . in a boy's pocket?" Chung-kin asked in disbelief.

Po braced himself. His money had changed the
sound of his mother's voice.

Au accepted his son's innocence and worked forward from it. "Ay-yah!" he laughed. "With that new
cane . . . with that cane they think . . . they think he's
a beggar!" he laughed. The mystery was solved.

Chung-kin, shocked, waited for Au's smile to fade.
It didn't. The pleasure in his eyes became a calculat-
ing glint, one that defied what she was thinking. "You
wouldn't," she challenged, stopping when she saw Au
understood but Po still didn't. But Au's eyes still said
he would. "You wouldn't permit your son to beg?" She
felt a cold prickle go through her body as Au's eyes
looked right through her. Out of habit, and to avoid
looking back at Au, she began raking the coins into a
neat pile. "Your son," she moaned to herself. "Your
son a blind beggar?"

"He wasn't begging," Au asked her to believe. "All
he was doing was standing there." The belief pleased
him. It helped wash away the year he had spent
smarting under his need for his wife's money. In Hong
Kong, as in Canton, scruples and honor were luxuries
—luxuries for the rich. His family was not rich. "You
weren't begging, were you?" he asked Po.

The question, carrying its own answer, came to Po
loaded with the mirthful sound of teasing, the sound
of two males joining in defense against the female. "I
wasn't begging," he repeated for his mother's benefit.
"All I did was stand next to the building. I couldn't get
away from them!"

Au drained some of the tension from the air by
laughing at the irony of the situation. "Don't be so

selfish," he teased his wife before she had a chance to poison her son's mind. "If Po can make people happy by giving them a chance to . . . to feel good," he explained carefully, "then we should be kind enough to oblige them. He doesn't have to beg. All he has to do is stand in one place so the people will have the chance—if they want to take it—to give him something. If he doesn't let them put money in his pocket they'll go somewhere else to get rid of it." He leaned to punch at Po and was rewarded with a smile for doing it. "It'll give him something to do . . . "

The words trailed off, out of conscious hearing, as Po's mind occupied itself with the implications of what he had heard. It wasn't begging. It was work! It was a place to go, a thing to do, a source of money, an opportunity to make other people happy. To make people happy was an honor, a privilege, and sometimes, like this time, it came hidden in the disguise of getting money for it. Most of all it was a revolution that might bring life to his blind death. "I wasn't begging," he mumbled to himself.

The solemn voice of Po ended Au's argument with his wife. The boy suspected the disgrace of begging. That was enough. There was no strong reason for him to be a caged animal because of his blindness, a creature unable to give to others what he had to take from them. "The boy has nothing to do all day," Au said, begging for Chung-kin's approval. "We can't afford to send him to school. He has no friends, no playmates. It isn't healthy for him to go on as he is now."

Wrapped in Au's argument, Chung-kin could not resist. She too begged that Po might live a useful life. With no better suggestion as to what Po might do, she let her eyes concede.

28

"We'll buy him a cup," Au went on, his enthusiasm watered only slightly by Chung-kin's silence, "and then find him a good place to stand. Some place where he'll be safe." He paused a moment to give Chung-kin the opportunity to object, and to give himself time to think. "We'll do it after we move to the new flat. There's no reason for Cousin Liu to know what Po will be doing."

During the following week Po's mind exercised its newly acquired right to reason. His thoughts, centering on the plot growing around him, stretched to examine the good of what was about to happen and shied from the reasons why others thought begging was dishonorable. The thought of helping people by taking their gifts of money was novel, however mysterious. But since Au openly accepted the idea, it had to be honorable in a way others refused to see. Po felt fresh with importance each time he reminded himself of this fact. His mother's objections were rooted somewhere in her desire to keep him young, an infant, a baby needing her help.

On the day of the move to the new flat there was an outward display between the cousins that exemplified the sorrow expected at a time when kin must part. The false emotions turned the minor move into a major one, and helped make the day memorable. The affections the cousins had once shared were now stoked in the safety of knowing the test was over. Liu's wife insisted Chung-kin take along, as a temporary loan, the necessary dishes and utensils for the first few weeks, and Chung-kin, falling into the spirit of an amiable parting, definitely refused. Liu and Au made several attempts to establish a regular night of the week in which they could meet, as good cousins were expected to do, and failed successfully as both wanted to do. Liu's nights were busy with work and Au's were subject to work without notice. To keep the idea of regular meetings alive they made reckless plans for a reunion without mentioning a date. They took turns putting off the appointment until the date was far enough in the future for them to forget or to feel the friendship would be sufficiently healed to guarantee a good time. The parting was made with grace. They parted close relatives once again.

The Au family spent a week in their new quarters before any of them admitted openly that living without the cousins was a rather easy adjustment to make. Au and Chung-kin pretended it was hard. Each felt they had to for the other's sake. But for Po it was hard—not hard to live without the Lius, but hard to live out the first week while waiting to begin his work. For Po the week was eternal.

At last the week came to an end, and Au followed through with his promise to get Po started on the new business adventure. He bought a gaudy, bright, yellow plastic cup—a cup impossible for anyone with eyes to miss—and took Po along while he scouted the city for a location. The common goal, that of getting money and making people happy for giving it, welded father and son together as never before. It gave the father thoughts of what might be done if the son's venture proved successful, and gave the son's life a most precious gift. He had a family, he belonged to the family, the family accepted him, and now he had the gift of being able to contribute. No longer would he have to beg from his family.

After several days of experimenting Au found a location he thought would be satisfactory. Next he studied the proper time for Po to sell what the cup offered. It must be in the morning that people needed the luck they expected to come from their donation to the cup, for it was in the morning that most of the coins dropped. People begged for a sense of goodwill early in the day, as though by starting early the goodwill they felt must continue longer. By evening the trials of work and of Hong Kong had changed them. By evening their hopes of luck and good fortune had vanished. By evening they became selfish and inward looking.

Au used his discovery of peoples' habits to settle the silent objections of Chung-kin. He told her Po wouldn't be out roaming the streets at night when evil lay latent in everyone.

CHAPTER TWO

Old Chen grabbed angrily at the stack of newspapers tossed so carelessly at his feet that some of them were torn and unsalable. It was the same every morning. The boys on the delivery truck played life as a game. Cursing them, he fanned out the papers and decorated his corner of the sidewalk with their display. The edges, left exposed, revealed only the name and headline. Nothing more need be given free to casual observers. Habit directed his regular customers take the same newspaper each day just as habit directed others to search for the most provocative headline. A smart man, Chen made a good living by helping people keep their habits. Habits were hard to overcome, if, indeed, a desire to overcome them existed. Habits were dependable, safe, honest. So it was his habit to cater to the newspaper habits of others.

While assuring himself his display neared perfection, this morning, like many another morning, he tucked a few of the headlines deeper under their folds. The headlines were not scrupulous. Hong Kong had too many publishers fighting for the business of the few who were both able to read and rich enough to indulge in this luxury. Headlines had their own habit, that of exaggerating. And some people had the habit of browsing, trying to match the headline with its accompanying story. When they failed to find a similarity they dropped the newspaper in disgust. Chen preferred they make their discoveries elsewhere, after paying for the right. Their wrath should be vented on the publishers, not on the salesman. The crafty, red-inked headlines had but one purpose: to tickle man's gambling instincts. Everyone knew it.

Chen was considered by some as a strange little fellow. Actually he was neither strange nor little. It was his ability to understand and to capitalize on the habits of others that made them suspicious of him. And if he seemed little, it was just that the new generation was growing so big—and old men shrink and curl with grandparenthood. No one could do anything about the monstrous youngsters, and Chen knew he could do nothing about his own size including forget about it. So he worked to use his size. Squatting in a fetal curl on the sidewalk alongside his newspapers he was not only comfortable but also the correct height for keeping a wary eye on his tin change box.

Chen's most acute irritant was the customer who, in either haste or disrespect, threw his coins on top of the loosely arrayed newspapers instead of dropping them safely into the confines of the tin box. All too often the coins got lost. They slid or rolled away, tucking themselves, hidden, in a newspaper fold. There was no way of knowing how many of them were given away as a bonus to some lucky customer. Not a man to give away anything, especially his money, Chen told himself that one day he would rise to the occasion and scold all those who tossed their money so recklessly. "Drop the coins in the box," he would demand of them, "or take your business to some other stand!"

A poor man, however, lives by his patience. Until the day when Chen's riches arrived there was little he could do other than keep his heart from overbeating during the morning rush when customers came so fast he had no time to chase down all the errant coins. Often while scrambling across the pile for a single coin he got splashed with another handful. Some men, he knew, did it on purpose.

"I'm going to buy a pistol," he growled to Po one morning. "If I shove a pistol into the bellies of those coin throwers . . . " He stopped. Imagination would not permit him to dream beyond the threat. Besides, the predicament could not be explained to Po. An explanation would have to begin with his size, and he preferred not discussing his littleness and how others took advantage of him for this reason. Such things degrade a man, rob him of respect. Remembering belatedly to disguise his size, Chen squatted; Po must imagine him to be much larger.

Covering his hesitation, he said, "Some men take newspapers and walk away without paying. They know I haven't the time to chase them and beat them. If I had a pistol they wouldn't tempt me like they do. I wouldn't have to use the gun," he bragged, beginning to believe the story himself. "It would be enough if they knew I owned one."

Po's mind spun with the thought of a gun getting shoved into someone's belly.

And Chen interpreted the thoughtful silence as objection. Silently he agreed to the objection. All men had handicaps and all men had to make adjustments. He secretly accepted his body as old and small and delicate and subject to abuse from larger bodies, but compensated the acceptance by telling himself his body was well-formed, well-proportioned, and in good condition. Morning calisthentics did it. They kept him small and agile. Big people were clumsy freaks. Look at the white people with their big hands and feet and noses. Hairy animals the whites. In bed with a woman they must be like elephants. Thinking about that, however, brought back worries. He turned his mind elsewhere.

The portable portion of Chen's newsstand hung from the open steel-bar fence surrounding the front yard of the stately Shanghai Bank. The twin frames hinged in the center for folding represented an early mistake. When other newsstands operating directly in front of the ferry gates combined magazines with their daily offering, Chen was quick to follow. He had one of his cousins make the fence-hung rack. As it turned out, his customers, unlike those preparing themselves for a sit-down ride, had no time for magazines. They were the grab-and-run type of buyers.

Rather than sink good money into keeping up the façade of success, Chen let the old magazines deteriorate instead of renewing them monthly. But rather than go so far as to take the rack down so all could see his mistake, he left it up and put the blame on his customers for not being clever enough to change their habits. The expansion was not all a loss however. The magazines, in spite of their age, were colorful, had pictures of pretty girls on their covers, and comforted the dream-filled days of old age. Besides, the wooden boards fanned open and made a good windbreak.

Although shrewd enough not to admit it, Chen knew his stand had been good to him. From its profits he had bought a wife, raised three children, and managed it all walking on the outer edges of Hong Kong's poverty. Still, problems had the habit of creeping in and spreading in the lives of older people. And, for older people, the solutions often hid somewhere outside human control. When solutions were found, Chen, like all Chinese, accredited them to the strength of his family. Family was indestructible, and Chen had a proud, large family. His years at the stand had not been wasted. He had two sons, a wife, a daughter, brothers, grandchildren, and cousins beyond counting.

With this morning's papers spread, ready on the sidewalk, Chen got up and took a position from which he could judge his display as it would be seen by his customers. This habit his eldest son had developed for him. The eldest had a good head for business. Knowing it made Chen proud. The boy had solved a problem for him just a week ago when a couple of strangers had surreptitiously eyed both him and his stand. The strangers had stayed too long and looked too carefully to be innocent sightseers. From the corner of his eye Chen had watched as they paced the wooden walk and concluded their sortie into his territory by drawing chalk lines on the wood at the ferry tunnel's mouth. The spot they had selected was not a good place for a newsstand. People coming out of the dark tunnel did not trust their adjusting eyes to count money. Nevertheless, another newsstand on the lane, no matter how poorly positioned, would be bad for business. In the lazy heat of afternoon Chen had tried to muster the necessary courage to attack the threat before it grew. He considered walking past the strangers while loudly lamenting the difficulties of making a living by selling newspapers, but he gave up the idea, sure that the strangers would neither believe nor listen to him. He was a poor liar and he knew it. So he said and did nothing. But before going home to his family with the problem he had mustered the courage to erase the chalk marks.

His eldest son, of course, came up with the answer. The following morning he took half of his father's supply of papers and opened a new stand on the exact spot the strangers had picked for themselves. He backed up his strength by having two burly cousins accompany him. Within the week, the show of Chen-family power had put down the threat.

The result pleased Chen in two ways. The threat was gone, and the new stand was a loser as he had predicted it would be. Moreover, his son was still roaming around as a bodyguard in case the strangers came back and wanted trouble.

Evil continues to threaten those who have the habit of waiting and watching for it, and Chen had developed just such a habit. He lowered himself to the curb base of the fence and drove his elbows deep into his stomach. Then he wrapped one thin leg over the other before pulling both legs in close to his body. In this accustomed position, he lit a cigarette. Resting, he looked like an old fetus, long overdue, smoking away the years and stubbornly refusing to leave the safety of the womb.

The serenity that came from an unsurprising

morning was anchored by the familiar sound of Po coming around the corner through the dusty morning light. The metal-tipped red and white cane clicked on the hard cement before mellowing into a rhythmic drumbeat as it touched the softer wooden boards.

Chen smiled. The recent threat of a competitive stand had turned his family's attention to him, had made him the focal point of their concern. At home he pretended the threat was still there to insure the attention would still be there. The past week, when he got home at night, the family surrounded him and flooded him with worried questions. It made him feel young, devilish, in a mood to play tricks. So this morning he remained silent as Po came near. Except for moving his eyes he was motionless.

Chen's impish trick went wasted, appreciated by no one. Po came slowly forward, his head bobbing in jerks as he directed his ears, until he was within reach of the news display. The morning breeze crawled through the fence bars, rustling the newspapers at his feet and carrying along the scent of Chen's cigarette. This morning was no different from any other. The twitches of his face synchronized into a smile as he asked in a whisper, since quiet was what Chen wanted, "Did they come back?"

Chen turned and spit wetly through the fence to the grass behind him. Shame flooded his body—not for having tried to trick a blind boy, but for having failed. Failure made the trick seem mean. Worse, he could not explain to Po what he had tried to do. To explain would be to confess failure. A confession would ease his conscience, but admission of failure would puncture his ego. He decided to accept the shame. "No," he said. "We chased them away."

"Good," Po said, letting his smile reveal the happiness he felt for having the confidences of a strong friend.

Chen's deceit was compounded. "We frightened them away," he added, rationalizing the lie by telling himself it would bring him the respect an old man should have. If one must beg something from a beggar, the least he could beg would be respect. Age takes from a man the respect given to the strength of the young.

"Is your son still watching?" Po asked, his excitement growing from the confident sound of Chen's voice. He danced in small, nervous steps, ready to leave if the son were still around, for Chen preferred that Po stay away when his son was there.

Chen watched the shuffling, awkward feet and resented them for calling attention to Po's blindness. Po was young and blind, and he was old and sighted. Po had little family, he had a large one. At times Po seemed suspiciously close to wanting to adopt another family as his own. No family wanted to embrace blindness even if a clever boy came with it. Chen used an unnecessary rearrangement of the newspapers to pull away. It was safer for him to keep separate the strangers of his work day and the relatives of his leisure nights. "My son has other work to do," he scolded, yet being vague. "He can't waste his time watching me work!"

Po jerked stiff at the unexplained reprimand. But Chen was his first friend outside the family. It was possible all friends treated each other with strange reprimands occasionally. "People will be happy because the weekend starts tomorrow," he said, venturing on a new subject.

39

Guilt stricken by how his need for respect had driven him to lie, Chen argued obstinately. "No one will be happy," he concluded positively as he picked up a newspaper. "The headlines say the water shortage is getting worse. The government wants to give us only four hours of water each week!" He groaned and took a moment to appreciate the deep sound. It made him sound big, heavy, authoritative. Still, the discontent he meant to instill in Po settled instead deeper in himself. One bath a week. At bath time his flat was crowded with impatient relatives who ignored the privacy his age demanded. The price of a large family was often as large as the family itself. If his ancestors had not left China in favor of Hong Kong he would have had a whole house all to himself. "No bath for a week," he moaned helplessly.

"I once went two weeks without a bath," Po remembered happily. "We walked for two weeks. Every night. We slept during the day," he whispered, "so the soldiers wouldn't find us." He paused, twisted to aim his ears, and listened for sounds of others who might be trying to sneak up and overhear the conversation. "Some days we didn't even have any water to drink. Those were the days when my father couldn't find a stream," he remembered.

After giving Chen several moments to comment, Po began to feel foolish. Chen's silence indicated talking too much was a mistake. Still, the story of his walk into Hong Kong was the only story Po had to tell. It was too precious to be left hanging. "I got wet when we crossed the river," he added.

Although Chen knew Po had never seen the big land, he still resented the boy for having lived there. Hearing Po tell over and over the tale of his flight renewed Chen's shame for being so old a Chinese and never having visited or lived in the land of his ancestors. He, like all Chinese men, yearned to live and die on the soil where his ancestors were buried. It aggravated him to be reminded by a boy that he had done nothing about returning home. The young beggar had lived in both places, had walked from one to the other, had mocked over and again the dangers in doing it, and could tell of experiences that would chill the wrinkled skins of many old men—if only the pride of the aged would allow them to listen.

Irritation over hearing the same story still another time caused Chen to shuffle his newspapers angrily and bang his empty tin box. Disrespect. Po treated him with disrespect. The belittling was intentional.

Chen's prolonged silence, capped by the ominous banging of the tin box, startled Po. He had erred, he decided, by pulling the subject away from where Chen wanted it. "The water shortage won't be hard for you," he went on amiably. "With your big family you can send five or six, maybe even fifteen or twenty of your relatives to get water when they turn it on. You'll have more instead of less!"

Chen preened as pride slipped back into his small body. No one checked how many of one family went for water. "I'll tell my family to buy more buckets," he said, as though the idea was new.

The voice coming up from the squatting man again had a pleasant tone. "The weather's warm," Po said, encouraged by the change. "With the weekend coming I think you'll sell out early today."

Chen sat straighter, more at ease. Po was clever. The boy knew what to give people when they begged something of him. "If I sell out . . . " he began, then stopped cautiously. "If I sell out early, as you predict," he said carefully, "I'll put someting in your cup." He thought again about what he had said and elected to like it. But then confusion set in. To part with money and get nothing for it—the thought alone hurt. Or did it? Deep inside his promise a touch of satisfaction came to life.

Po giggled, aimed his smile in the wrong direction, and shrugged at the offer's seriousness. With such a large family, and with so much money gained over the years, Chen had no reason to need anything from the plastic cup. Besides, the cup was not meant to be used by friends. It was reserved for strangers. Chen knew it was. Over the months of their working together, Chen had never given the cup anything just as Po had never purchased a newspaper. The more Po's mind played on the reasons for Chen's offer the more the offer sounded like an attempt to build strangeness instead of friendship between them. "It's late," he apologized, wanting instinctively to leave. "I have to go to work."

"Yes," Chen agreed, "it's late."

Both had to be prepared for the heavy load of workers coming off the early ferries. There was no way to replace the potential of those who passed before the cup was offered or before the newspapers were spread.

Po took a methodical count of his steps away from the newsstand, and on the count of twelve he shuffled sideways until his shoulder pressed solidly against the wooden fence. He pulled the cup from his pocket and then faced the direction from which the crowds would come. By shoving the plastic cup at arm's length into the path he obstructed as much as he dared the width of the lane. His shoulder, leaning against the solid fence, blocked the one side and forced the commuters

42

to detour around the arm offering them the cup. The stance caused congestion, and congestion gave the people time to find their money. The cup was held at waist level where coins could drop without drawing attention to those who dropped them. Sometimes people were ashamed of needing something from the cup.

Chen's eyes followed as Po walked away. He encouraged distrust to lessen his suspicious anxiety. Their acquaintance was shrouded, guarded against where it might lead. The boy was a beggar. Worse, he was a professional beggar. Perhaps a beggar not above trying to beg a loan from a friend. For more than a year no such thing had happened, yet caution seemed wise. Po had talked of a father and mother, but never of brothers or sisters or cousins. Without such relatives, he would have to go to friends for money, and he must need money or else he would not beg.

The ferry's first cluster of workers bought little from either Po's cup or Chen's newsstand. They seldom did. They had time, they knew it, and they enjoyed using it. They stopped to look at the boy's cup until deciding he was a fraud and didn't need their money, then proceeded to the newsstand to look and read as much without buying anything that their nerve and time permitted. It was the usual morning.

Chen kept his eyes on everything going on in front of his stand but his mind stayed on Po. When the boy first came to the lane he emerged as competition for the attention of pedestrians, attention Chen wanted exclusively for himself. One way or another, over his many years of selling papers, Chen had managed to shoo away territorial intruders. But Po was blind. A young, blind boy. The combination was too much to fight. No matter how secret, every man has a gram or more of sympathy for the blind. Who knew how much should be granted to others as compensation for such a handicap? It was confusing.

That day, the first day Po came to the lane, Chen could only watch and suffer. He hoped the boy and the man with him would walk the lane and disappear around the corner, taking their problems with them. But they did not. They stayed. An alternate choice then was for Chen to believe the man was a professional who hired blind children to beg for him on a commission basis. Coping with professionals was simple. Sympathy for the blind could be quickly, and gratefully, converted into hatred for those who used the blind for their own gain.

This means of moral escape, however, soon closed. Time and talk with Po indicated he was not being used by someone else. The man he was with the first day was his father. For Chen, the discovery was distressing. It ruled out family force just as it ruled out summoning help from the police. No one wanted to be guilty of turning a blind beggar boy over to the magistrates, authorities who were white and might not understand.

From Po's expression as he tried to hurry past Chen each morning and evening in those early days, Chen knew the boy was afraid. Po's fear built Chen's courage. It was no longer Po's presence threatening Chen. It was now Chen's presence threatening Po. So Chen used his new courage as an excuse to extend his patience with the beggar. He was the master between them as he once was the master of his own family. Having a problem of his own, a problem wrapped securely away from his family, and a problem he could solve if he wished it solved, gave him a sense of power. He could afford to be patient.

As the weeks rolled by, Po learned to work with precision. He never missed a day—other than Sundays when the offices were closed and the ferry crowds both smaller and less predictable—and his movements could have been used to set the ferry tower's clock. To Chen's chagrin, the boy had developed a pattern of begging so successful that control of the situation might have escaped Chen in his patience. Po's grin while begging never changed. Morcover, he was the quiet, inoffensive type of beggar. Too smart to say anything that might give his donors reasons to get angry with him, he refused them a release from their consciences. Other than a polite nod of thanks he did nothing to get money beyond making the cup accessible to those inclined to buy from it whatever they needed it to give them.

The boy was both clever and well trained. His fear of passing Chen remained until Chen's conscience yielded. In this world of individual minds nothing is given without reason. Not even a morning salutation. When it was granted, Po jumped in surprise at the sound coming up to him from the squatting newsman. And his shocked reaction hurt Chen. It shamed Chen for having waited so long to break the strangeness, for it was he who was in debt to Po and it was he who had delayed in balancing the books of gratitude.

Chen's newspaper sales had doubled since Po had been sharing the lane with him. With his own eyes Chen had watched how the people who usually passed his newsstand without seeing it now had to watch their step to keep from falling over it. The beggar's position on the one side of the lane jammed the people to the other side where newspapers were spread, blocking their path. The sudden obstacle snapped their lazy minds into work. Forced to think, they were forced to use their eyes, and many decided to buy what they now saw. Po's position and what it did to Chen's business might have been accidental. It might also have been planned. Whatever its origin, unless paid for, the situation might change.

Since midmorning and midafternoon business was slow, Chen spent those periods dreaming of many things. Always concerned about improving sales, he studied the faces that passed the beggar without giving and saw the same faces pause in front of his display to look worried. It was as though buying a newspaper from an old, white-haired newsman could somehow quiet the guilt that pricked from passing the beggar's cup without giving a sacrifice. Such sales held a hint of charity. Nevertheless, to encourage them, Chen aimed at such people a face that begged for pity.

The only way Chen knew to rid himself of his obligation to Po was to offer the boy his friendship. But friendship is sentimental, unmanly, and, when given to someone suffering a handicap, is defenseless against accusations of condescension and suspicions of self-interest. Still, he argued with himself, were not all friendships born out of what they gave to each party? Did not everyone expect something in return for what he offered? So Chen steeled himself against sentimentality by remaining suspicious of Po. By deciding that Po must know how newspaper sales had picked up and be aware of Chen's debt, Chen found it easier to offer the friendship.

Over the months the friendship flourished. In the quiet mornings Chen caught himself anticipating Po's arrival, but still he allowed his ambivalence to linger. At times he told himself he could walk away from the beggar without returning and feel no remorse, no pain. At other times he vacillated—there was no answer. He and Po were alike. They both begged, but they both gave something in return. After giving to Po people smiled—it was worth the price of a coin. Chen used his age to beg sympathy from the young men, and for their money they got not only a newspaper but a sense of well-being. With the older customers he snorted and complained and pretended not to need their business. They liked him for it. It proved to them that when their time to be old came they need make no sacrifices to age.

Words were kinder to Chen. He was a business-man while Po was a beggar, and that gave Chen permission to feel superior. And being superior, he felt the pressure of having to find a way to salve the hurt he had given Po that morning. If Po wanted to repeat his story of walking out of the Mainland, a superior being would have let him. A superior being would have been more patient, more tolerant.

By the time the day had spent itself, and Po approached the newsstand on his way home, Chen's conscience demanded he erase the morning's error. "Why did you leave Canton?" he asked Po amiably.

Po beamed his delight. Sharing secrets with a friend was delicious. He slid sideways, cautiously, feeling his way closer. When his ears could not discern any unwanted sounds, sounds of intruders, he offered, "We didn't have enough to eat!" He let out the statement carefully, fearing it might draw an argument. "The government didn't have enough food."

"People shouldn't expect the government to feed them," Chen noted scholarly, elderly. "Families should take care of themselves." He moved about, closing the stand. "You should have stayed in Canton with your relatives," he added. "Families must stay together and grow."

Chen's voice grew and faded—the old man was shifting positions below. "My father wanted me to stay," Po remembered. "He thought if he left me the government might take care of me. We have no relatives . . . in Canton. My mother wanted us to leave so we could eat."

"You should stay with your father," the old teacher proclaimed, his sternness weakening in pity to one without relatives. But Hong Kong had too many people. It struggled under the refugee influx. "Your father should have stayed in Canton," he added, fearing Po would uncover his tender heart.

Po shifted awkwardly. The decision for which he was being blamed had not been his to make.

"Your father should have stayed with his father," Chen went on, safely since the lesson was ancient. "He should have stayed to take care of his father."

"My father," Po repeated cautiously, "had nothing to eat." He considered Chen's lesson. Why hadn't Au explained family obligations to him? Perhaps such rules were made up for some people and did not apply to others.

Chen curled his lips over a silent curse when he

realized that the absentminded recitation had told a blind boy to be responsible for his father. Did Po's blindness excuse him from his duties to his father? "I have to go," he complained. "My family needs me home early tonight. They do nothing without me." He watched Po, subconsciously wanting the boy to leave first, wanting the boy to strand him unjustly to equal the cruelty in the conversation. But Po remained. "I must go," Chen repeated, begging Po to leave. Chen closed his stand quickly and called back "Goodnight" when he was already on his way.

"My father had nothing to eat," Po said aloud, as the sound of Chen's footsteps grew fainter.

The following morning Po was awakened by the whistling scratches of Chung-kin's cardboard slippers on the cement floor of the flat. She was sliding here and there, working to get the day started. Po knew it might be possible that her slippers had been scratching like that for hours before he heard them. He cocked an ear toward the table. Clicking dishes and rattling chopsticks. He had not overslept.

Chung-kin caught Po's movement. "Breakfast," she ordered.

Po resented his mother for telling him the time. She treated him like a deaf baby. If only she would accept the fact that he would soon be thirteen, and that he was a working man. He sighed. Perhaps it was his growing into manhood that she resented. Perhaps she preferred having a baby. With a minimum of calculated effort he raised himself off the cot and shifted his backside onto the chair at the table. To keep from becoming a drudgery, getting up each morning had to be a game. Sometimes he used only one hand. This morning he stretched out a bare leg and tried to hook his clothes with his toes.

Au's heavy, even breathing pervaded the room. Au had spent the night either working or playing Mah-Jongg. Whichever, it was better not to disturb him. Po wished his father were awake. Breakfast was more fun when Au was bright and stimulating. Au was also safer. Au wanted him to work. Au knew how to talk to Chung-kin. She no more accepted the possibilities in Au's Mah-Jongg games than she accepted the possibilities in Po's working. When she was irritated, she carried on about the evils of gambling and the evils of accepting donations as if they were worse than the evils of hunger. She still called it begging. She closed her mind to its good. Women were strange Au once said. Life was strange. Remembering what Chen had said about sons taking care of their fathers, Po wondered how a man could have sons without first having a wife to tolerate. Au would know. Au was smart. Au handled Chung-kin much better than Cousin Liu handled his wife.

The prodding, extended foot failed to find the clothes, so Po turned to his breakfast before Chung-kin became cross. To keep from aggravating her he ate obediently and in silence. When breakfast was finished he went to the cot, slipped lazily into his trousers, forced his feet into the canvas shoes so darkened by age that they were cooled with holes. He snaked his arms through the sleeves of a shirt that had been cut down to his size when Cousin Liu had discarded it a year ago. The shirt and trousers were patched so discreetly they allowed a man to take pride in his frugality. That's what Au said. Po had better clothes, but Au said wearing the good clothes would hurt business. Po, however, had once thought better clothes would make the people think his cup had an abundance of luck to sell. The controversy ended when Chung-kin insisted the good clothes be saved for Sundays and family outings. Au had agreed with her.

Po buttoned his shirt by matching the top button with the second button hole. It was wrong. He knew it was. But it was right too. By mismatching the buttons he proved, to those who needed proof, that he was blind. It had become a habit. If people needed to think a blind boy had trouble buttoning his shirt then they should be allowed to think it.

As a final effort he slipped into a man's old, pinstriped suit coat so long it hung down just inches above his knees. Chung-kin complained the coat was much too big, but Au maintained a good fit would not keep the boy as warm. The coat's cloth, like that of the shirt and trousers, was tired from overuse, but clean and pressed. What Po overheard about the coat made him undecided. When he heard that other children did not wear coats like this one he was against it. It tended to make him different, to draw attention to his handicap when he was off the job. But then Au said all businessmen wore coats, and that this particular coat was good because it had big pockets, and Au was smart, even when he made decisions that were hard to take.

Chung-kin delayed Po's departure. "If you must go," she began out of habit, stooping to whisper in his ear, "then I hope you do well today. The rent is due next week. We're still a little short." She brushed her hands tenderly, possessively over his shoulders.

"Yes," he agreed and pulled away from her.

51

His mother was truly strange. She objected to his work but waited for the money he brought home. It was his father who realized he needed a goal, and it was his father who set the goal at sixty dollars a month to match the rent. But Chung-kin laughed right along with them each time he achieved the goal. Chung-kin could be fun when she wanted to be. But whenever he failed to reach the goal Chung-kin was quick to use the opportunity to plead with him to give up working.

"I asked your father," Chung-kin went on, stooping to tighten a shoelace that did not need tightening, "to try to get us a flat in one of the Resettlement Centers. The women at the shop tell me the flats there are only twelve dollars a month. If we could get in, one of these days you wouldn't have to beg any longer."

"The Resettlement Centers are far out of the city," Po whined, the first objection that came to his mind. "They're too far for me to go to work!"

"With rent at only twelve dollars a month you wouldn't have to work," she answered, closing the trap. She smiled as Po pouted and patted him gently on his behind. "We can discuss it later. Don't tap your cane until you get outside. You might disturb your father."

"I don't beg," Po growled once he was outside the door and she couldn't hear. Although anger urged him to slam the door, he clicked it shut obediently. On the steps he aimed the cane sideways, preparing to rap it antagonistically against the cement wall. He held the pose until good judgment prevailed. Revenge on Chung-kin would be offset by Au's anger.

The family needed cheaper rent about as much as he needed the cane. Except for supporting the cup at the right height and giving his arm a rest, Po considered the cane useless. Worse, it was negative. It told everyone he was blind, a thing they might not see if he had no cane. He could walk without it if he wished!

Do not beg. Do not wake your father. Do not slam the door. Do not rap the cane. Do not pay sixty dollars a month rent. There was only one way to make his mother sorry for the way she treated him. Die! He would die and then she would be sorry! He held his breath as he began circling down the stairway, testing his decision. By the time he thought he could feel the cool outdoor air strike his face, Po knew he had to find another way to die. This one was too painful. He gasped for air much too soon and filled his lungs with the odor of stale urine coming off the walls and dark corners of the cement steps. Small children living in the building used the stairs rather than leave their games. Each mother knew her child would not do such a thing, each thought it terrible that the other children did it, and each found it someone else's duty to scrub away the culprit's waste.

The hallway emptied into Lyndhurst Street between the stationery shop and a small clothing repair store. Once past the clothing store Po's nostrils began marking off his progress by a memorized sequence of odors. Dust seemed always to be swept to the street from the floor of the tea shop. The tiny particles bothered his nose until the smell of hair oil coming from the three-chaired barbershop on the corner drenched them with fragrance. The identification of the barbershop had changed recently. It's odor had gotten more demanding. "Bay rum," he had overheard someone say. It smelled as though the shop's owner was trying to cheat his customers by using an inferior product. Perhaps the salesman got the profit instead of the barber. Chen often talked about asking more for his newspapers, but never did. His customers could see the price.

The street of small shops was the most difficult section of the journey. As crowded with merchandise as with people, the sounds and smells and changing voices melted together, too mixed for identification. Po walked through the confusion concentrating on keeping a straight line. At night the little shops sucked in both merchandise and families and held them crowded inside, protected against thieves and external evils. Then, in the mornings, the whole pack exploded onto the sidewalk as though the ambition growing in sleep could no longer be confined. The sidewalk became littered with baskets, goods, pans, small stoves cooking breakfasts, people milling, working, cooking, and children running carelessly free of parents too occupied to correct their antics. Going through it all was next to impossible, yet necessary. Po had been knocked off-balance so often he took the hazards as part of the day.

As he trudged along, concentrating on what Chung-kin had said about Resettlement Centers instead of thinking where he was going, he took a careless stride and the canvas top of his shoe slid underneath the huge buttocks of a woman squatting on the walk. His forward motion landed him against her back. When the shape of what the foot was touching registered, Po pulled it away quickly. His toe teased the woman as much in leaving as it had in getting there.

The woman yelped. "Walk in the street, beggar!" she bellowed angrily. She struggled for composure as she salvaged some of the breakfast rice that had spilled onto the sidewalk. "You're no good!" she insisted.

"People have to keep you! People waste half their lives looking after you. Punished by the devils, that's what you are . . . "

Po shuffled rapidly in side steps until his foot felt the curb. He walked in the gutter, her ire fading as he went. The sound of her pot bouncing on cement and the remembered feel of the large contours of her bottom struck him as being exceedingly funny once he got safely away from her wrath. Yet he did not laugh. She had been too quick to identify him as a beggar. Some people hated beggars just as they feared the blind. "I don't beg," he mumbled, "and I pay the rent," he insisted to compensate for the shame her revenge demanded. Still, he let what she had said frighten him into stretching his cane far in front and banging it noisily to warn those still in his path. As a reluctant concession he hid his cup. A coin or two before getting to work would not be an omen of luck this day.

When he figured the vociferous woman was out of earshot, Po gave up straddling the curb. The curb was more dangerous than an angry woman's shouts. Not only the raceway for fast walkers, the curb was also the home of huge piles of refuse the morning sweepers accumulated for the collection wagons. A woman's anger could be forgotten but the smell of gutter garbage stayed in his clothing all day.

As he turned to walk down the steps of the next street he relaxed. On this "ladder street" shops were lined with small, busy, temporary stalls selling everything anyone could need or want. Here the bargaining voices came pitched high, here no one hurried, and here there were no trucks or automobiles. Speed was less important than getting the better of a bargain. No words, or combination of words, had not been used on this street. Here Po heard words of filth and sex and questionable ancestry that were used nowhere else. He descended the steps, dropping to one after the other in leisurely rhythm, his ears alert to all sounds from both sides. From each stall he took a little knowledge. Then the street leveled at Queens Road.

On the corner he waited as the sound of shuffling feet gathered around him, and crossed when the moving feet told him the light was green. Staying in the center of the sound he continued on to Des Voeux, a more orderly street that allowed him to hurry. Closed stone and glass fronts gave no hint of what these buildings contained. Tapping his cane alternately between building and sidewalk to maintain a straight line yet be aware of emptying arcades or street corners, he walked on to the alley by the huge Shanghai Bank. This corner, running east and west, predicted the weather by letting the morning sun come to the ground. The early sun, peeking over the bay, explained the air was clear and the sun wanted to work. To stay both safe and inconspicuous while letting the sun's rays penetrate his coat, Po faced the building and raised his hand to brace himself against being jarred.

The morning sun was warm, welcome, stupefying. Po absorbed as much of it as time allowed. By midday its warmth would be forgotten, burned away with a heat that could drive a man wild for water. But there was no water. The rainy season had come and gone again, misnamed. In fact, three rainy seasons had been that way. The spell had lasted so long that the reservoirs and underground wells had dried, and the citizens had forgotten how typhoons could uproot trees and blow out glass windows. The city had been too long without a bath, its citizens reduced to washing by a cloth rinse from a small pan.

At night the winds returned, strong off the water, and tempered the day's heat. There was little consolation in the cool nights however. The winds eddied the city's accumulated dirt and drove it into sweaty skin where it had to stay until the next water day.

So Po used to advantage the good morning sun by letting it drill into his back until he felt flush and lazy and ahead of nature, and until the clock of conscience nagged him away. Leaving the spot, he walked across the final intersection to round the corner that lifted him to the temporary wooden sidewalk.

"Morning, Mr. Chen." It came out methodically.

"Don't give me any of your cheerfulness," Chen scolded, determined to keep the previous night's ruptured conversation from healing too fast. "The newspapers report four more cases of cholera were found last night!" He glanced over the top of his bare kneecap to see if Po's expression was as worried as it was supposed to be. It was. Pleasure at having Po's attentive ear conflicted with Chen's desire for misery. "How can you be cheerful when there's so much cholera?" he asked, taking his choice of pleasures.

Cholera had been mentioned in overheard conversations before, but it remained a mystery and had been pushed aside for being meaningless. Po wrinkled his nose, disgusted with himself for letting Chen steal from him the morning's subject. He had come prepared to discuss the depth of a woman's crack; Resettlement Centers at twelve dollars a month; the lack of water and the heat of day. "What's cholera?" he asked politely.

"The disease of the devils," Chen warned dramatically, "that walks around in the loose dirt!"

A calculated side shuffle took Po out of the center of the lane to the fence where the magazine rack was available to his searching touch. "What color are the devils?" His fingers worked from the rack's outer edge, behind the strings holding the paper books on end, to the glossy surface of a cover photograph. "What do they look like?" While his ears stayed tuned to Chen's stories of fire-red bugs with many small legs, his fingers brushed inquisitively across the picture's smooth surface. Somewhere on the gloss there was a picture, a girl's picture, Chen had said so. It all felt the same. Nothing round or big and no deep crevices. The bugs hid themselves in wood and dirt. They hid so well Chen found it hard to describe where they might hide. Chen once said men liked to look at pictures of girls. What was a girl's picture like? It was very bad indeed when the bugs got inside a person. A girl's picture must be very different from a man's picture. When the bug got inside you, you died! You died!

Po's fingernail picked at a ridge across the center of the hard picture, a ridge made by someone's folding the page. Inside the book the paper was rough. He could feel the imprint of the letters. The cover, except for that ridge, was smooth. No marks, it all felt the same.

" . . . if these devils get inside one man, and another man touches him . . . " Chen sucked deep a wind of disaster, "the other man dies also! We might all die," he went on, encouraged by Po's silence. "We wouldn't have to worry about making money any longer," he offered, trying to cheer himself against his natural pessimism.

Po smiled his appreciation at Chen's ability to exaggerate a story until it became interesting. Exaggeration minimized the danger. Death-bringing bugs were frightening if one concentrated on them too long. Everyone knew how difficult and dangerous dealing with devils could be. Why didn't someone make a picture the blind could see?

Chen had run out of stories; he looked at Po tilting his head in anxious thought. Whatever was occupying the head, it seemed willing to stay inside. Worried that he might have injected unnecessary concern in this innocent mind without truly intending to do so, he tried to reduce the sting of his rantings. "We can wash away the dirt and get rid of the bugs," he conceded, "if they would give us enough water."

"Hah!" Po barked. He knew it. It was less dangerous than Chen made out. Someone had already found a solution, now all they had to do was find more water. The time seemed at hand; the silence from Chen indicated he had said all he wanted to say. "Why is rent only twelve dollars a month in the Resettlement Centers?"

Chen smiled, fatherly. His story of bugs and death had fallen on deaf and unafraid ears. He straightened, unseen, to the position he thought a squatting professor might assume. "Because the people in the resettlements pay no taxes! They're refugees! Warts on our society! The government has to build the resettlements to keep the refugees from building tin shacks on the hillsides. If the shacks burn or fall down"—he found it necessary to pause for a breath indicating disaster—"they'll fall on top of all of us!"

The answer pleased Po. Before accepting it as truth, however, he needed to test it. "Can only hillside squatters move into the resettlements?" He wanted to ask if people who could afford to pay sixty dollars a month were eligible, but that would have narrowed the subject and given Chen more information than he had a right to know.

"Yes," Chen mused, feeling authoritative. "You see," he began, pointing at the cardboard shacks climbing dangerously the nearby hills. But Po wasn't looking. Nevertheless Chen kept the pose. Others might be watching. "The government has to stop the fires and keep the cholera bugs from spreading among the people living in the shacks." He stopped to enjoy the sense of ultimate wisdom tingling his small body. The preserved long nail of his small finger went searching for wax in his ear. "That's why they build Resettlement Centers."

The clear answer needed only a final certification. "My family couldn't move into a Resettlement Center, could it?"

"Hah!" Chen laughed. Po's secret had escaped. Someone in Po's family was entertaining the idea of moving. "Do you live in a hillside shack?" he asked laughingly.

"No." Po answered, and laughed back. Chen didn't know where he lived.

"Then you can't move to a resettlement," Chen assured Po. He watched the young face for a hint that the answer was the desired one. It came. "Even the squatters have trouble getting in. The list is long. It takes money to get to the top of the list. You have to know the right people, have to offer the right amount. A gift. The refugees come in faster than the government will build Resettlements for them."

"Hah!" Po exclaimed, this time falsely imitating the sound Chen had made earlier. He turned sideways. His mother lacked the money for an official gift, and Au would not use his influence among his friends to take Po from his work. "Hah!" he repeated doggedly, letting the sound precede him as he walked down the wooden platform.

Jackhammers rattled in rapid puffs, and falling bricks bounced dull against the ground as workmen tore away at an old building on the opposite side of the protective wooden fence. Po leaned, refreshed from what Chen had taught him, and geared himself for the first sound of commuters forced onto the wooden protection by the destruction so near.

The day ahead held problems about Resettlement Centers, cholera bugs, angry women, and a host of other thoughts. Since none of them were particularly pleasant, Po concentrated on the vibrations coming off the wooden boards and into him through his feet. Footsteps. Still far off. Many of them. The ferry had docked, had unloaded. In spite of lingering in the sun and talking to Chen for so long, he had reached his post on time. He pressed against the wood and shoved the cup out sideways, into the lane. The cane supporting the arm under the cup was as bright and as noticeable as the cup and Po's smile. The door to another day of business opened. He raised his arm several times to tap the cane on the wood for attention.

The morning came, lingered, then left normally. Each time a five- or ten-cent coin dropped into the cup Po brought it in, snatched it from its container, and quickly returned the receptacle to its working position so no conscience would escape. The coins were stored in the left coat pocket, the pocket pinned against the fence by his body. As the morning wore on, boat arrivals became less frequent and less full. During the slow periods when he exercised his arms and shoulders he remembered always to guard the coins. The pockets and cups of the blind were targets for the unscrupulous. Idle money attracted evildoers, Au had warned.

A lone policeman passed that morning. The police of Hong Kong were cursed by having to wear heavy boots with equally heavy leather putties; a tradition handed to them by the bigger white foreigners. The heft strapped into the policeman's walk such a resounding thud that Po had long since learned to distinguish those vibrations from all others. On hearing the blunt sound, Po swung his cup quickly inside his coat and turned to face the wooden fence. He held the pose as the vibrations neared, stopped, waited in front of him, left, diminished, and were safely gone. It was time lost, an unfortunate part of the game.

The colony's laws only frowned on Po's business. Without a written complaint against a particular beggar, the police could do little. Some of them bothered to chase the beggars to another officer's district, but most did nothing more than display the threat of their authority and hope it would keep the beggars from becoming troublesome or abrasive. Occasionally a beggar would collect the wrath some officer had been saving for his wife, but when it happened both sides understood and parted feeling better.

Out of shyness and ignorance Po played innocent. His every move had been planned by Au to push luck as far as it could be pushed without creating a nuisance. When the policeman's boots stopped, stamped unnecessarily, accompanied by several coughs in case the victim was truly blind, Po more than got the message. The sounds left Po with the impression that all policemen were large, surly, and certainly above tolerating nonsense.

Lunchtime began around noon, about the time coolies balancing trays of lunches on their heads started marching by. The rattle of their dishes and the tantalizing odors of the food was as much a noon whistle as the bell on the Ferry Terminal Tower. Po let the aroma whet his appetite for a few minutes and then pulled from his pocket the rice cake Chung-kin had wrapped. Sliding his back down the wall to a sitting position, he ate, a little piqued that customers might be passing unable to buy from the cup while he was at lunch.

Children running by often stopped to witness the scene of a blind boy having lunch, and most hung their mouths open for better vision. They watched until learning nothing unusual would be shown, and then went on with their errands. Po heard their quick steps, knew from the sound they were children, knew from experience that whatever children gained from looking at him they wouldn't pay for, and thus returned his mind to the day's issues.

He kept his head low to keep the children from trying to peer into the slits of his closed eyes.

This day he thought about Resettlement Centers and about how to approach his mother with the news that it was impossible for them to apply. Next he wanted to examine all Chen had said about cholera, and further wonder at how devils could hide inside something as small as a bug. He allowed his mind to envelop the hideous subject until he felt bugs crawling up his arms and legs. He brushed wildly at them, but felt nothing. The itching stopped when he stopped thinking about it. Thinking too much about anything was bad. Au had said so.

All of Po's thoughts were abandoned at the feel of vibrations coming from the wooden walk. The office workers, released from their stone prisons, were taking their noontime exercise. Po bunched to rise. While waiting for midday business, he counted the coins as he passed them through his fingers en route to the opposite corner of his pocket. One dollar and fifty cents! Twenty cents better than average for noon. Perhaps he might, after all, make the month's rent. Perhaps Chung-kin would forget about Resettlement Centers and would laugh with him if he got even more than sixty dollars this month.

CHAPTER THREE

Victoria Bishop was one of Hong Kong's unmarried English women. Although well beyond the normal age for marriage, she claimed she had no desire for it. She claimed also her years in Hong Kong without a husband had been happy years. Unlike the single, younger Chinese girls who wasted their youth in pursuit of rich, single men, Miss Bishop had devoted hers to her work. She was employed by the government's Department of Social Welfare.

Reared in an English village so small it granted peace and happiness only to conforming conservatives, Miss Bishop automatically practiced what the village had taught. Her proper mate would come unsolicited at the proper time. She was expected to wait. As the years passed and her age edged dangerously higher her pride edged her toward clinging to the early belief.

Her pride would not allow her to marry just to avoid spinsterhood. As time passed she began to believe that fate had conspired against her. During those supposedly glorious days when love has the power to overwhelm, she had been a student at Sussex County's Roedean College. The school was close enough to her home for her actions and emotions to be monitored.

Fortune had also dictated that her college days be spent during World War II when all the young boys had been swept off to camp and battle. Of course, there were those among her classmates who picked husbands and lovers from Brighton's handicapped and aged, but she thought such compromises vulgar. A life spent with a leftover seemed worse than prolonging a virginal wait. So, to the delight of her instructors who had wasted too many years training girls who simply married and raised families, Miss Bishop plunged into study of social work with a missionary's zeal. Her dedication put her at the head of her class.

After her graduation, the faculty steered her toward a career in government welfare work. The war had ended, Japan had surrendered its conquered areas, and England had to rebuild its empire. In Hong Kong the postwar government reestablished its policy of hiring only Britons to fill the colony's supervisory governmental posts. Everything was in short supply, including workers willing to leave England just when thousands of soldiers were doing their utmost to return. Hong Kong job openings were advertised in London, and telephone messages went out between friends, including those at Roedean.

It was thus that Victoria Bishop learned of her future. Hong Kong begged for the services she needed to give. Out of school but a few weeks, she had already been subjected to questioning eyes. Her neighbors, influenced and frightened into silence by her four years of education at college, still wondered why she was not married, not engaged, not involved with men or a man. To prove she was normal, and to hide until the new world's changes allowed her to escape the mold of the past, she accepted a job in Hong Kong on a temporary basis. Hong Kong, after all, was part of the empire.

She left for the East, and, like most single girls with her training, began a career in child welfare. That was eighteen years ago.

When she first arrived in Hong Kong she sacrificed everything in favor of proving herself on the job. She let work take the time she might have used to think of herself, and gradually the artificial zeal she had used to silence her classmates and neighbors began truly to engulf her.

The years, however, had been used prudently. With the continuing, crushing workloads, and the increasing importance of her assignments, she maintained the vitality of youth. The years brought her seniority, and she recalled them precisely when seniority had the power to win an argument or a pay increase. Her seniority often beat down her male supervisors.

When she finally gave herself enough time to study the inner neglect bothering her, she discovered that much of her love was still unclaimed. It might have been a love inherent in women, a love saved for husband and children, or a love that needed use for growth just as did zeal. She did not know. And it was rather late to find out. Her youth had evaporated. The British soldiers in the colony got younger as she got older, and there were fewer of them. Economy dictated that London trust its Asian influence to the fiercely protective abilities of the cheaper Nepalese gurkhas. When one totaled the remaining Britons in Hong Kong, and subtracted from the total the women, the married men, and the men either too old or too young in spite of Miss Bishop's more generous assessments, very little remained. The misfortune that plagued her days at Roedean stayed with her.

Sex and marriage between the races was a subject discussed but not freely and not with outsiders. The English women, and married English men, agreed those little Chinese girls were dolls, perhaps subservient for a price, perhaps also fun to live with—but to marry? The girls were still Chinese. When these giggling little girls married into the kingdom without love of country, Miss Bishop knew they would always be more Chinese than British. Happiness for their husbands would be short-lived. The husband would someday return home, and the wife would never understand what it was that made an Englishman proud to be an Englishman. Other than their bed, there was little an interracial couple had to share.

At times Miss Bishop trembled secretly at thoughts of interracial sex. Yet she never found the nerve to approach a confrontation that might teach her whether differences existed anywhere outside the stealthy confines of her imagination. Perhaps an inner fear of learning that there were no differences kept her from attempting to solve the dilemma, and perhaps believing there were differences was too stimulating to be wrecked by discovering the truth. The problem bothered her mostly at night, when she was alone, but less and less lately. When she lingered too long on the subject she began to feel like a refugee from her own country. It was distressing. It made her want to cry. Luckily the English men often discussed marriage to a Chinese girl but never an English woman's marriage to a Chinese man. It made it seem her dilemma was not a reality within the social group.

During her years with the department Miss Bishop rose past all the minor posts—posts lately given over more and more to the Chinese she had trained—and into the exclusively British administrative position of Assistant Director, Kowloon District. She commanded a salary sufficient to enable her to rent a nice flat in the better section of Tsim Sha Tsui, a downtown district near her office. It was only seldom that she crossed by Star Ferry to the island side of the colony. She avoided all but the colony-wide conferences, for the others were a waste of time and effort.

The meeting this day, however, could not be avoided. The continuing water shortage endangered the people. Her clients. A joint departmental conference had been called to acquaint all branches with the problems that would arise if the water shortage led to a cholera epidemic. Unable to escape, Miss Bishop convinced herself the meeting would be a good chance to see if any new English faces had appeared in other districts. And her search would seem accidental, circumstantial. Most of the old-timers remembered she was still unmarried, and although she pretended to loathe their matchmaking efforts, she had come to pay attention to them.

After lunch she took a short but brisk walk to the Star Ferry and boarded for the ride to the island. The boat docked at Victoria pier as though sucked to it by an underwater current. An eight-minute ride, Miss Bishop timed. The shuttle disgorged its passengers down the ramp, under the terminal's covered passage, past the Royal Jockey concession selling lottery tickets, through the Connaught Street tunnel, and into the open air to cross Chater Road. Hurried by the crowd, Miss Bishop was drawn into a confining tunnel of wood. Workmen were demolishing an old building. To protect pedestrians from falling objects, the contractor had built a wooden walk, a high wooden fence facing the old building, and a roof over the whole thing. Only one side remained open, the side facing the fenced, open grounds in front of the Shanghai Bank. It was atrocious how long it took Chinese workmen to demolish an old building. They worked as though they enjoyed the dust and noise and disturbance they made.

A few steps into the wooden lane brought Miss Bishop to an abrupt halt. Shocked, she stared ahead, submitting slowly to transfixation.

"My God!" she said aloud so those nearby could share her astonishment. "A blind boy begging!" The sight, even at a distance so pathetic, mocked all the good the government had done in the colony over the years. This one beggar, only a boy—as pitiful as the hopeless old leper the Department had struggled to get off the streets—shamed her many accomplishments. What would people think of Social Welfare—what would the governor think if he saw blind child beggars still operating as though the government agencies offered no help?

She steadied herself against the fence while contemplating the next move. To give the problem undisturbed thought she waited until the ferry crowd had dispersed and she was alone. Since this side of the channel was out of her district, her first notion was to save the subject for discussion at the conference. There had always been backbiting and friction, competition between districts, and satisfaction when inadequacy in someone else's territory was accidentally discovered. The impulse became a decision. In the meantime, until the island district became aware of this boy, an initial approach had to be made. Somehow this poor child must be told he had friends, that his misery would end, that someone cared for him, that someone cared enough to love and help him.

With her intentions established, Miss Bishop approached the yellow cup with a slow, cautious pace calculated to warn the boy that someone was nearing him. The department's book explained how the blind suffered traumatically from sudden shocks. Several years ago a blind man had actually attacked her. She recalled how he had swung his stick wildly, searching to hit her, and the scene he had created was her fault. She had come too suddenly upon him. She had surprised him.

As she walked closer she pulled a dollar coin from her purse and held it ready. Money. Money was the answer since it was money the boy needed. His clothing, although clean, showed very well indeed how much he needed money.

Stopping in front of Po, Victoria Bishop studied him sympathetically a moment. She reached slowly out to touch the hand that held the plastic cup ready above the cane. By caressing the hand she wanted to send a silent message of compassion.

Just as she touched the beggar, however, his hand jerked in surprise. It pulled back a few inches, hesitated, then cautiously felt its way out again, prodding the air for what had disturbed it.

When the hand had returned to its position Miss Bishop again touched it gently, but this time she let the coin slide over the boy's thumb hooked over the cup's top, and dropped it into the cup. When the coin hit the cup's bottom it triggered the arm inward so the coin could be extracted quickly by the other hand.

After dropping her dollar Miss Bishop felt a tide of satisfaction flood her body until it prickled every pore. She pulled back her shoulders to suck in the feeling. In exchange for taking away a portion of the beggar's troubles she was granted an outlet for her unspent sympathy. The cup, by uniting their handicaps, tried to make them secret friends.

So pleased over what the cup had given her, Miss Bishop walked away seeing neither the newspapers spread in her path nor the old man cuddled next to the fence.

"Mr. Chen?" Po called in a whisper when all had quieted on the walk.

"Yes," Chen called back. "I saw her."

"It was a woman?" Po asked foolishly.

"A white woman," Chen added. "She stood in front of you and watched a long time."

"She grabbed my hand!" Po argued, expecting Chen to scold him. "I thought she wanted to steal my money! I thought I might have to use my cane to beat her off!"

"How much did she give you?" Chen asked suspiciously.

"A dollar!" Po announced. "A whole dollar!" It was the first time he had felt anything so heavy touch the bottom of his cup. Its feel and sound were repeated in his imagination until fixed there.

A bit jealous over Po's getting so much money for doing nothing, Chen puzzled to fit together the pieces. "Be careful of the white people," he warned, since no acceptable solution came to mind. "They govern the city and find pleasure in getting themselves involved in the lives of the poor Chinese."

The dollar, already his, made the white woman's involvement magnificent. "Why would she give me a whole dollar?" Po asked without truly caring. Apparently the woman needed so badly what the cup had to give she paid high to assure getting it. This automatic conclusion, however, worried Po. Was the cup capable of giving so much? "Why a dollar?" he repeated.

"I don't know," Chen answered skeptically.

Never mind. The dollar was now his, not hers. "Hah!" Even if it never happened again, this dollar was his. The woman had already left. He used his memory to re-create the sound of her heels carrying her away. But why must it never happen again? Excitement welled in Po at the possibility. An extra dollar would buy ideas from Au and bring Chung-kin to forget about resettlement centers. That lone dollar would help weave his life into the lives of his parents.

As the afternoon dragged on Po imagined laying the large coin on the table at home and relating what had happened. Good news must be told in a way to make it sound ordinary to keep it from being followed by bad news. Po wondered if he should wait for Au to ask if anything special had happened, or if he should tell of the dollar without waiting. Au might not ask.

But Chung-kin surely would! The rent was due. Still, neither Au nor Chung-kin ever direcly asked for his money. Both waited until he was ready to give it.

The excitement brought by the dollar and the anticipation of the evening made the balance of the afternoon drag on endlessly. A five-cent coin, an occasional ten-cent piece. Po could tell by both sound and weight just what had dropped into the cup. Intentionally fighting to keep from making a mental, running count of the day's proceeds, Po folded his left hand into a fist to rest atop the coins instead of fondling them. Even so, the dollar seemed to touch all of his fingers. The proper course for this day would be to let the whole family share in the count when he got home. The pleasure of doing it had to be shared, and shared with family.

After an interminable time, long enough to worry Po into thinking something had gone wrong, the clock in the Ferry Tower pealed off four bells. He shook nervously with the clanging of each, waited forever to be certain the fourth ring was the last, sweating out his fear that he had stayed too long, and then slipped the empty cup into his pocket and began the trek to the flat. His mind was so engrossed in his good fortune that he passed Chen without a farewell comment. Au had told him many times to be home before the streets swarmed with office workers. During the late night rushes no one got sympathy and no one got help.

This journey, always slow and tedious, was worse this night. Po faced the nearly impossible task of concentrating on where he was going while concentrating still harder on keeping his coins from rattling inside the pocket. Noisy coins drew attention and teased evil minds into plotting.

Po completed his trip without incident, without drawing more attention than usual. So happy with his success once he entered the safety of the flat, he suddenly forgot all the courses of action he had considered during the long afternoon.

He burst into the room. "This has been a most lucky day!" he shouted.

Au and Chung-kin slid their stools noisily to explain they were present, seated, willing to share.

Po, savoring every sentence, gradually released his excitement by going over the whole day. It began with the woman who spilled her breakfast on the sidewalk and shouted at him, continued with the conversation about cholera bugs and how mysterious they were, sketched cautiously the rules Chen had given about entering the Resettlements since this news might embarrass Chung-kin, and finally slowed for breath while searching his mind for hidden importance in happenings without importance. He took a final sigh, preparing himself for the major event.

Au caught Po's signs of delight. Teasing the childishness with equally childish exclamations of disbelief, he joined in Po's pleasure. Chung-kin, on the other hand, examined all Po had said with a motherly instinct to tone down his glee. To keep her son from getting too excited she attempted to extract the truth from his exaggerations.

The moment at hand, Po brought out his story of the white woman and the dollar she had given. Silence from Au and Chung-kin told him he had capped his revelations magnificently. To prove his story he pulled from his pocket the fist wrapped around the bundle of coins and splashed the lot onto the table.

The story had not been exaggerated—the coins

were there. And no matter how alluring to the eyes were the many small brown coins, the huge silver one dominated the scattering as a single lotus blossom dominated a watery field of mud. Both parents added the amount rapidly with their eyes, but said nothing. Po was counting with his fingers. It was his happiness, his right to reach the end first.

"Three dollars and forty-five cents!" Po shouted. His eyelids opened unconsciously in his surprise.

The shout bothered Au. It had been loud enough for the whole building to hear.

"Don't get so excited," Chung-kin admonished. "After this, what you get tomorrow will be like nothing."

Po flinched at the sour note. This day was meant to never end. His mind discounted her pessimism as his hand lingered on the dollar. It had bumps and ridges, a heavy circle. The bumps had a pattern; a picture begging his fingers to see.

The three remained at the table wondering what next to do. The excitement, so long in building, was over. They knew it. "Everything over two dollars," Au said, attempting to resurrect at least part of the dream, "we can save to buy something in the future." He left the coins untouched, waiting for Po to finish caressing them.

The evening meal was eaten in the disheartening silence of post-celebration. Po grunted his frustration after struggling with the slippery noodles, a food too thick to be drunk from a bowl and too soft to be felt with chopsticks. Sometimes he got them to his mouth and sometimes he did not. The anticlimax got the better of him and he pushed away the bowl, clanging it against the dishes in the center of the table.

The small room, made still smaller by filling one corner with saved buckets of water, was too crowded to hold three people struggling with diverse thoughts. As Chung-kin cleared the table and began the dishes, Au and Po escaped to the cool breezes flowing across the building's roof deck. A place for after-dinner talk, the two used it to dream and wish, to find solitude, to scheme secretly about the future their imaginations created.

More often than not, however, the roof was crowded. Not especially crowded with people, but crowded with clothes hanging from wires strung in all directions. Each flat had its own clothesline, and following water day, each clothesline was attended by a watchman. Spies also roamed in search of lost shirts, socks, or underclothing, or whatever was believed missing from the previous washday. When a missing piece appeared strung on someone else's line the normally quiet roof became a battleground.

Au and Po strolled, ignoring the others on the roof, until reaching the corner of the building. There, safely away from it all, on the rising edge of the adjoining building, came a solitude in spite of the roof's visitors and the noises reaching for the sky from the street below. The air was filled with odors of spices and frying grease, with the rattle of chopsticks, soup spoons, and dishes, and with the high-pitched hums of voices. Smoke from a million fires cooking a million dinners choked the air, obscuring the lights of Kowloon across the bay and elongating into red shadows the colored neon tubes of the shops on Lyndhurst.

Without his cane, Po held Au's hand. He slid his feet across the cement until his toes touched the familiar brick rail. Au, already sitting, spread his legs until his knees touched Po's. He looked at Po and was pleased in what he saw. Work had reached into the vacuum of the boy's life to bring forth a human being. Now he had something of his own, something to share. They sat together, each respecting momentarily the other's right to silence. Au took a cigarette from his blouse pocket, lit it, and blew the smoke skyward.

Po, holding the silence for as long as he could bear it, broke the spell by attempting to encourage what he was afraid to encourage in front of his mother. "Do you think the white woman . . . she might come back?" he asked.

Au sighed. "I've been wondering about it myself," he confessed. "Each night when you count your total I see you have almost always the same number of five-cent coins and almost always the same number of ten-cent coins. The difference each day is . . . perhaps one or two of each."

Po let seconds pass, but Au did not continue. It bothered him. Whatever Au had said, it slipped by. "Yes?" he wondered aloud.

"Don't you understand?" Au scolded quietly. "It could mean that the people who gave you a five-cent coin today are the same ones who gave you a five-cent coin yesterday. And the same ones who will give you a five-cent coin tomorrow. It's possible they save their five-cent coins just for you. It's possible they think about you every time they get a five-cent coin. Oh," he qualified, "it's also possible that a few of them leave each day and get replaced by a few others, but not enough to make a difference. People live by their habits. You've become a habit to them."

Po moved in an awkward symphony of uncontrolled jerks. "Then," he reasoned, willing to accept

Au's conjecture because he wanted to believe it also, "if this woman passes me each day she might give me a dollar each day!"

"Only if she passes each day," Au warned, seeing a need to answer as Chung-kin might. "Since she was a white woman it's possible she was just a visitor to Hong Kong. She might only stay one day. Or only a short time." But he could not bring himself to let go of the dream completely. "We'll just have to wait until tomorrow," he reasoned.

Silence again separated the two minds.

Au's cigarette, now too short to be held with extended fingers, was held pinched at its very tip. He took one last slow pull then carelessly tossed the stub over his shoulder to fall to the street below. "I had an eventful day myself," he mused. "Cousin Liu told me the man who owns the tea and noodle shop is having a hard time making money. His expenses are greater than his profit. The cook is overpaid and the waiter steals too much. People come in for tea and then sit all afternoon without buying anything else. Cousin Liu thinks the owner might have to sell the place before he loses all his money."

The distance between Au's new subject and the one still wanting to dominate Po's mind was great. Po's concentration failed to handle both, the excitement of the day had made him too tired. Au's puzzle was unworthy of solving. Po waited for the opportunity to theorize over the white woman's habits again.

"Do you know which shop I'm talking about?" Au asked.

The direct question forced Po to think. "Yes," he decided. "The one down the street.. I pass it every day."

"What do you think of it?"

"In the morning it smells of dust being swept to the street. At night it smells of stale smoke."

"No smell of food?"

Au's persistent voice sounded intent. Po prodded his memory. "No," he decided slowly. "I can't remember smelling food." The puzzle was being forced together. "If he doesn't sell food how can he make money?"

"He can't," Au assured him. "Perhaps the food is so bad no one will eat it," he hinted and waited for the twist of Po's lips to tell him there was an understanding. Nothing changed on Po's face. "Your mother is a good cook," Au teased further.

Roof talk was restricted to man talk. Au's so freely mentioning Chung-kin had widened the conversational gap. Po shifted, now tired and growing uncomfortable, and yawned as though his mind wished to escape his body. He struggled to bring it back. The bumps on the silver coin. They might have been a picture of a girl. Could the picture on a coin be felt, but not the picture on a magazine cover? He must remember to ask Chen to describe the white woman.

Au kept silent while watching Po's face for an indication of reawakening. Fearing he might lose his listener altogether if he did not unravel his own riddles, he asked, "Do you think we should try to buy the tea shop?"

Po stiffened and held the pose as the query browsed around his sleepy head. Of course! The dollar, and more of them! The puzzle, when glued together, left an important corner open. "If we did," he extended his thoughts, "would I still have to work?"

"You would have to," Au guessed for the correct answer. "At least you would have to work as long as the dollars came, and until we have enough money to pay the loan on the shop. We could give up going to restaurants on holidays, and . . . and save a little more from your mother's pay." The dream bubbled and began foaming into life. "We could save enough money of our own first, and then get a loan to cover the balance."

After waiting a few moments for Au to say something to indicate the plans were a joke or future dream, Po searched for Au's intentions. "Should we visit the shop? We could go now . . . if you like."

"That might not be wise," Au warned as he reached to keep Po from giving up the railing seat. "The tea shop owner might get the idea that we're interested in buying. He'd tell us stories about how big his profits are, and how many customers come to spend their money. He'd try to tell us his business is so good that he isn't thinking of selling . . . unless someone offered him much more than the place is worth."

It was all a joke. Po grew suspicious of the logic. "How else can we learn how much he wants for the place?"

"First, I think," Au said, breathing deeply and wisely, "we should get some more money. Money always influences the seller." He smacked his lips, pleased with his wisdom. "Then, maybe through some friends, we can get a message to the owner. We can let him know we have money and are interested in buying a tea shop . . . somewhere. Not his shop. In that way the owner would have to come to us. He'd have to make his price lower than what he thought the other shops were worth." He thought a moment more. The plan sounded good. He nodded his head in a positive motion.

To Po the idea was overworked and overinvolved. It was not Au's way of doing things. In spreading the plan to cover other people and other shops it got lost. It became the possession of too many others. Po fell silent as he raked together the pile of words, and then searched the pile for Au's unstated intentions. Secrets were no longer secrets when spread so thin. Dreams were the same.

Slowly the motive behind Au's plan emerged. "My work isn't . . . it isn't honorable," Po dared to guess, "is it?"

Au frowned. The hint had been caught, as hints were meant to be, but it had also been opened to exposure rather than saved. "It's all right," he argued mildly, "but you shouldn't be thinking of doing the same work all your life."

Po consigned the advice to memory. This also. For pride's sake he must force himself to sell the cup rather than beg. It was all he could do.

As Au watched, trying to read from the small face what went on inside the large mind, he hoped the honor lost was a sacrifice to manhood. "I think we would need your help inside the tea shop very soon. Someone would have to sit behind the counter and collect the money from the customers as they left. The shop has a glass cage in one corner. As the customers leave they hand their money to the man behind this counter. He makes change for them when they give him too much." He paused, debating the value of keeping dreams alive, and wondering if he had gone too far to stop. "We could work out a secret scheme for marking the bills. Only you and I would know how much each customer owed. Maybe we could fold the corners of the bills or make up a secret language." A flinch stopped him again. The more he said the more he realized his trap was engulfing him instead of releasing Po. Yet the dream was grabbing Po. It was giving him a future. "The people would be surprised at how well you could work!"

The suggestion of a secret scheme, one known only to him and Au, enraptured Po. It so delighted him he refused to speak of it. He mulled over what it might mean if Au was not joking. His head began swimming with unanswered questions, with all the mysteries of working in a tea shop. In the confusion he got off the railing and started to walk back to the flat.

That night Po tossed on his cot for hours while re-creating the goodness and complexity of the day. Much of the good rested in what would happen the next day, but he had no way to speed the next day's arrival. Nervous anticipation finally snapped the strength of his curiosity and he fell asleep.

CHAPTER FOUR

The colony-wide conference did nothing to allay Victoria Bishop's excited concern over what she had seen—the blind beggar boy. Instead of being a conference, as she had assumed, the meeting turned out to be a well-organized, elaborately staged presentation with a minimum of audience participation. The huge crowd, invited from all branches of government, filled the auditorium. To Miss Bishop's dismay, she was pushed hurriedly into a seat of silence between two Chinese strangers instead of being allowed to select a seat next to someone who might listen sympathetically to her troubles.

Armstrong Harrington tried from several rows away to get her attention, but she pretended preoccupation and ignored him. Armstrong was another one of the old-timers who had allowed his years in Hong

Kong to turn him into a lush. He was married, furthermore, off and on, to a Chinese prostitute; that was the fact, even though his social group denied, for the sake of its own pride, that the girl had lived that way before her marriage. Armstrong was also not the kind of man Miss Bishop expected would take seriously either her problem about the beggar or her consternation over her maidenhood. Armstrong supervised the government's motor pool—a garage full of drunken, greasy rowdies —and sported the colony's wildest mustache. He bragged about getting smashed at night and then racing the governor's Rolls-Royce to the top of Victoria Peak in record time, and did it openly, as though his listeners should find something commendable in such behavior.

The afternoon's official presentation was dedicated to defining inter-agency duties should a cholera epidemic break out in the hillside shacks. Doctors gave tiresome talks on the finer points of identifying cholera symptoms and on the disease's wearisome causes and effects and then screened horribly vivid color slides to show the viewers what to expect. Miss Bishop squirmed uncomfortably. When hints were given as to how Social Welfare might help, she perked to attention and dutifully took notes. Her field workers, those with close client contacts, would want the information. She imagined they would also want her to prove she had not wasted her afternoon by attending the conference.

The medical team singled out yu sang and yu sang chuk as the foods most apt to contain the germ and small public restaurants and dirty food carts specializing in fish foods as the likely starting places. The English members agreed that there was no way the government could stop the Chinese health inspectors from accepting money in lieu of seeing that these dirty places were washed, so an English team was assigned the task of checking on the checkers. A brave Chinese man, one unknown to Miss Bishop, dared to stand up and suggest that the colony also might have a few Englishmen whose eyes could be blinded to dirt and germs if covered with enough money. His suggestion drew the token number of polite laughs.

After the color slides had gored all the complacency out of the viewers the conference disintegrated. They all needed freedom to vent their queasiness. The English renewed their poise through humor. They told stories of Chinese theatrics, Chinese behavior in the face of calamity. The Chinese renewed their strength by telling themselves alienation was a national dream.

After members of both races finished their self-assurances and saw the need to go their separate ways together, the meeting reorganized. A compromise to their unspoken differences was offered. Together they agreed that, in the event of an epidemic, only those inside of government would stay level-headed. The resolution restored their pride and opened the door to cooperation at administrative levels. It was in administration that the many groups dovetailed in duties, and it would be in administration that each department stood a chance of making or breaking its reputation among the other departments.

The orphan among the departments was Social Welfare. All too often welfare was chalked off as a luxury, a place for government to drop its money without due return, a well without a bottom. Any gain

Social Welfare made against the wave of incoming refugees was likened to a hand holding back a typhoon. Social Welfare was further handicapped by not having money enough to prepare beautiful charts with colored statistic lines for presentation to the governor's table at fund dividing time. The hospitals drew graphs of cases accepted and saved, and the police did the same with their arrests and convictions. But a request by Welfare for enough money to meet the problems squatting in the hillside shacks would so bludgeon the colony's budget that all the other branches would have to work for free. So Miss Bishop and her colleagues labored under the embarrassment of helplessness.

The meeting closed with a request for volunteer workers to participate in the newly organized cholera prevention program. Nervous when confronted by a hypodermic needle, Miss Bishop offered herself to the inoculation centers. This, she concluded, made her contribution greater than that of those who picked enjoyable work. She would have preferred a role in the prevention educational program, but most of the volunteers accepted for such assignments came out of the Educational Department.

It was long past the normal quitting time when the meeting ended. Miss Bishop watched with a sinking heart the scramble for the exits. She had no where to go. Her evening was young, unfulfilled, no one waited for her. It was not often that she got the chance to meet with these people, and less often the opportunity to talk with them. Elbowing through the rush she searched for Harry Leong, her Welfare counterpart on the island side. But Harry was gone. He had a large family and a habit of leaving early in order to spend more time with them. Her search for him, nevertheless, continued until she was the last to leave the auditorium.

The line of taxis had rushed their loads away from the Magistracy Building long before Miss Bishop got outside. She stood alone, growing exasperated with each wasted signal sent toward the corner. The taxi laggards lingered, cruising the emptying business area as though not caring to catch the waves of a single woman. They were much too independent for their own good. They sold rides illegally, often refusing to put down their meter flags so they could bargain over the fare and keep it for themselves. Whenever the opportunity to scold them for breaking the law presented itself, Miss Bishop jumped at it. But when she did the drivers laughed so mischievously that she became still more upset. They had an inner sense that told them who could hurt them. They never did anything illegal when there were white police around. It was time the government took action against them.

Trams were cheaper. A fixed ten-cent fare. And the trams stopped when someone waited. Yet in the crowded cars the bodies rubbed suggestively together in the heat, and in their summer clothing Miss Bishop easily distinguished every bend, dip, and protrusion of those sliding by behind her. She put up with the ride by convincing herself that by joining the masses she would somehow emerge wiser and more able to understand them. She nursed this thought until the rocking car docked in front of the lane where she had last seen the beggar boy. The tram steadied with patience as she dismounted, as though its engine knew there was a white government employee aboard.

The beggar was gone. Miss Bishop stopped at

the newsstand and fingered carelessly the magazines racked in front of her. It gave her a reason to be where she was, an excuse to scan the moving crowds while looking for someone smaller, slower, perhaps obstructive, trying to work his way free and needing help to do so. But the boy was not to be seen. Saddened, Miss Bishop stared dreamily down the lane where he had stood. She stared until feeling the burrowing eyes of someone watching. It was the small newsman, standing, waiting obediently at her elbow.

"Your magazines are very old," she told him curtly as she returned to the rack the one she had been holding. Her criticism failed to budge the old man. Perhaps he spoke an unusual dialect. She watched him as he rudely occupied himself with cataloguing her features. White people all look alike to the Chinese. Perhaps he had never been so close to one before.

"You should replace them with newer issues," she scolded, hoping to help him forget that he had caught her daydreaming. "Nothing but girls!" she scoffed. "Pictures of girls! Is that all you sell? Pictures of girls?" As she dominated the offense she wondered if the small man knew where the beggar had gone. Still, it would be useless to ask. The Chinese loved their secrets too much. Keeping something secret from anyone outside their own race was delightful for some reason. She guessed it gave them a feeling of power. Mysterious power. They enjoyed mysteries also. Sighing her loneliness, she left for the Star Ferry resolved to return the following day. It would be better to do without the help of the stupid little newsman. Why give him reasons to think he knew something of value to her, reasons to believe himself superior?

Because of the emptiness away from the office,

Miss Bishop arrived at work early the following morning. She spread papers over her desk so those coming in on time would see she had already started. After scouting the departmental phone book for Harry Leong's number, she attempted to call him. No one answered. Not too unusual. Harry, feeling his job was secure, was more dedicated to his family. It was disgusting how little loyalty the Chinese offered.

Later that morning Miss Bishop learned Harry Leong would be out of his office until noon, and although she seethed a little at having to make an appointment to see him, she nevertheless did. It could not be helped, something had to be done about the blind beggar. Throughout the morning she made notes and judgments on the case reports crossing her desk, and was stimulated into writing a directive insisting on neater files and more accurate records. Next she jotted a reminder on the calendar to schedule a group meeting to discuss the cholera conference.

Her brisk walk to the Star Ferry began immediately after lunch. En route she encountered a dirty little tyke standing in a doorway, naked from the waist down. Chinese mothers thought it easier and cheaper to keep their youngsters naked than to wash soiled panties. The child needed attention, his nose was running. She stopped to put a paper napkin to the nose. "Blow," she ordered. When he did she hugged him possessively, a reward for good behavior.

Inside the ferry terminal Miss Bishop struggled her way up the cement steps, became mentally transfixed by the repetitious advertising painted on each riser, and was quietly angry at having to climb the steps. First-class passengers paid more than second-class, yet had to climb the steps only to descend again before boarding the ferry. Second-class passengers walked directly on. The Star Ferry's management was a nondescript Chinese group, so remote from the government that there was no place one could go to register a complaint.

When morning came to the Au flat Po was already awake, already anticipating the unknown of this important day. He lay still to let the thrill of being alive soak his body with excitement. When he heard Chung-kin shuffling the dishes he spun toward the table with a grand gesture. Au was also awake. Although he knew his mind was open to Au, exposed by what they had discussed together the previous night, Po made no mention of what had transpired. Their discussion of the tea shop, made a half-truth dream by his tiredness on the roof, was clear as a bell's ring. This day would either kill the dream or authenticate it. A breakfast that might have been noisy was stilled by the intent of both males to hold their secret.

In his eagerness for the day to begin Po walked the streets with an intensity that brought on many mistakes, misjudgments, and minor accidents. Yet all were forgotten soon after they happened. This day would be either eventful or regrettable. By arriving early at the newsstand Po made still longer what would soon prove to be the longest day in his life. Nevertheless, to rush the day he clipped short his usual greeting to Chen, hesitated a moment to establish the exact spot from which to count the twelve steps, and walked on.

The morning stretched painfully long. Po tensed each time he heard the sound of another ferry discharging, and again when he heard the load drumming its way onto the wooden boards. The sound he waited to hear was uncertain. He scolded himself for letting it slip away. The previous day's event had come so unexpectedly, so shockingly fast, and was followed by so many possibilities that the beat and pitch of his new benefactor's feet had been lost. He recalled hearing clicks as the woman walked on, but now his fear made him wonder if the sound he had heard belonged to the right person. There must have been others watching, listening to the exchange, their personal marks mixing in with the woman's. In the quiet he resurrected the sound as best he could. Metal heels, tiny, hitting the wood smoothly. A sound similar to that of the steel plates the policemen wore, yet ever so much more delicate and gentle. It was a tap associated with friendliness rather than with the threat of authority.

By lunchtime nothing unusual had happened inside the plastic cup. As a matter of fact, the only unusual thing was the shortness of breath Po experienced from worrying that among the hundreds of gentle clicks he had singled out during the morning was the sound of the white woman passing, forgetting, proving that yesterday had been an exception for her as much as it had been for him. The thought had to be rejected—at least until the day ended.

As a precaution, Po ate in a standing position with the cup out, receptive, working. Twice during lunch he shoved his coins to the pocket's corner preparing them for a midday count, and twice he refused to make the count. The total might be so small that the dollar, should it still come, would make the day only average. The third time, after fortifying himself, he counted. The day was average. He sighed.

Shortly after lunch Po began fidgeting uncontrollably in response to nervous tension. There was no way of knowing, beyond just waiting, if the woman had passed or was yet to pass or would pass at all. And waiting was so exhausting. Each time the terminal bell pealed off a signal he tried to recall the time the woman had made her appearance. People lived by their habits. Chen had said they did, and so had Au. Au guessed those who gave the same each day passed each day at approximately the same time. Po thought the woman must have passed him early in the afternoon. He remembered how long after getting the dollar he had waited to go home. After a few more minutes, however, this estimate had to be rejected. To accept it meant to accept the fact that the woman was not coming.

All thoughts were suddenly left far behind as Po heard another group thunder its way onto the wooden path. With the gift earned over years, he singled out the particular sound, lighter, somehow sharper, than the noise of the other heels hitting the wood. He froze, his body tightened by muscle knots. The sound stopped directly in front of him.

"Good afternoon, young man."

The words floated as tenderly through the ether as had the sound of her steps. He felt the tingling touch of her fingers on his above the cup. Alert, he waited. The great moment had arrived.

Clunk! The dollar coin skidded heavily over his skin and made the sound that encouraged wild dreams. A sound now memorized. The impossible had happened a second time!

"Good afternoon, Ma'm!" Po sent the greeting blasting out of his throat as he spun to smile at her guessed direction. He waited, his smile getting heavy in wondering if it was being seen, being appreciated. He held it until hearing her leave, and after she had, he still smiled without trying. The cup with its magic contents stayed tucked under his coat until he regained his composure. When all was calm he extracted from the cup the day's fulfillment.

Chen, whose afternoon seemed filled with excruciatingly slow business, looked up from his stand at hearing Po's loud greeting. He stared negatively at the determined look the white woman wore as she walked past his stand. Her face was strong, intent. It worried him into believing that he had better do something about those old magazines she found so distasteful and inadequate. Twice she had passed, and twice at the same time. She might be a new customer. She was white—she had money.

It was with mixed emotions that Miss Bishop surveyed the austere Causeway Bay office of Harry Leong. Everything she saw met the established requirements of English tradition, but the building was too new for tradition to have etched its grooves deeply. There was something deceitful in its appearance. Maybe the deception arose from all the Chinese she saw working there. Still, the confluence of headquarters in one building produced many Englishmen, and there was nostalgia in seeing fellow countrymen bobbing in this sea of foreigners. As she waited for Harry, she felt the aura of home whenever a white man passed the open door.

The Chinese practice a graceful way of wasting small talk before slipping sideways into a meeting's subject. At times this made Miss Bishop suspicious. When Harry returned to his office she took advantage of the English atmosphere to speak immediately of her trouble. "Harry," she began, "twice now, yesterday and again today, I saw a young blind boy begging just where the ferry empties between Chater and Des Voeux. Along the construction path for the new building. I thought we had done away with this nasty business of begging."

Leong struggled to keep from grimacing at this source of wonder. He had known Victoria for years. As a matter of fact, now that she was in front of him, he remembered that it was in her district and under her supervision that he had begun his career with government. Apparently her naivete, even after so many years, was still with her. But then, European women came out of a different culture. They were notoriously thin-skinned, a characteristic often useful in welfare work. He smiled weakly, friendly, wondering if her concern over one beggar came from worry about the boy or from finding him in someone else's district. They were equal in rank, but the color of her skin opened doors above him. Considering his reply carefully, to guard against upsetting her, he asked, "What do you suggest?"

"An end to it, of course," she answered quickly.

"Of course," he agreed. The next step was to determine how. "Did you get close enough to hear if the beggar was asking for money?"

She furrowed her brow as she turned away to look out the high window. There was action in the yacht basin. Pleasure-boat owners would be cursing the working junk masters for blocking the channel this weekend. Everyone in government knew there were enough welfare organizations, both public and private, to support the few blind. Giving to beggars just kept them on the streets. It encouraged them to stay away from official sources of help. She glanced back at Harry. He was waiting for her reply. She sighed. The only sound to come from her memory was the wonderful reward of excitement her coin had brought to the boy's voice. She let both the picture and the sound return to touch her as strongly as it had the first time. "No," she elected to say. "He just stood there. Begging. Holding out his cup."

Leong cocked his head to take his turn at looking out the window. "You know he wasn't begging, don't you?" he suggested meekly, trying to feel her out. After a moment, a moment in which she refused to commit herself, he turned bravely, straight in his chair, folded his hands, leaned forward and stared at her. From the way she refused to look at him he knew she understood the law. "A man must ask for money before he's guilty of begging," he reminded her nevertheless. The words had no sooner come out than he regretted saying them. He was forcing her to either admit that she did not know the law. or that she did know the law and was searching for something else, something she wanted him to guess at. "Did he ask," he began again, "either with some physical motion, some personal contact, or . . . or in some verbal, solicitous way?"

She glanced alternatcly from her lap to the window. Harry had explained what she already knew, and now he was moving in the direction she had thought she wanted him to move when she first came in. No longer sure she wanted him along, she remained silent.

"There's a case on record," he went on, trying to ease her embarrassment, "where a beggar held a sign that read 'Help thc Blind' but said nothing. Remember it?" he asked, reaching for a stack of folders and pretending to go through them as if the case might be among them. "The magistrate ruled the man wasn't begging." The recollection amused him. "And we thought we could use the law to get him!"

To hide her feelings Miss Bishop feigned anger. "Harry, I'm not out to *get* anyone! All I'd like to do is *help* someone."

He breathed deeply, then let the air escape slowly. The laws often made it difficult to do what was right. Just as often the same laws made it easy to do what was wrong. "Perhaps there's some other way," he compromised. "Maybe we can help the boy some other way. Is that what you want?"

A tinge of desperation flicked through her. She had been foolish to burden Harry with her problem. Legally there was nothing either of them could do; she should have considered that fact before coming. Her case rested in her emotions, and emotions were neither used nor understood by the Chinese. The Chinese acted as though revealing one's emotions was both sinful and inhuman. "Maybe a school," she suggested, trying to escape the increasing pressure. "Didn't we make attendance for a few hours a day a mandatory requirement?"

"I don't remember," he lied amiably. She was grasping for a release. If she were Chinese instead of English he could change the subject and let her escape. "Perhaps he goes to school in the morning and begs in the afternoon. Did you ask him?"

"No."

He sighed, wishing her to be Chinese so he too might escape. "When we first started the schools . . . on the Hong Kong side . . . we tried to get cooperation from the parents. We couldn't. These people never keep in touch," he moaned, hoping she would see him siding with her race against his. "Too busy trying to earn a living I imagine. A poor excuse. They should think more of their children's futures. The children beg because their parents want them to beg. When the parents aren't interested in talking about it . . . what can we do? They move to another shack so we can't find them."

"I know, I know," she mumbled, warming to his begging for her understanding.

"Did you get his name?" he went on. "Is he registered?"

The question shamed her. Officially she knew nothing about the beggar. "He had a red and white cane, the same type the Junior Chamber gives at registration," she said, remembering, "so I assume he's in the books."

"Was he dirty? Did he look like he's been living in the streets?" he went on, attempting to force her either to open up or give up. If she was as concerned as she pretended to be, she needed help. Hong Kong had its professionals the same as every port. If she had wandered the battery at night when the sailors were in and had seen all the kids begging she would have had reason for concern. Along the wharf the children did more than beg. They pimped also. Professional beggars and pimps did better with professional travelers. They understood each other's moods and needs.

"He was poorly dressed," she said, redrawing a mental picture of Po, "but clean. Very clean. So neat as to be attractive." She smiled, pleased at remembering so accurately what she had seen. "His efforts to keep up his appearance made me think he'd welcome some help."

"He doesn't appear to be a regular," Harry decided. "Unless some new organizer is cleaning his kids up and spreading them out. Fifty percent of nothing might be forcing some of them into giving the kids clean clothes and working them downtown. Did he have any money? Were people giving?"

The two silver dollars clanged noisily in Miss Bishop's conscience. The coins took an imaginary trip from the boy's cup to some fat, greasy, greedy, smiling organizer who was using the boy's blindness to make himself rich. The scene sickened her and made her determined to do something to stop it. But Harry could be wrong. This beggar was different. This one needed her. "No," she told him, "his cup was empty."

Leong leaned back in his chair, cupped his hands and held them to his lips, and stared at her while he concentrated. She had gone close enough to the boy to see the empty cup, close enough to hear if he spoke to anyone, and close enough to describe his clothing vividly. She knew the laws and their helplessness in such situations. There was no need for him to suggest that the boy might be faking blindness, she would fight him on that.

When his re-examination failed to uncover whatever it was she wanted of him, he pleaded with her, "What's wrong, Victoria? Is this boy a friend of a friend? A son or relative of a particularly unworthy client, one who should not guardian him? Is that it?"

She breathed deep her consternation. "No," she hummed slowly, "it isn't anything like that at all. I don't know him or about him. I just think he should be helped."

"I agree," he answered quickly, sympathetically, "but how? You know how it is. When you see the first beggar . . . you suffer. After that you tell yourself you can forget them as easily as you see them. It isn't true, of course, but when you can do it, it doesn't hurt so much anymore. We have enough organizations to help such children. They don't need us," he added, begging her to leave him alone. "Most likely the boy has already refused official help. Perhaps he thinks he can make more money by begging than by working in some factory for the handicapped. Maybe his family wants him to earn money so they can go back home, up north somewhere." He paused, then continued, remembering other cases. "Besides, he needs something to do. He'll probably beg for a couple of days and then give up when he finds he's not making as much money as he thought he would."

And again the two silver dollars squeezed Miss Bishop's conscience painfully. "I don't know about that," she confessed. "Harry, maybe for the first time I'm seeing a welfare client as a human being, an individual, one who needs me. Not as a statistic, not as a black name scribbled on a piece of paper." She sighed, defeated. Harry was asking her to describe a woman's feelings rather than a beggar's right to be helped. "Harry, are we getting too hardhearted? Are we getting like . . . " she paused to wave an arm in a sweep to include the whole outdoors, "like those people out there who have given up and don't care any more? Are we getting ourselves so wrapped up in our own lives that we haven't the time to suffer the trials of someone else's life?"

"Conditions do that," he argued defiantly, feeling a racial demand to defend his people. "They're too poor to help each other."

"I'm sorry," she said penitently, yet knowing what she had said was true. Harry was different. Accusing him through a generalization was unfair. He had worked in government so long he was almost English. "Somewhere in my past I've missed something. I don't know what. Seeing this boy has brought it out." She relaxed, enjoying the relief her confession had brought. "I've seen a lot of child beggars, regardless of what you might think," she guessed, and saw his nervous flinch tell her how accurate the guess had been. "They're bad to have around. They leave visitors with terrible impressions."

The confession, so distasteful for revealing a weakness, yet so understandable for a woman, turned Leong to worrying about being as hardhearted as she had accused his people of being. He had tolerated the young beggars by not comparing them with the fate of his own children. Perhaps she needed to worry about all children. "Would you like to have one of my men go back with you?" he asked, suspecting her pride would keep her from forgetting the boy. "He could follow the beggar home and bring a charge against the parents for being mendicants."

"That wouldn't help the boy," she complained methodically. "That would only teach him to mistrust his parents. He might need his parents as much as he needs us." She stopped talking to let a hint escape from what she had just said. It was possible the boy had no parents. No parents existed in her mind when she dropped the silver coins. On sight, he was an orphan who begged for money to buy food, money to keep himself alive. Why had she not expected he might have parents? "And there's no need for your man to go with me," she added coolly. "The boy won't be there any more today. He goes away early."

Harry lifted his eyebrows in open surprise. She

knew more about the boy than she wanted anyone to know. "All right," he agreed, willing to let the case close itself. "Are you going to pursue it?" he asked cautiously.

"Perhaps," she answered, trying to sound undecided. She wore a false smile while getting out of the chair. "Perhaps I'll come back Monday afternoon and take you up on that offer for help."

After leaving the office Miss Bishop felt relief. Sharing the problem had helped just as refusing to give it away had helped. By the time she reached the tram station outside the Magistracy Building she had relegated her relationship with Harry to a distance reserved for strangers. Years ago they had been rather close. At least she had thought they were. When Harry learned she was coming to Hong Kong to be his boss he had invited her to his home for dinner and to meet his family. It was a nice thing to do. It seemed warm and friendly—at the time. His children and young cousins called her Auntie Victoria. They were so cute and lovable.

But then the years of experience taught her caution. Chinese took friends like they took money; their purpose was to get something in exchange for friendship. Although she never learned exactly what it was Harry's family wanted to get from her, she suspected it was employment in the government for more family members. They had not "adopted" her, they had just used her visits to test her. Before a single member of the family could have a friend, even Harry, the whole family had to pass judgment. When she learned what they were doing she resented it, resented them for it, and most of all resented Harry for trying to use her. When Harry transferred to the Hong Kong side, her visits to his house soon stopped. He said he wanted the transfer because his new office would be closer to his home.

Now she worried that she had revealed too much in the way of incompetence to Harry today. The boy was begging in Harry's district. A phone call would have fulfilled her duties. She shrugged, bravely telling herself she had nothing to fear from Harry. He would not fight her and he would not take her problem to his white superiors. Chinese just did not do such things to other whites. Most likely, she decided, he would not discuss it with his family either. Some of his children might still like her in spite of what she suspected he might be teaching them. For Harry to explain what had transpired in his office would require him to first accuse her of being prejudiced against the Chinese, and that would be hard to do since the beggar was Chinese. She could get Harry's help, one way or another, if she needed it. The closeness of their past friendship had earned her that much.

And, she decided, since she was feeling better, the blind beggar had no parents. He kept himself clean because he was a naturally clean child. Instead of taking the tram she elected to walk back to the city. During the walk she might accidently find the boy curled in some corner, alone. He had to live nearby. He earned too little money to spend it on trams, and being blind he would not walk very far.

From the moment the second dollar touched the bottom of Po's cup his anxieties vanished to make room for his zooming spirits. The heights of last night came closer. The second coin had dropped at approximately the same time as had the first, and it had

happened on consecutive days. This woman, the dollars helping him forget that she was white, could be
the customer of habit that Au had dared to suggest she
might be.

Po's delight was infectious. Donors, touched by
the happiness radiating from a face reason said should
be somber, reached into their pockets a second time to
see if they could buy a little more from the cup. Many
who passed regularly without giving the beggar a
second glance found themselves digging for a small
coin that might enable them to share whatever it was
that so pleased the beggar. Associating with someone
experiencing luck was a wise thing to do.

To Po, everything over the first two dollars that
day brought the dream of the tea shop just that much
closer to reality. During the afternoon's waning hours
his left side got weary from pushing itself against the
fence. Yet he took fewer breaks. He dreamed away the
endless minutes by teasing himself. He let his imagination build the tea shop. The shop had to have living
quarters. All shops had living quarters. Or did they?
Never mind, this one would. If they could sleep inside
the place at night there would be no need for sixty
dollars a month rent money. There would be no need
to work anywhere outside the shop. No one worked
elsewhere when their family owned a respectable tea
shop!

The busy mind concentrated on the glass counter
and how it must feel under his touch. Was there more
than just a glass top? Did the glass hide something?
Something he was to guard or to sell? His unanswerable questions piled one on top of the other until he
feared he would forget them before seeing Au again.

Better still, why not ask Au the questions—inside the tea shop! Tonight!

When his work day finally ended, Po's mind had no room for any thought other than the dream of visiting the tea shop.

Chen was also stimulated to new ways of thinking by the repeated appearance of the white woman at his newsstand. When his evening customers had lingered, read as much as they dared without buying, and finally left, he fingered through the long undisturbed piles of magazines and sorted out those old beyond belief. Those with the most vividly suggestive pictures were worn from excessive handling and got wrapped into a bundle. He took them to the used magazine stalls along the waterfront where they could be sold by someone else to the coolies working the sampans and junks, coolies too poor to have wives, concubines, or the money for a prostitute.

Sold in bulk, the old magazines brought only a fraction of their original cost. He chalked off the loss as a necessary part of keeping his customers happy. New magazines might lure a few new customers. The editions bought as replacements were selected very carefully. Lesser known publications, their aging was not apt to be recognized for some time.

CHAPTER FIVE

The coolie pulled his wheeled shop along the curb, in the gutter, empty. The bright red rickshaw, with him so long, would have been as incomplete without him as he would be without it. As he walked he peeked back toward the strollers on the sidewalk. A mischievous smile told him he had recognized what his eyes saw.

The girl, hiding behind the darkness of sunglasses, played the expected role—that of a virgin experienced in being accosted by devils. Still, she shot quick glances at the coolie and allowed a bit of business to interfere with the pleasures of her performance. Pretending to be a virgin or innocent or a wealthy man's mistress was fun but it brought her no money. And being without money was no fun.

She continued her sidewise glances while trying

to judge the rickshaw coolie's expertise. Some coolies brought tramps, cheap sadistic animals looking for a thrill without wanting to pay what the thrill was worth. The right coolies had a knack for finding the right men, men willing to pay without being too demanding. This one she studied carefully since she was tired of walking the streets to advertise with her eyes, smiles, and body. To have customers brought to her would be an improvement.

The coolie was too poor to play games. He appraised openly what he saw in the girl. He needed a girl capable of making a man happy enough to come back again and again. He needed a girl beautiful enough to entice good money, yet not so beautiful as to steal away a customer by living with him. This one looked young, yet tired. He smiled appreciatively at her act; no innocent virgin walked with the unconscious moves this girl had. She might be useful. His regular customers were seeing too much of the same girls. The feel of youth, the thrill of conquering, and the education in new methods were over. His customers were begging him to find someone new for them. And, unless he appeased them soon, they would go to new coolies with different contacts. Also, some of the old girls were taking advantage of his long friendship. They stalled their kickbacks. They even tried to pleasure him out of the money they owed. Yes, he needed this girl.

Po, in his hurry to get home so he could spread the good news of the second dollar, heard no squeaking wheels or the sounds of bare feet slapping on the pavement. He stepped carelessly off the curb. The coolie, still undecided as to how he should approach the girl without destroying her game with his frankness, was looking back. Coolie and beggar collided, sprawling recklessly on the street.

The girl walked on, laughing. The accident made her decision for her. Only an idiot would walk into a blind boy. The coolie got off the pavement, pulled his rickshaw in close where it belonged, and cursed the lost opportunity as he brushed dirt from his clothes.

The beggar got up angrily and quickly walked away, firmly clutching the coins in his pocket. He dared rattle the coins while checking them. They were all in the pocket where they belonged.

"You tore your trousers!" Chung-kin scolded as soon as her son came in the room.

"I fell," he whined childishly. After a moment, however, her power to reduce him to childhood angered him. He paid the rent; there was no need for him to cower in her presence. Yet, Au would also scold him if he irritated her. "I'll be glad," he said, attempting to appease her, "when we get the tea shop. Then I won't have to walk the streets any longer."

"What tea shop?" Chung-kin scoffed.

He jerked in recognition of his stupidity. Had he let slip the valuable secret he shared with Au? "Didn't father tell you?" he asked, feigning innocence.

"Your father tells me many things," she joked while running her finger through the torn trouser leg and wondering how to fix it. "Some of them I believe and some I don't."

"But the tea shop would be good for us," he argued, wanting to build her enthusiasm to where it might support his. No longer wanting to deny her the right to share the dream, he added, "I think it's a good scheme."

She backed away. His face, tilted downward, expressionless, said his mind was busy. He had talked to her as though still a child. Perhaps he was, or perhaps it was her attitude toward him that forced him to act so childishly. Out of her fear of the compounding of his difficulties as he grew older, she might be denying him his right to manhood. When he got older she would no longer be able to help him. Now, at least, he had dreams. Denying him dreams would be denying him his right to happiness.

"Many of your father's schemes are good," she conceded, "but they are also impossible. Where will he get the money?" Inside the torn trouser his leg had felt muscular, hard. Food and exercise had put meat around the bones that had carried him into Hong Kong. And the feeling of usefulness that came from begging had expanded his mind. He was a son to be proud of. She allowed her pride to flow, knowing he would feel it although unable to see it.

"Mother!" he barked, suddenly remembering. "The woman came back this afternoon! She gave me another dollar!" He reached anxiously into his pocket and pulled out the handful of change, and again, as he had the previous night, he splashed the coins in the middle of the table. He smiled, pleased and proud, his head held alert to the sound of her movements as she approached the table.

Chung-kin sat silently on the stool while the coins, lying there, teasing her obstinacy, worked on her doubts. Was it possible? A dollar a day? Certainly nothing to a rich, white foreign woman. Although it would take more than a dollar a day to buy a tea shop, the possibility, if all three worked to realize the same goal, was still there. She stared down at the silver coin, trying to see in it a change of luck for the family.

Surely to save money was good, even if the reason for saving was questionable. It was also possible that the luxury of wild dreams might change the family's luck. She and Au might need the dream more than Po did.

Not quick to voice optimistic conclusions, Chung-kin decided to calm Po's enthusiasm, to keep a false dream from harming him later. "This is good news," she agreed calmly, "but let's be patient. Let's not spend the money before we get it," she recited maternally as she patted his arm.

The change in her attitude, however intuitive, encouraged Po. She had hinted a desire to join his dream. It was better now to leave the subject. She had granted him the privilege of thinking about the tea shop. If he persisted verbally, she might withdraw the concession.

When Au came home he knew what had happened that day by just looking at Po's face. The face had a subdued, complacent smile. The table was set for dinner with the dishes spread in a circle around a small, unstacked pile of coins. The silver flash told Au he had guessed correctly. He watched as Po's hand reached nervously out to feel the coin, assuring himself that the coin was there for Au to see. The movement caused Au to smile. His was a good family. It shared. He walked to the table to touch both the coins and the small hand alongside the coins. "We'll put it away," he suggested.

No reference to the coin was made during dinner. All three, allowing themselves to be guided by inner fears, aimed the conversation to safer grounds lest their hopes be uncovered and squashed. Both Au and Po revealed their emotions through nervous actions, while Chung-kin cloaked her happiness in a sullen pretense. Each told himself he was doing what the others expected of him.

When the meal was finished Po went quickly to the hallway, hurrying the nightly routine. Hearing Au follow, he waited until the door clicked shut. "Father!" he whispered excitedly.

"Let's go to the tea shop," Au suggested immediately, knowing Po wanted to hear. He pulled at Po's loose fitting coat to lead the boy from the doorway, and stayed close as they took the steps. "When we get inside the shop we must remember to say nothing that can be overheard. Rumors spread fast among those with nothing to do. We cannot give away our secret!" Au emphasized, thus hoping to give the dream an extended life.

On the busy sidewalk it was impossible for them to walk abreast so Au went first, reaching behind to guide Po and keep him from getting bumped. Noise kept both from trying to speak as they went. To keep nervous excitement from getting the best of him, Po concentrated on matching Au's short, dodging steps. Au's speed, plus his own preoccupation, confused Po—he was lost until a cloud of disturbing, dusty air broke his rhythm and he stumbled to the pavement. Somewhere inside the smell hung the answers to his daytime questions. He struggled for footing until Au's hands reached him.

Au pulled Po upright and half slid him to the protection of the curb where the pillars supporting the upper levels of the building slowed foot traffic. "The shop is dirty," he noticed immediately. "Poorly lit. They have very few customers, not many people eat their dinners here. The man behind the glass counter must be the owner. He's fat, reading a newspaper, picking his teeth. Some of the unused tables have dirty teacups and bowls standing," he went on, knowing he was encouraging both himself and Po with what he observed.

Po, engaged in a losing war with his patience, began tugging at Au to lead him closer to the shop.

Au waited until a reasonable opening appeared in the walking traffic, then signaled by calling, "Now!"

Feeling composed under Au's leadership, Po walked into the shop so naturally that his handicap went unnoticed. To stay inconspicuous Au squeezed Po into the first available bench, one next to the wall. Sitting together, facing the empty bench on the table's opposite side, they had reached their goal without drawing any unwanted attention.

Secure in being pinned tight between his father on one side and the wall on the other, Po settled quickly. The wall stretched upward as far as he dared feel. He sucked in a deep sigh. All the answers to his questions were before him, waiting to be dug out from the terrain of the enemy. The table had a hard, smooth top with a rough underside. A common piece of wood, like that used on the fence in the lane where he worked, but covered with something hard. The bench had been made of two pieces of wood nailed together, carelessly, since the crack between the boards was wide and easily felt. The wall had the touch of plaster over brick like the walls of the flat. In roaming his finger-eyes over the table's surface, Po found only an overfilled ashtray and a small glass supporting upright toothpicks. When curiosity within reach was satisfied, he searched beyond. "What's inside the glass counter?" he whispered. "Can you see?"

Au glanced at the cash desk beneath the owner's

spread newspaper. "Cigarettes and old newspapers," he whispered back. Leaning forward, he rubbed his hand over the back of his head as an excuse for pulling near his son. "The cigarettes are cheap brands," he added. "Several packages have been opened. I guess they sell one cigarette at a time."

"Old newspapers aren't worth anything!" Po said, remembering what Chen had told him. "What's on top of the counter?" he asked, searching further. "What does the man have with him for his work?"

Au looked back once more. "A small pad for writing. Probably uses it for adding. I don't see an abacus so he doesn't have much to add," he said and smiled at this observation.

A stranger came out of nowhere to disturb the plotting. When he sat on the empty bench facing Au and Po his knees touched theirs under the table. When Po jerked at the touch, it drew the stranger's attention and caused him to straighten his slouch.

Po, holding himself both speechless and motionless, was convinced the intruder was a spy. Their scheme had been uncovered. He stiffened in defense while waiting for Au to say something, anything, either to him or to the stranger in a way of explanation. As the seconds of silence passed he gave up a second hope—that the visitor was a friend of Au's. Time caused his head to bob in tiny searches as it tried to discern small sounds. Slowly his hands came up from beneath the table to renew their search, prodding the unknown without realizing they could be seen.

The stranger's eyes went from the peculiar actions of the boy's hands to the face. He dipped slightly to look up into the hidden features. From the closed eyes that failed to follow the movements of the hands, he drew his conclusion. In seconds he decided the abnormality was unpleasant and he got up to find another table.

"He's gone," Au said.

"Was it the owner?" Po wondered, sure by now that they had been discovered.

"No," Au answered calmly. "A stranger joined our table for a minute. He left when he saw a friend across the room," he lied.

After a time much too long for good business, yet too short for anyone wishing to observe without being observed, the waiter came. He sauntered recklessly, bumping into chairs and tables, until, an unkempt figure of impatience, he loomed at Au's shoulder. Guessing beforehand that a pencil and paper would not be needed, he left both in his apron pocket.

"Tea," Au told him tersely, trying to establish his authority.

"Is that all?" the man asked, obviously unimpressed.

"For now," Au explained, holding his pretense by not looking up.

The waiter radiated scorn downward until convinced it was being wasted, then walked away, peering with indignation over his shoulder, hoping to score belatedly.

"It's best to make them think we might order something more," Au instructed. "The service should be better if he thinks we'll buy something more after we finish the tea."

"What does he look like?" Po wondered.

"Like a relative," Au answered quickly and laughed. It fit. "His apron is dirty and his hair isn't combed. Not the type of man anyone should hire to improve business. He looks like a cousin," he decided, and laughed some more.

The tea came spilling out on the table as the waiter in passing roughly set down the pot. Au turned the two glasses right side up and began pouring.

Po's hand stretched automatically to touch the sound teasing his ears. He felt the glass and felt the heat of the tea. The glass was greasy—too many hands had touched it before his without their touch having been washed away. The glass was chipped dangerously around its upper rim. His prejudiced tongue found the tea too weak to be of any medicinal or nourishing value. Still, in the silence of that first sip he discovered the satisfaction he needed. In it was the novelty of doing something in secret. Once again the finger scouts explored the table. The waiter had brought no sugar. Sugar was meant to be free. Po preferred tea without sugar since sugar could spoil his teeth, but when it was free it was meant to be used.

"How many people will the shop hold?" he asked after the warm liquid had had time to excite his stomach.

Au began a whispered count. "There are three tables in the center of the room with four stools around each. That's twelve. There are four tables along each side. Each table has two benches, two people to a bench. That means thirty-two people can be seated along the walls, plus twelve in the center of the room . . . forty-four people!" he totaled in astonishment. It was much higher than he had guessed before counting. "No, two people on a bench like we're sitting on is too much. One person to a bench or eight people along each wall, with twelve in the center, would be more comfortable and more accurate. Still, twenty-eight is a pleasing total."

As Au had thought, two people on one bench was too many. To prove it, Po had allowed himself to suffer from being crushed between Au and the wall. If they stayed two on one bench the people would stare at them. "Move to the other bench," Po said, pushing an elbow against Au, "so no more strangers come to sit with us." The wood wiggled as Au moved out to the other side. Their knees now touched beneath the table. It was better.

Whispering secrets across the table presented too many problems so both stayed silent. And in the silence they calculated. Knowing only the maximum number of customers that could be served at one time, their guesses were worthless. The variables in both number of customers and amount each would spend were variables the imagination could distort, either way. In Po the figure exploded. It grew so large it had to be discarded. His answer was too big to fit his hope of the owner's going bankrupt—he came on this mission to find failure, not success.

Au played with guessing the shop's profit but gave up quickly. Buying the place was a dream to be kept alive for its intrinsic use. Instead of telling Po there was no exact answer to the problem, he allowed Po to do as he wished, as he had to do to keep the dream valuable. As he stared across the table at Po he wondered what the stranger, just moments ago, had found so unpleasant about the boy's face. Po was handsome. His face was not off-balance as it might have been had the blindness come from a prenatal accident. It was also a happy face. Po's delight in the secret mission was ill hidden.

As Au continued staring, he became blessed with Po's pleasure. It was infectious, it made Au happy to see in his son what he wanted for himself. The smile, reaching across the table, penetrated, explaining Po's success as a beggar. Au let the feeling of happiness build recklessly, until shame crept in also and injured the feeling. People with a lot of money to give, gave to institutions and not to single beggars. There were contradicting stories, but they came from opera and not from truth. The white woman's dollars would stop. Au knew they would. But he did not have the strength to tell Po. Buying the tea shop was a subterfuge, a comic opera, an escape from reality. His shame hardened. He was the weaker of the two since he was leaning on Po's vulnerability to brighten his hopes. Instead of lightening Po's life, he was begging Po to lighten his.

To stop his thoughts from further pricking his conscience, Au waved for the waiter. The waiter's speed, explained by his efforts to promote a tip, gave Au an outlet for his self-disgust. Everything about the man was wrong as he touched with his moving pencil the two empty cups of tea.

Po's turning an ear instead of his face to the sounds of the pencil clicking against the two glasses and then scratching on the pad drew the waiter's curiosity. He stared down long at Po, then appeared dumbfounded at discovering the blindness. He allowed the oddity to produce a small smile, and, like all unusual events, it had to be shared. As though uncovering a trick meant to deceive him, he spun around to punch attention into a few friends sitting nearby. When the deception had been explained, the friends laughed also. They too had been fooled.

"Let's go," Au instructed Po angrily. He grabbed the check out of the waiter's hand and led Po toward the counter.

When they reached the glass counter perched at the sidewalk's edge Po stealthily ran his hand along its top and corners to determine its size. The appraisal was stopped midway as Au jerked him out into the street.

"He didn't even look up from his newspaper when I dropped the money!"

Hearing that made Po happy. The owner had laid himself open to cheating. In this knowledge Po found a way for the man to lose his business. "How much was the tea?" he asked, searching for a means to strengthen his dream. For not concentrating on walking he got kicked by a pedestrian.

"Forty cents!" Au growled, another target on which he could vent his disgust. "Forty cents for two teas coming from the same pot!" He silently scolded himself for not having the courage to sit longer without buying anything. "At the shop next to the poultry market I get a whole pot of tea for twenty cents," he complained.

And Po chalked up still another reason to expect bankruptcy.

Au's disgust lessened as he watched Po's excitement increase.

By the time they reached the flat Po learned that the tea he had detested for its weakness and expense was nevertheless soothing to his nerves. Happy with how his mind was willing to let this night end, he crawled into bed and fell asleep. The night had been extracted out of the silver coin. He dreamed of the joy the silver's power had brought him.

Pleased with himself for having brought some excitement into Po's life, Au let his contentment overcome his sense of guilt. He waited for Po to fall asleep and then he went to share Chung-kin's cot. He ran his hand over the swell of her body where the new child was growing. The night was dedicated to deception. He had fooled Po, had fooled himself if only for a few hours, and now wanted to believe the silver coin could justify bringing into this world another member of the family. "If the next one is as wise as this one," he whispered to Chung-kin, "and has eyes . . . we'll not have to work in our old age." As he lay next to her he allowed his wishes to infiltrate reality. One day, after many more were born, they would all go back north to the land of their ancestors.

On Sunday Au and Po stayed late in bed, secretly attempting to stretch the holiday's luxury. Chung-kin moved around carefully to keep from upsetting the daydreamers. For breakfast she cooked Shanghai cabbage mixed with slender pieces of pork, steamed fresh rice as a treat to those whose happiness made her happy, and smiled at seeing the odors pull the two lazy bodies closer to her. The breakfast had been planned to entice them to open their secrets to her, yet she suspected their secrets might not survive the reality of daylight. So she refused to ask.

Po waited until he heared Au get out of bed before doing the same. They washed together and saved together the dirty water to use in flushing the toilet. The building's underground well had gone dry and the family, along with most families on the island, had given up trying to guess how many inches of rain would have to come to fill the empty cavities beneath the city. The government had its figures, but the citizens chose not to believe what the white people handed out to the yellow people who wrote news-papers. It was safer to assume that the foreigners had secrets to keep just as everyone else did.

The good breakfast worked its intended purpose. Loose talk cracked the curtain of resistance between male and female as Au openly discussed the visit to the tea shop, the discoveries, the surmises, the future dreams, and the confirmed prejudices. He watched pleased as his dreams embraced his wife. She con-tinued to fight outwardly what she also needed to accept inwardly. She exaggerated the difficulties of owning and operating a small shop, and Au suspected she did it because she knew both he and Po needed someone negative to offset their foolishness. The work involved, the gamble, the trials unknown to all of them, were elaborated by Chung-kin with gleaming eyes that belied her voiced doubts. She shyly refused Au the pleasure of laughing into her eyes by hiding them from him, and laughed along with him while he explained to Po what was happening. Merchants lived in beautiful flats outside the city on the income they received. They tried to hide their financial wealth just as Au and Po and Chung-kin were trying to hide their wealth of happiness.

The meal and its subject were linked; to end one was to end the other. So both were sustained with cup after cup of tea until the tea became as cold as the subject. Au and Po in unison teased Chung-kin's efforts to belittle the silver coins and the possibility of getting an extra thirty dollars a month. Teasing, it seemed, was what she wanted them to do. She poked back at them until she could control herself no longer. She laughed.

She laughed until she choked, and choked until it was abnormal.

The enjoyment, fondled so carefully, drained away. Chung-kin, pale with nausea, began to remove the dishes. Her illness, a plague crawling beneath the surface, threatening the family's blossoms, ended the happy mood of breakfast. To prevent the oncoming depression, Au concluded the old subject by saying all extra money would be put into the tea tin until it grew high enough to support a hope. Yet, with Chinese caution, he quickly warned the money must be kept covered, hidden, the door locked, and they must all be quiet about what they had lest outsiders learn of it and try to take it from them.

Thus the subject of the tea shop was closed, while its promise was kept open so it might creep through lowered guards.

To get back into the safety of habit, the balance of the morning was spent washing heads. The task became painstakingly slow as each member of the family made an effort to be falsely loud and falsely content. Evil devils lurked in empty lives, but they shied from lives strong in family union and contentment. Neither Chung-kin's upset stomach nor new sources of wealth were mentioned. Po tried to ignore the many questions that kept creeping into his mind. While Chung-kin worked to make a good, clean part in his freshly scrubbed hair he wondered if the tea shop had living quarters in the rear. Au had said nothing about it, and he had forgotten to ask. After Chung-kin set the part he tried hard to keep his hands from going up to feel it.

By afternoon the battle of strength versus hidden evil had become tired. To get away, Po went downstairs and sat on the last step facing the doorway. Since it was Sunday, the sidewalk was more congested than usual. Babies wanting to crawl over him kept him from concentrating on unfamiliar sounds. To escape the children before they messed his hair, he took a long walk up and then down Lyndhurst—but was careful not to be seen near the tea shop.

It was not until the day had reached its end that Po realized how he had wasted it. Instead of sauntering away the hours he should have been concentrating on devising a scheme that would allow Au to mark the customers' bills in the tea shop so that only Po could read them. The customers would cheat him because of his blindness just as they must be cheating the present owner who blinded himself by inattention. The search for a solution stayed with him, exhausting him for sleep.

The next morning, Monday, was late in arriving. Daylight had to fight to break the grizzly dark, foggy sky, and the air swirled dust in little eddies as the winds whipped around the corners of the cement city. In spite of the dark, fast-moving clouds no one bothered to look up hopefully for rain just as no one bothered to carry an umbrella. The rainy season had ended. Even if it had not, too many promises brought by damp mornings like this in the past had been left unfulfilled. Hope had died. It was safer to assume rain would never come. If a typhoon was developing somewhere in the vast China ocean the event of its birth would be great enough to be heralded in the newspapers.

Those with places to go grumbled their way, getting a mouthful of dust with every audible curse. The streets were ripped open over the many places where sewers had clogged from too much waste and not enough water, and the wind lifted the loose dirt and stacked it in secluded corners. The employed, those able to own the prestige of a cloth handkerchief, covered their faces to keep out the dust and filter out the repugnant odor of the open sewers. The poor turned off their senses. To the white-collar workers, Monday meant the beginning of another week. To the majority of workers, those who worked seven days, Monday meant nothing. The past week had neither begun nor ended, just as this one would neither begin nor end.

The morning was marked for Po by its peculiar beginning. This morning he had not been awakened by the sound of Chung-kin's slippers shuffling, or by the rattling of breakfast dishes, or by a reminder that he had better get out of bed if he wished to be on time for the arrival of the early ferry. He just awoke. Startled by the strangeness, he sat up, listened, and wondered if it might still be night. Sounds familiar to morning came to him through the open window, but the sounds in the room remained strange. There was choking in the corner. The gurgling barks produced a rancid odor and were accompanied by Au's whispers.

"Is something wrong?" Po called out.

"Your mother is sick. You'll have to take care of yourself this morning."

"Is she very sick?" Po asked, then wondered how sick that might be.

"No," Au answered. "It's not unusual for a woman in your mother's condition being sick in the morning."

It was morning. Po turned to get out of bed. What condition? He didn't remember Au saying anything about his mother's condition. The bedclothes felt damp from the foggy air seeping through the window all night. He dressed and reached for his stool at the table. It was gone. Au must be using it. He touched his hair gently, worried about the damage done to it by the night's sleep. The room's odor got stronger as he concentrated on it. The choking of Chung-kin continued until the smell made him feel like choking himself. The water buckets were kept in the corner by Chung-kin's cot. He wondered if he should go after one, or if he should give up washing. "Can mother talk?" he asked, feeling no dishes spread on the table. He shuffled to the shelf for a bowl and scooped into a handful of cold rice kept in a box since yesterday.

"Of course," Au replied. "She'll be all right."

"There's some cabbage in the small bowl," Chung-kin called, begging Po to eat.

He did. He ate standing. His fingers had already found the cabbage. The smell of the cabbage mixed badly with the odor in the room so he ate only the rice. To end the trial of having to eat under such adverse conditions he raked the food into his mouth and then felt the table's surface for a damp cloth. He stood, waiting, hoping Au would remember what he always did next.

"Take this one."

The pushed water bucket bumped his leg. It was one of the odorous ones. He held it at arm's length while negotiating his way down the hall to the toilet where the smell might be flushed away along with the smell of what he had to leave. With concentrated effort he finished quickly and discovered in his speed a fear of being late for work.

In his preoccupation with haste Po overlooked the exceptional cold of the morning until he turned down the ladder street. But when the cold at last got through his coat and into his body he began to think about it. The missing warmth of the sun by the bank's corner confirmed what he already knew. Nevertheless, he stopped out of habit and bemoaned the cold, his mother's illness, the indecent breakfast, and the probability that the flat's odor was sticking to his clothing. After putting all these evils together he had to add the fact that people knew his cup held no power to affect the weather. The day's total would be small.

By noon he garnered his courage and counted the day's take to prove that the morning prediction had become a fact. The total, less than average, even for a Monday, even for a cold day, was near disaster. And now it had to be subtracted further. He had forgotten to take a lunch, the lunch that his mother always put into his pocket.

"Mr. Chen?" he called quietly as he walked toward the old man's stand.

"Yes?"

"I have no lunch," he complained. He lowered himself to the curb beneath the bars of the fence. It was a bitter world. "When the boy comes will you buy something for me?"

"Ribs and rice," Chen recited. He watched Po's hand explore the magazine rack. "Every Monday, ribs and rice. Thirty-five cents," he warned, alert and suspicious of the unusual visit. "Why aren't you begging?"

"I don't beg," Po admonished angrily.

"Working then," Chen rationalized.

Po grunted. Getting angry solved nothing. It made him feel worse instead of better. To expect the bad day to change by changing his habits took more strength than he cared to spend. He dropped a hand into the pocket and singled out seven five-cent coins to hand out. "Here," he called as he waved the coins in the air in the direction of Chen.

Chen sat on his heels alongside the stand as he ate. "Bad day?" he asked, prodding Po and interrupting the boy's lunch. He eyed a few office workers who were promenading away their lunch periods in the threatening weather. Negatively he concluded they were not worth watching. "Bad day for me too," he noted when Po failed to answer. Sure enough, the walkers refused to buy any newspapers. They never did on dark days. People bought when the sun shined and saved their money on dark days.

While Chen spit out the small talk of his miseries, Po dwelled on his loss of income. He was particularly upset about having to pay thirty-five cents for lunch. If he had had a good breakfast he might have been able to bypass lunch. He leaned back against the bars. Steel bars, widely spaced, fencing in nothing. He could squeeze through them if he tried. Chen had said there was nothing but grass on the other side. Just grass. No buildings, no shops, no homes. Only grass. It was foolish to build a fence to keep people away from nothing. Foreigners were foolish that way, Chen had said they were. In Canton there were fences also. High fences topped with broken glass embedded in cement. Fences that kept the poor people away from the rich people. High fences were deceiving. A rich man could build a high fence around nothing and everyone would think it hid something. In Canton the fences were solid, solid like walls. Strong too. So strong and solid and high that no one ever found out the secrets their opposite side held.

He put the empty bowl and chopsticks on the newspapers so Chen would see them when the delivery boy returned. People could feel through steel bar fences. He felt. Grass. It was senseless. Like today. Today was senseless. This was a day to be forgotten. Surely there were ways to live through such days as this one without having to know about it. He struggled to his feet, counted the twelve steps, and returned to work.

By midafternoon the strength of his exaggerated miseries became so great in concentration that they helped him close his mind completely. He operated mechanically and concentrated on the mechanics. The good things that might come if sought were not sought. Working on perfecting his apathy, on closing his mind to everything so nothing would harm him, he managed to bring on a trance that left him totally unprepared for anything.

Including the arrival of the white woman.

Miss Bishop disembarked on the Hong Kong side of the ferry in a mood as dark and sour as the weather. Her weekend had been wasted. Beyond knowing she had to see the beggar boy again, the weekend had passed without fixing her intentions. It had been wasted on dreams, dreams of filling the void in her life by protecting the boy. Perhaps even housing him herself if necessary—and she considered ways in which to make it necessary. But such thoughts were foolish since they were acceptable only to her dreams.

She came forward in a slow, pensive walk, expecting the last minute to produce the miracle of a plan. She allowed the walking newspaper readers, the arm-in-arm lovers, and the coolies carrying heavy loads to precede her. Dropping behind gave her time to think before facing the wooden path and the problem of the blind beggar that the path held. Her gait, slow and erratic, was indiscernible to Po's deadened nerves.

She stopped directly in front of the beggar to stare at him a moment, subconsciously expecting the sight to warm her. It didn't. He was like a statue, rather than like a friendly animal begging for her assistance. "Good afternoon, young man."

The young mind emerged slowly from the self-inflicted trance. The voice sounded different, troubled. It was not as gentle as it had been. "Good afternoon," Po recited as he tried to form a smile. It took time. The day had brought too many troubles for a smile. He remembered to stand straight and to square his shoulders to face her. This also took time because it had to be done while the cup reached out at the sound of the wind moving her dress.

Miss Bishop stayed in front of Po, sighing her indecision. He was not as happy as she had expected him to be. His attitude was not transforming hers as she wanted it to do. Had he forgotten about her already? Had he forgotten all she had given him? Did he not realize how much more she could give? Deciding his attitude reeked of Chinese pride and ungratefulness, she let her anger flow. "I have a dollar coin here," she teased him. "Would you like to have it?"

Po wiggled nervously, undecided. Her question broke the pattern of habits he had ascribed to her behavior. He waited, but the coin failed to drop.

"Why don't you ask for it?" she persisted, then winced in surprise at how her disgust had permitted her to ask such a question. The question was unkind. Yet, no other course of action would give her the privilege of helping him. "Why don't you say, 'Please give me the money'?"

He felt no touch of fingers on his, and the cup still had not jiggled from a dropped coin. He stayed squarely, curiously facing the sound of her request while leaning his back protectively against the wooden fence. Natural shyness kept him from answering, and he dipped his head while his ears listened for sounds.

"Why don't you say, 'I'm a blind beggar, will you please give me money'?" she continued her course, using his obstinacy to rationalize her misbehavior.

With the prior tenderness gone from her voice the question came at Po as a demand. He was frightened. In fear, and without the coin, she loomed large and dangerous with all her white, foreign differences. She was the woman who built steel bar fences around nothing. She talked his language, but with a noticeable accent that erred in word pitch. Some of what she said was hard to understand. Why should she disguise her words in a monotone when her open fences exposed her foolishness? "I don't beg," he mumbled in an angry, yet frightened voice.

His perfect answer hardened her need to make him

law abiding, even if doing it might hurt him. She folded her arms across her stomach and rested her weight on one leg. "If you aren't begging," she demanded to know, "then what are you doing?"

He pushed his back hard against the fence and shifted the cup to the left hand so the right would be free with its cane to fight her off. Questions. So many questions. What did she want from him? Were answers what she wanted from his cup? He considered just walking away from her, but worried as to where he should go and what he should do if she tried to stop him. She still had given him nothing. In the waiting silence he stretched his cup out once more, farther this time, in the direction of her voice, thinking perhaps she had refused to give because the cup had been out of reach.

"Who do you work for?" Touched by the cup coming closer she yielded to a desire to hate someone other than the boy.

But Po did not hear her question. His ears were being distracted by the sound of change rattling violently in a tin box. Chen. Chen was sending a warning. Po pulled back the cup and stayed speechless, motionless against the fence. Now there were no sounds—to play dead was a good move. As he relaxed, his ears sharpened. He heard footsteps coming toward him from all sides. The woman was still there! She was drawing a crowd! The people were stopping to watch what the foolish foreign woman was doing to him. Instinctively he dipped his head further to keep them from looking into his face.

The beggar's small movements of self-defense were easy for Miss Bishop to decipher. They increased her frustration. He was well-schooled. He understood her trap and knew enough to stay out of it. His knowledge pulled him farther from her help. The trap, set for him, had caught her instead. "You shouldn't beg," she scolded mildly to keep his mind occupied while she bent low to look up into his tilted face. He was a professional, perhaps not even blind! He could be pretending. Someone had taught him how to pretend so he could steal money for his cup.

As Miss Bishop bent down she felt sick. She prayed silently for him to have eyes so she could escape. She prayed for him to be a heartless little rascal faking blindness just to get money. She prayed for the strength to forget him, for reasons to forget him.

The muscles both below and above his eyes had overdeveloped from his many years of pinching them nervously together, blinking, holding the eyes shut, trying to hide from others what he knew was missing. The large muscles surrounding his eyes made the sockets appear sunken.

She stooped still lower, dominated by her need to know, and kept watching until an unconscious twitch opened the slits of his eyes. She had to know—and then she knew. He was blind! God, he was blind! The truth robbed her of the protection she needed for emotional control, the British game of life. His blindness reached out to clutch the pity she needed to give it. But now she could no longer give him pity or sympathy or love. The harsh, cruel questions that had attempted to snare him could not be withdrawn. He had stiffened against the fence in protection from her, and he did not know how close she dared put her face to his.

After several soul-searching moments Miss Bishop knew she had to yield to him. Frightened by what she had seen, she backed away. What had she done to him? What could she do now to help? Was he begging for what she begged to give? In exasperation she reached into her purse and pulled out a dollar. In keeping with the character she wanted the onlookers to see in her actions she threw the coin hard into the cup without touching the boy's hand. Then she left, rapidly, pushing a path through the gathered crowd.

Although petrified over his frightened inability to go to Po's aid, Chen nevertheless came to attention as the woman left the beggar, almost running toward his stand. In his silent wait of the afternoon he had kept a watchful eye for her. He wanted to use this woman for her money just as Po was using her, but he preferred Po not know he was sharing something good, but dangerous.

When Chen had spotted Miss Bishop bringing up the rear of a ferry crowd he had reached under his pile of newspapers to extract a late edition of a magazine as his answer to her complaint. Its cover was decorated with a large colored photograph—not of a girl but of a very large, strong white man, wearing shorts, flexing his muscles for women to see and behold in wonder. He kept the new magazine hidden, yet readily available, while watching her leave the beggar. As she neared him he mustered the courage to shove it into her sight.

In her frustration, and preoccupied with leaving the proper impression on the onlookers, Miss Bishop strode away so fast she passed the newsstand without seeing either the display, the magazine, the photograph, the old man, or the helpless frown worn to attract her money.

The forced frown disappeared when the woman did. Chen clenched his fists to hammer the new magazine. Boiling with the conviction that the white woman was some form of devil revisiting earth to antagonize both him and the beggar, he decided he would never sell her so much as a newspaper even if she begged him to do it.

CHAPTER SIX

Embarrassed at having lost her composure among so
large an audience of Chinese, Victoria Bishop hurried
past the slower walkers, the streetside vendors, and
the playing children with a speed that threatened
their safety as well as hers. The crowd still watched
her, she could feel their eyes cutting into her back. To
show them she was a government worker, that the
time she had spent on the beggar had injured her
schedule, that her pride had not been damaged, that
foreigners worked to hold Hong Kong together for the
Chinese, she looked anxiously ahead as though troubled over being late, yet hardly saw what was in front
of her. She kept the pace until reaching the entrance to
the Alexandria House arcade, the first opportunity to
get out of sight. Inside the arcade she quickly turned
the first corner, and, at last, feeling out of sight of

those who saw her encounter with the beggar, she stopped in front of a dress shop where mannequins filled the sequined clothing Hong Kong made especially for tourists.

Selecting a gown tucked in a corner, one she could study without showing her face to the arcade strollers, she stared until the sequins became watery blurs. She had acted foolishly. Ever so foolishly. Her impatience and frustrations had taken from her the chance to help the boy. Her attack on him had been cruel, crude, personal. He had every right to be suspicious. He would now guard himself against her, perhaps against all white people. He was a good boy. She should have worked first to gain his confidence instead of charging at him as she had. The Chinese were like that. Help from anyone other than a relative or friend obliged to give it was studied very cautiously. Help had to be taken as though taking it was a favor to the giver.

Under the pretense of wiping her forehead she dabbed a handkerchief at her eyes before walking out of the arcade to wander aimlessly while thinking. Harry Leong had offered help, but Harry's solution was to send a truck-sized man to crush the beggar until there was nothing left but a statistic; a case report, a piece of paper work for the police and courts. Harry's solution was guided by Chinese subservience to English rulers and the safety of observing the prescribed English codes. The blind beggar boy was her case. A case living inside of her rather than inside a government folder. But her sentimental motives had to be secret. Lately the Englishmen in government acted as though they were tolerating her. As they might be expected to tolerate an ancient freak, a tradition. They were polite of course. They had to be. She was just as

English as they. They could no more get away from her than she could get away from them. But being with them meant she had to play by the rules, and sympathy for blind beggars was not in the rules.

A red sign blinked alongside a small restaurant to attract her attention. She stopped to let the sign's message penetrate her preoccupation and hint that a pot of tea might be both calming and stimulating. Much to the chagrin of the attendant idling outside the door, she turned toward the entrance.

The attendant moved aside to make room for the determined white woman and then followed her inside. His customers were local people, wary in the presence of strangers and wise enough to know foreigners meant special prices. High prices aimed at vulnerable foreigners and tourists drove local customers elsewhere. In this neighborhood one foreigner did not lure others. To keep this foreigner from taking a table near the entrance where she might be seen from outside, the attendant led her to the stairs going to the upper floor.

Miss Bishop climbed the steps, glanced about the room, and was pleased to spy an empty table. No matter how comfortable she pretended to be when joining a group of Chinese, her efforts were always one-sided. Their small awkward moves, forced quips, and frightened glances told her of their subtle determination to keep the West from joining the precious mysteries of the East. To them, it was important to keep their motives—whatever they might be—secret. They acted as though afraid they might be laughed at. She felt as uncomfortable as they appeared. Today, however, she was in no mood for their nonsense, and in no mood to cultivate fractured companionships even at shy distances. She needed to think. To do it, she had to be alone.

The signs flashed noticeably nevertheless. Chopsticks hung in midair while heads turned to watch, and when she used chopsticks to pick a peanut from the center dish those who saw shoved elbows into those who were not watching. The young waiter, anxious to impress the foreigner, hurried to fill the table with unnecessary equipment and then perked to importance as he handed her the dirty, much-handled special menu printed in a peculiar array of misspelled English words. The cardboard was worn from low-paid waiters who used it to improve their English. This waiter was onstage. He acted out his role bravely.

Without looking at the menu Miss Bishop held it aloft, above the busy hands of the waiter who was brushing crumbs from the table to the floor. His actions, strictly for tourists, irritated her. Such excess motion would be considered ridiculous in the restaurants where she was well-known. The local Chinese would never accept the English as citizens or residents. They acted as if the colony belonged to them. When she wore Western clothes she was treated like a tourist, and when she wore her *cheongsam* she was treated like a high-priced Eurasian streetwalker.

God! What horrible thoughts. She glanced at the waiter to see if he was reading her mind. It had to be the weather. Or the beggar. Or time. Yes, it might be the passing time. The local restaurants she once thought quaint and delightfully different were becoming more revolting each year. Food stains covered everything. Perhaps they always had. She wondered how much "gift money" the owner of this restaurant paid the health inspector each month. She ordered tea, and after telling herself there was not much they could do to spoil tea the thought had the reverse effect. When the tea came she could not drink it. She had changed. She was slowly giving up her valiant efforts to join these people.

That was it. She had changed. Women of her age often changed. But she had not felt the signs of change—not yet at least. Were there recorded cases of change that weren't felt? If not change, then what was it that bothered her? This, she suddenly realized, was the second time in less than a week that she had manufactured excuses to leave the crushing workload of the office to come to see the beggar. Was it change or a new tendency toward dereliction? Was the old spirit gone?

Whatever the cause, she decided she had only two choices. She either had to forget the beggar or settle matters in a way that would put him out of her mind. The boy would be better off in a school. Schools explained the dishonor of begging. Even Chinese schools did that much. Perhaps a Chinese school would be good for him, for he seemed the type who would never believe what a foreigner told him. Most Chinese were like that.

A school! Of course, a charitable institution was the answer! The beggar boy must be made to attend a school. Harry Leong had mentioned schools. Even he would agree. The private schools, more crowded than ever with the recent refugee invasion, would prove a real challenge, an honest proof of her good intentions. Perhaps the boy had wanted to go to school but could not get in! Perhaps she could show her love by getting for him what no one else could get. If this were true, he would have no reason to be afraid of her.

By the time she turned her attention back to the tea it was cold. Cold and distasteful tea in a filthy restaurant. A trap. The type of restaurant that would charge unreasonable prices to foreigners because they knew foreigners would pay rather than fight back. To get away from the embarrassment of haggling and from hating herself for yielding without an argument, she dropped two ten-cent coins on the table and quickly walked to the steps. Tea was twenty cents and this place had bloody well not ask for more.

From a desk inside the Court Building where she had requested the use of a government telephone, Miss Bishop could look directly across the open ground in front of the Shanghai Bank and see the beggar still at work. She silently thanked the government for having the foresight to fence in this small island of green in the middle of the hard city. The boy stood still, his cup extended, the same as always, as though nothing had happened. What she had done to him appeared forgotten. She dialed the number.

"Protestant Home for the Blind," the voice answered.

"Is Mrs. Hoff there?" Miss Bishop asked, then turned cold. She had given no thought to what she might do if Mrs. Hoff were gone, off on a vacation somewhere.

"Just a moment, please," the voice answered.

Miss Bishop sighed to help push off her fears.

"May I ask who's calling?" the question, delayed, was an oversight, a rule forgotten except when the caller had the voice of a foreigner.

"Victoria Bishop, Social Welfare here." She tried to picture the operator. It was marvelous what the school could do. The operator, a girl, was blind, a graduate. The line hummed, dead for a moment, then burst with a false excitement.

"Victoria! How nice to talk with you again. It's been so long!"

Mrs. Hoff's voice sounded old, tired. The connection was wasted in silence while Miss Bishop worried how to approach the subject. Over the years friendship with Mrs. Hoff, a German, had been difficult. Mrs. Hoff was older, so much so that courtesy forbade calling her by her first name. She was the widow of one of those missionaries who had stayed in China through the war, the Japanese occupation, and the civil war, losing a little more of their life's work day by day until the communists threw them out. Even their churches had no idea of what to do with them. Many of them settled in Hong Kong with the hope of living long enough to return north and begin over. They refused to admit, however, a need to begin again. As the Nationalists on Taiwan were sure the Mainlanders had not turned communist, the missionaries were sure the Mainlanders had not turned atheist. Both expected a triumphal return.

Although Mrs. Hoff was always pleasant at the standard Sunday social dinners, her presence nevertheless cramped the conversation. As she was German, she could not join in the revival of the grand old British traditions. The memories of home that welded the English together in pride excluded outsiders. When Mrs. Hoff was around everyone had to remember she was a religious woman with a background different from theirs. Curious and open questions about the differences kept her apart in spite of her tolerance.

"I'm sure you wouldn't call at this time," Mrs.

Hoff offered, "unless it was about something important. You're always so busy, Victoria. Is there something I can do for you?"

"Sorry to keep you waiting. They won't leave me alone here," Miss Bishop lied. Recollections of their past meetings yielded nothing to talk about except the subject of the blind beggar. So she began. She admitted she was talking unofficially since no case report had been opened on this particular boy at Welfare, and in an effort to win a favorable response, she confessed a special interest in the case. The purpose of her call, she added, was to search out a school that had an opening for a blind boy. Placement in the school could be used as an objective when the case was opened. Rather than ask if the Protestant Home had such an opening, she asked politely if Mrs. Hoff knew of one. The question placed Mrs. Hoff above all the directors of blind schools in the colony.

Mrs. Hoff's answer stayed with the script. She said there was no need to look further since the Protestant Home had an opening. This was a half-truth justified by necessity. The home had a waiting list of poor and desperate, but charitable contributions were never sufficient to cover costs. Victoria Bishop was with government and government could pay. Rather than ask outright if government funds would accompany the boy's entrance, Mrs. Hoff asked if the boy had parents who might object to his entering school and, thus, might not be willing to pay for his keep there.

Parents? Miss Bishop tensed. The possibility of the boy having parents had been locked out of her mind. She had allowed herself the pleasure of believing he was alone, as alone as she. Ashamed of her unpreparedness, she apologized for going ahead in a manner that might appear premature. She alibied the mistake by cloaking it with departmental secrecy, and forgave Mrs. Hoff for not understanding since there was no reason for her to understand. "It's an unusual case," she half-lied. "It simply does not fit the customary procedures. That's why I've assigned it to myself. Could I ask you to hold that opening for a day or two, at least until I can formulate the details?"

Mrs. Hoff's consent came slowly, slowly enough to indicate a return favor might someday be called for. Still, she was careful to keep the opportunity from slipping away. To avoid a bureaucratic delay, she requested an early decision, and underlined the suggestion by referring to the church's desire to help the most needy, regardless of where they came from.

Miss Bishop sighed, relieved. At last she had found the direction in which to work. She agreed mechanically to the request for speed, hung up the receiver, and floated out of the Court Building. Outside she stared through the steel bar fence and across the open mall at her charge. Conditions remained favorable, the boy was still there.

The afternoon was about gone. Miss Bishop watched the boy from across the mall, telling herself that he would leave soon, certainly before dark. Anticipating her next encounter with him, she waited unmoving, until her legs ached and turned to criticizing the government for not putting benches around its oasis. Tiredness leaned her against the steel bars in an unladylike stance until the terminal tower clock sounded out four rings. Then she stood straight. The clock's bell might be a signal to one who had no eyes.

On the fourth ring of the bell Po put the empty

cup in his coat and left for the flat, glad this day was over. Although another silver dollar clinked its offer to fulfill his dreams, its glory was tarnished by the warning that had come with it. The new rattle was ominous. It called for repayment, for something he might not be willing to give. Au might insist the dollars be refused in the future if taking them meant being involved with the foreign woman.

When he reached the open end of the lane Po barely paused to wish Chen a good-night. Chen, always negative in speech, could do nothing to brighten this frightful day. As Po tapped his way around the corner he worried about the problem that awaited him at home. His mother was sick. Perhaps Au had gone out for some medicine. Perhaps Chung-kin's illness would keep the family from having dinner at home. Another meal might have to be purchased from the day's profits.

With the accuracy of fate's touch Miss Bishop stepped in front of Po just as he turned out of the lane into the open sidewalk at the corner of Des Voeux. To warn him in advance that something was about to happen, she put her hand gently on his shoulder. "Good afternoon, young man," she said pleasantly, sure now of her intentions.

Po recognized the peculiar accent and stopped immediately. Surprised by the breech in her habits, his mind became too crowded to think clearly. One by one he discarded hazy explanations until a final thought remained—silver dollars. If she had wanted to give him two dollars in one day why had she not given both at the same time? He sidestepped automatically toward the building, away from the fast walkers who might be tempted to push him. When the wall touched his back he leaned against it. There he waited. The woman did not speak again. Was that all she wanted to say? Was it a casual passing on the street? Was she gone?

The wait seemed endless. What more could she want? Would she make another scene? Draw another crowd? Would she put him on display a second time? Chen was around the corner. Po listened for the warning rattle of change in the tin box, but there was nothing. Chen was too far away. He let the strangeness engulf him until it brought fear. This was the wrong time for work, the wrong place for work, the wrong time and place to hear the woman's voice, and the wrong time to be standing idle. Minutes at night were valuable. Each minute increased the size of the going-home crowd, and the greater the crowd the greater the hazards of his journey.

Po's fear increased until his body began to shake. Finally, he heard the woman saying something, but he could not distinguish her words. The sounds of the street, the blasting angry barks of cars and taxis, the clicks of leather heels hitting sharp on cement, and the ripples of her voice blurred in his brain. The sounds mixed like colors flashing wildly inside a kaleidoscope with none staying long enough to tell its story, but all meaning danger. Although Po pushed harder against the wall for protection, he remained vulnerable.

Then, not knowing what else to do, he pulled the yellow cup from his pocket and inched it out cautiously, feeling toward the source of the white woman's voice. Perhaps she wanted to see the cup if she needed so badly to give it her dollars.

The sight of the cup drawing nearer, waving, feeling for its target, cut through to open Victoria

Bishop's weakness. People slowed, smiling as they passed, watching the woman's love flow out to meet the boy and approving of what they saw.

Aware of what the onlookers might see in her relationship to the blind beggar, Miss Bishop stooped to be certain only he would hear what she had to say. "Are you alone?" she asked, knowing how distasteful the word orphan was to a race that emphasized the importance of family, "or do you have parents?" When he refused to answer, she instructed, "I'd like to talk to your parents."

Po held himself motionless, caught by the fear of her face being so close to his. She was so near he could smell her. In low tones he mumbled the first prominent thought her words brought to mind. "My mother is sick."

Miss Bishop straightened. The watching crowd was forcing her back into playing her role. It was time to face the possibility of his using lies to put her off. If a mother existed, the mother was supposed to be too sick to be bothered, or a sick mother was meant to be an excuse for the boy's begging. Steeling herself, she waited to hear him say he forgot where he lived or that he did not live with his parents. She used the time to paint a mental picture of a professional beggar, one who had learned to play on the sympathy given him. The attempt failed. She needed him too badly.

Since nothing had been given to his cup, Po began to revise his thinking. Apparently the cup had failed in its mission. Now she might want her money back. He reached into his pocket and was not surprised at how quickly the silver came to his touch. Giving up his dreams, he held it out to her. In a moment, after she had refused to take it from him, he began trying to believe she had gone. And not really believing it, he nevertheless put the coin back in his pocket. He needed it too much.

"Keep the money," she told him. "We'll see about your sick mother."

She was still there, behind him as he walked.

In the first block she made several attempts to talk, but discovered she had little to say. Yet, if she did not talk he might think she had given up. Each time she touched his shoulder to guide him he jerked, most likely in disappointment. His pace, so slow and tedious, stirred her sympathy until she began giving him gentle, guiding shoves. One such push put him into the path of oncoming traffic and she had to grab frantically to get him back to the curb. Less than an aid, she felt like a hindrance. Still, she could not resist touching him.

The journey reached the quiet ladder street. "My name is Miss Bishop," she told him. "What's your name?"

She was still following. "Po," he answered.

"Po what?" she asked pleasantly.

After a moment of thinking he managed to excuse her. Only a foreigner would think his name to be Po What. "No, ma'm," he corrected. "Au Po-tong."

"Well, now, Po," she began, warming to the new communion, "have you ever thought about going to school?"

He frowned, angry at having surrendered his name to her. Au said to tell people only what they had to know. Now it was too late. If she had wanted to believe he was Po What, he should have let her believe it. "No, ma'm," he stammered. She was touching him, making him answer. "I mean," he worried, "yes, ma'm." Having to guess the answer she wanted frightened him. He hurried. Since she refused to leave he had better get to Au quickly. Au would know what to do.

"You should, you know," she suggested. "Go to school, that is."

He breathed relief. This statement held the answer she wanted. "Yes," he agreed politely. His upset nerves were making the walk tiring, and the weight of her presence was embarrassing. He heard people stop talking when he passed.

He walked too slowly for Miss Bishop to follow without being conspicuous, and the way he refused to accept or return the friendship she offered made her feel awkward. Ashamed for having forced herself on him, she began to imagine she was being misled. He would go in circles until her nerves and patience ran out.

At the top of the ladder street Po turned right onto Lyndhurst. As they passed the corner everyone in the barbershop stopped working to see the white woman following the blind boy. Heads on both sides of the street studied the strange procession. Miss Bishop tried to maintain a running, smiling, pleasant conversation—to prove the boy was not being harried into something against his wishes—but found it impossible since Po contributed nothing. There was always the possibility of racial animosity in this all-Chinese neighborhood. She tried not to think about it. It was still daytime, she was part of government, they would attempt nothing against her.

The owner of the tea shop lowered his newspaper to watch the unusual parade, and the owner of the clothing repair shop looked up from his sewing to observe the two of them hesitate at the foot of the steps leading to the flats. He overheard his wife whisper to a customer that the boy's mother was sick.

In order to call attention to what was happening to him before he entered the building Po rapped his cane hard against the cement steps. This was friendly neighborhood territory.

So as not to rush Po into another near accident as she had done on the street, Miss Bishop let him get about five steps up before continuing after him. She curled her nose at the smell of stale urine and tried to concentrate on how to approach Po's parents with the idea of sending him to school. Surely a Chinese family would not deny their son the opportunity for an education even if it meant giving up a few pennies a day from his begging. School, she decided, so precious to the Chinese, had to be her introduction. If that failed she would fall back on the laws and the courts. It was important to remember the threats had to be aimed at the parents and not at the boy. Threatening the boy might damage him for life.

On the first floor landing Po paced off the correct number of steps to the flat and then kicked open the door. Walking in, he left the door ajar so his persistent follower could enter also if she chose.

Miss Bishop stayed back from the open door, wanting to be announced before showing herself. An intrusion, with older people, called for an invitation. She carefully avoided the open flat so as not to seem to be peeking, perhaps at scenes not meant for her eyes. The dark hall rang with the busy sounds of dinner preparations in other flats.

Weary from the ordeal, Po sighed relief as he

dropped on his cot. "Father," he called, "this woman wants to talk to you."

Pleased at overhearing Po's polite message, Miss Bishop remained in the hall out of sight. Waiting properly, she prepared a smile, a smile calculated to disarm whoever appeared in the doorway. She waited longer, growing concerned over the silence in the room. Minutes passed. Was the room empty? Had the boy escaped through another exit? Was he deceiving her? Her nerves played on her patience and won.

She leaned sideways to look into the room.

Inside a man sat on the end of a small cot, his back to the door, massaging a woman's legs. Miss Bishop pulled back quickly. Politeness dictated she not watch the picture of marital intimacy. Accustomed to living in a crowd, the Chinese were forced to do many things not meant to be seen.

Relieved by knowing the room was occupied, Miss Bishop renewed her patience. Husband and wife. The boy had both parents. Was the mother the type who could love the boy as she did? Would the mother do what was good for the boy instead of what was good for herself? Miss Bishop brought the image of the mother to mind so she might appraise her. The mother had looked strange. But other than looking strange no interpretation could be extracted from the woman's expression. She looked into the room again, more bravely this time.

The woman on the cot appeared cold, her skin dark purple. Alongside the cot there were a couple of buckets spattered with a white, rice-like liquid. The strangeness repelled Miss Bishop and she stepped back into the hall while her mind searched for an explanation. Out of the depths of her memory came another scene.

The two matched.

"Cholera!" she gasped quietly in recollection. She crossed the narrow hall to lean against the wall opposite the open door. "Oh God!" she cried. "Cholera!"

The man on the cot spun around at the sound of the ugly word. His expression told her she should not have called. After staring a moment he grimaced in contempt for having heard her.

Terrified now that the man had silently confirmed her fear, Miss Bishop stepped back helplessly until she stood pressed hard against the wall. The man glanced over his shoulder again. She interpreted the glance as a request for silence. The picture framed in the flat's doorway was horribly unreal. "My God!" she whispered. "Cholera . . . second-stage cholera!" The man was giving quiet instructions to someone out of Miss Bishop's sight. The boy! The moment, so critical, had made her forget the object of her visit. The boy had walked into the room without knowing, without seeing. It was she who had told him what was happening to his mother.

Au, tired and close to accepting defeat, turned wearily to look at the strange woman. She looked as if she wanted to leave, to run, but for some reason she had to stay. "Go," he encouraged her quietly. "Go call the hospital."

Miss Bishop responded eagerly to the instructions that freed her. Still stunned, but with a legitimate reason to leave the danger, she started for the stairs. Then, thinking more clearly, she went back to close the door so no one else in the building would be subjected to that horror. On the sidewalk she looked anxiously both ways, hoping to find someone quickly who might relieve her of her duty. But there was no one, no one but Chinese. The lights in the clothing repair shop caught her attention. The shop had to have a telephone.

Inside the shop the telephone sat on the end of a long glass counter, near the door, welcoming her. She paused to think what to do, then responded to the red-lettered sign pasted on the box. She dialed 999 for police emergency.

Someone answered immediately.

"Bishop here, Social Welfare," she identified herself smartly. "I've just discovered a cholera victim . . . second stage," she added, proud of remembering the terminology. "Send someone quickly!" As the receiver was on its way back to the cradle she heard garbled mumblings come from it. "Yes?" she asked, raising the receiver back to her ear.

"The address, Bishop, the address?" Then, more calmly, knowing the request was being heard, the voice said, "Don't get excited. Just get the address. I'll wait."

"It's . . . " she did not know. The transition from total shock was still incomplete. The blind boy . . . he walked up Lyndhurst . . . the horrible scene in the flat flashed back . . . was Lyndhurst the last street the boy took? "I'm sorry, just a minute, please."

"Don't get excited," the voice repeated. "Ask someone nearby."

She put down the telephone and walked deep into the shop, finally looking around the curtain marking off the living quarters where the owner and his wife had discreetly retreated so as not to be accused of listening to the foreigner's call. They told her the address. At the end of the call she felt exhausted, yet worried that something might have been overlooked.

Sidewalk strollers, their curiosity pricked by the white woman's presence and her distressed appearance, stopped to form an audience as she came out of the shop. They stood in a quiet semicircle patiently waiting for the show to continue. Old wives stood slightly behind their old husbands, their hands hooked behind their backs, giving little attention to the grandchildren clutching the pants legs of their pajamas. Younger couples, more dedicated to the excitement they might create themselves, slowed to look and wonder before passing. Middle-aged people, already bathed for the night, stood idly exchanging gossip. This was entertainment; activity to set this night apart, and it was free. It would keep the neighborhood alive and active with fresh rumors and speculation. The foreign whites intruded only rarely into this society, but when they did, it was worth watching.

The store owner's wife, who had overheard the telephone conversation in spite of her backroom pretense, waited for the white woman to move away from the shop's front door so she could slip out and spread the news. When she did, the ugly name of the disease was whispered through the milling mass, and over and over again there was the sound of air being sucked in through half-clenched teeth. A helpless sound, a sound that whistled man's inability to alter his fate. It produced excitement. The crowd moved back a safe distance from the white stranger.

Miss Bishop was left standing alone in the center of their circle. Their behavior reminded her she was a member of another race. It made her want to run from the feeling of rejection, to run to her own kind, but she knew she could not. No one watching indicated a desire to take her burden from her. For years she had embraced the problems of these people, and for years they had pulled away to let her do it. Their eyes, wild with excitement, were made wilder still with the fear of becoming involved.

She was tired of them. Her eyes saw deceit in scenes that had once filled her with compassion. Welfare had taught her to look for the evil in everyone. It had trained her to look until she found it. Now it existed in the poor, in their families, and in their city. She had no love left strong enough to overcome what she saw.

Tears of self-pity came to her eyes. The small blind beggar boy had not been evil. As much as she had suspected evil, and as hard as she looked for deceit, she had found neither. The thought made her look lovingly up to the first-floor window, knowing Po sat near it. But she saw only a curtain. He had walked like a blind lamb into the troubles she multiplied. She wanted to cry, but knew she couldn't. Everyone was watching. The crowd also looked up to the window, following her clue. She had told them exactly where the cholera victim rested. Her staring at the window had put a further curse on the boy.

"Can't you people do anything for yourselves?" she scolded quietly in English, hoping they would not understand. It made her feel better, superior. It returned the onus of her misery to its source and helped restore the mask she had worn so well the many years. It buoyed her spirits to see them retreat from her anger and stimulated in her the authority they expected to come from a white foreigner. She selected from among the faces the one most disturbed and smiled into it a look of complacent assurance. If she managed to cope with one of them, she might be able to cope with them all.

The selected face smiled back. A clever smile. A smile that sneered its belief that the cholera germ might be inside of her by now too. After transmitting its message the face backed through the crowd and went away.

CHAPTER SEVEN

A small, open police van arrived shortly after the emergency telephone call to relieve Miss Bishop of her responsibilities. She left the building's entrance and approached the van before it stopped moving. "It's second-stage cholera," she called out. "On the first floor. A woman. First flat on the right. Shall I go with you?"

Men in khaki uniforms trimmed with resplendent black belts and shoulder straps jumped off the van and fanned out as though not hearing the instructions. One uniform brushed by her to assume the post at the door she had just left while two others walked to the corner in search of the flat's rear entrance. The summer shorts, so heavily starched that the dark legs pumped inside them without bending the creases, looked like stiff canvas covers over walking pistons. The balance of the squad mingled quietly with the onlookers to disperse them before cordoning off the area.

The independent efficiency of the special Chinese squad relaxed Miss Bishop. As a part of the government team, she felt brave. Yet their ignoring her presence tended to make her feel insignificant and unwanted just when she needed to feel the opposite. She worried that her actions had somehow betrayed her fear, and that the betrayal had subtracted from her authority. The cholera case was her discovery, it became important that the official record carry her name. The whole department took pride in seeing a Welfare worker's name head a police report. To keep from being mistaken for a casual onlooker, and perhaps get pushed aside, she fought through the uniforms to edge closer to the police van. Still sitting on the front wooden bench of the gray truck was the sergeant, a white man, an Englishman.

"Your men certainly are well train—"

"You make the phone call?" he cut her short.

"Yes."

"You Bishop?" he asked somewhat curtly. "Social Welfare?" He kept his eyes on the report board resting across his bare knees.

"Yes." He looked hard, crusty, an element of lower London or Liverpool.

"You sure it's cholera?"

He was young, fifteen to twenty years her junior. His ears were much too large for his face, and his nose was so huge that his eyes looked hidden on opposite sides of a dividing wall. His head was all features, features topped by a cap of long, unruly hair. Hair grew from his bare arms and legs as it would grow on an animal. She continued appraising him while he continued to work on his board. She shivered. He was ugly compared to the smooth-skinned and delicately balanced bodies of the Chinese. The Chinese might rightly look at someone like him and wonder if it could possibly be domesticated. Her heretical thoughts forced her to sigh; she had been away from home too long.

Suddenly he lifted his eyes to stare impatiently at her.

"Well," she began, coming out of her dreams, "the woman appeared bluish." She grew doubtful under his cold scrutiny. He might be appraising her as she had just appraised him. "There was a white liquid . . . "

"Nasty business, isn't it?" he smiled. The notes done, he chucked the workboard to the floor while making a cursory check of his men. "I'll be glad to get off this bloody detail. Sit around for days doing nothing, then right in the middle of supper . . . " he paused to exaggerate his disgust, "exposure. My wife says she's had it with me on this job."

"I've had it too," she aped, wondering if his wife was Chinese. "I haven't had my supper yet either." She folded her arms, preparing to stay with him. He was becoming a touch of home in this foreign atmosphere.

Inside the flat Au gave up trying to ease the cramps in Chung-kin's legs. He went to the window to stare out at the street. The trouble inside the flat was spreading; the normally placid people outside were agitated. Turning his back to the cot, he watched Po turning his head to catch the sounds of the disturbance. "Your mother is very sick," he whispered. "Soon the people from the hospital will come. When they do, I want you to stay right here on the cot."

"What does mother look like?" Po asked, frightened.

"The same as always," Au lied, pleased that his son's blindness spared him from sharing the sight of the ugly contortions. "But now she has pain."

"Can she talk?" Po asked loud enough for his mother to hear and answer if she could.

"She doesn't care to talk," Au explained. "She needs her strength to fight the bug."

The bug! Po stiffened. The bug that lives in the dirt and rises to kill people. If one man with the bug touches another . . . where did it come from? Was it brought by the white foreign woman? Torn between going to his mother for consolation and staying with his father for protection, Po squirmed restlessly in indecision. The bug might be walking up his trouser leg or flying around, waiting to touch him without warning. When or where it would strike was unknown. The bug might have come to the flat on a silver dollar. A dollar like the one he still had in his pocket.

In the racing confusion of too many mixed thoughts Po heard his mother's groans deep under the din of the high-pitched, excited voices gathering outside beneath the open window. People flocking around the building to spy on him, to watch his movements, to see him without him seeing them in return, made him feel still more uneasy. He moved to the other end of the bed, away from the window. The audible wail of the ambulance was disassociated with what was happening to him until its siren came louder, closer, and eventually screeched below the window before dying. He could not understand the new, anxious, sharper cries coming up from the sidewalk until he heard them also in the hallway. The door clicked open and he shuddered at the sound of heavy police shoes coming into the room.

Disturbed by the attitude of emotional indifference that the sergeant expected, Miss Bishop steadied her courage until her contempt for hiding was greater than her fear of cholera. She went up the stairs and into the hallway where she waited beside the door of the Au flat. The medical officer was kneeling over Chung-kin to examine her.

An Urban Services inspector pushed past Miss Bishop, walked into the room, looked around quickly, then left to pace up and down the hall. He settled alongside the police guard at the door. "Keep people off this floor," he instructed. "If they knew what they were trying to see, they wouldn't be so anxious to see it."

From the color of Chung-kin's skin and the severity of her leg cramps, the doctor made his decision. "Send up a stretcher," he called out.

The stretcher coming out of the ambulance confirmed the rumors spreading among the street's onlookers. Helplessly fascinated by the presence of danger, those who had used their fortunate residence in the building to get past the door guard now decided to get as far from it as the outdoors would allow. They spied around the corners of the staircase before trying to rush past the first floor guards. Their decision to leave, however, had been made too late. The guard had been instructed to let the tenants in but not out again. They were shoved back to their own floors and their own flats.

Behind the closed doors joss sticks were lit.

Noting she was the only government woman present and the only idle government employee, Miss Bishop felt guilt stricken. She looked for something to do. There was nothing. In her search she let her mind retreat to the case's beginning. It was Po who had brought her here; it was Po who had needed her. She peeked into the room to see him sitting alone on the cot, forsaken because of his youth and possibly his handicap. His head was dipped in shyness of all the strangers.

She moved into the room slowly, secretly waiting and secretly hoping to be told to stay out. When she reached the cot she sat down next to Po. "Your mother is very sick," she whispered. "She'll have to go to the hospital." He refused to answer, but his blinking eyelids signaled he had heard.

After a few moments, during which Po failed to react to her presence, Miss Bishop put an arm around his shoulder. She pulled him into a gentle embrace that begged for him to respond. He was strong, and bigger than the oversized coat had led her to believe. Since he made no effort to resist, she allowed her yearning and gratification to increase until her head swam. Feeling herself losing control, she became frightened. Could the others see her weakness, her desire? Only the boy's father watched. She stared back into the father's expressionless eyes and pulled from them approval of her mothering the son. After a moment, when time scolded her for staring, she looked away.

The room was so small that the medical officer and government inspector had to leave to make room for the stretcher. The table was pushed back to open a space for the canvas next to the cot. Chung-kin's writhing body was transferred, and then carried out.

A dull thump rocked the frame of Po's cot as the stretcher went by. "Mama?" he called weakly and pulled loose from Victoria Bishop's hold.

The sudden withdrawal saddened Miss Bishop. It explained her inability to comfort him just when he most needed comfort. She put a hand on each of his shoulders to keep him from jumping up and drawing a reprimand in the crowded room. "Everything will be all right," she recited mechanically. "She'll come back. Your mother is sick, that's all." As his body settled back on the cot his jerking head indicated his mind followed the sounds going out the door and down the steps. "Your mother will be all right," she lied, telling him what he wanted to hear.

The medical officer came back to stand over Au who had taken a seat on the cot vacated by his wife. "How long has she been ill?" he asked.

"Yesterday," Au mumbled obediently to the floor where he had fixed his stare. "Yesterday morning. She didn't feel well. She coughed. We thought it might be from carrying another child."

The officer whistled softly, loyally, in recognition of someone else's loss. "How long has she been pregnant?"

"A couple of months."

The officer in his helplessness walked in small circles, an animal caged by the room with its ugly duties. He squinted, wanting to determine the depth of Au's sorrow and whether Au would give accurate answers. "Has she been out of the flat since yesterday morning?" he went on.

"No," Au told him. "Not for two days. She wanted to be careful."

"How about you?"

"This afternoon," Au explained carefully. "She asked me to go to her cousin's for some medicine."

"Have any of the neighbors been in to visit her?"

"I don't think so. We don't visit with the neighbors. We have no relatives in the building."

The officer frowned. Au's answer was weak, hard to believe. "Cholera is highly contagious," he warned in an attempt to dominate the interrogation with authority. "She'll be taken to the Infectious Diseases Hospital." His frustration was making the room smaller. With each pace he spun on his heel. "You and the boy," he said, nodding at the window cot without looking at it, "will be kept under observation for a short time. Long enough to determine if you're infected or carrying the germ. It's a precaution—for your own protection."

The situation out of his control, Au shrugged his indifference to it. He glanced at Po and saw that the boy's face showed what his heart felt. He leaned forward automatically to join Po, but decided against it since the officer blocked his path and Po's cot was crowded with the white woman. The white woman was staring back at him, her eyes sending him the same sympathy her arm around the boy was giving. He rewarded her with a nod of appreciation.

The officer asked, "Is that your son?"

"Yes."

After a suspicious glance at Au, caused by having noticed Po's blindness, the officer left the room. In the hall, however, the privacy he needed was invaded by the returning bravery of the tenants. Once more they were yielding to curiosity. They stood on the staircase watching him.

Turning his back on the rows of faces, the inspector told the medical officer, "I think we can confine our efforts to this floor if what the man inside told you is true. The toilet's filthy. Community property. No one cares. It smells worse than the stairway. We'll have to wash and disinfect the whole place."

"We'd better post another guard on the stairs," the medical officer decided, "to keep these people away. We'll take everyone living on this floor in for observation."

"Then it is cholera?" the inspector asked.

"Definitely," the officer told him. "Let's hope there isn't an epidemic." The thought of an epidemic renewed his fears. He stretched inside the door to ask Au, "How many people live on this floor?"

Suffering the loneliness of his loss, the question irked Au. "I don't count people," he growled.

The officer frowned his disapproval of Au's refusing to share his fear. He turned to the Chinese police guard. "Count the people on this floor. While you're doing it you can also tell them they're going to the Isolation Center. Don't tell them where they're going until you learn if anyone is missing in their family. Get help from downstairs if you need it." Surmising racial differences would make the task more difficult, he got angry beforehand. "Tell them," he added, raising his voice and pointing at the listening audience on the steps, "if they don't stay off this floor they'll be taken away too!"

After a moment of exchanged angry stares, the threat was believed. The watching faces pulled back, frightened, to go scrambling and shoving up, away, out of sight with the hope of being out of mind also. The white man ruled the colony. The white man was rich. If there was a gift price on avoiding the white man's laws, the cost had to be too high for those living on Lyndhurst.

The first-floor residents, listening from behind half-open doors, turned to pleading and complaining on hearing that the tragedy now involved them. When their cries failed to alter the foreigner's instructions they substituted resentment for helplessness. They blasted their wrath at the authority that was persecuting them.

The undignified shouts ricocheted off the hard walls and into the Au flat where the medical officer had to raise his voice to resume questioning Au. "We must make an effort," he said apologetically, "to determine where your wife contracted the disease. If she hasn't been out of the flat for two days, then where was she on Saturday, Friday, Thursday . . . " he went on slowly, implying he would go on forever if it took Au forever to cooperate.

"She worked at the poultry shop on the corner," Au cut in to stop the endless talk. "Six days a week. She bought our food at the same corner."

"Cholera spreads fast," the officer reminded himself. "You saw how fast it worked on your wife. We owe it to the colony to stop it. What type of work did she do?"

"She cleaned chickens."

"Ripped off the feathers or cleaned out the insides?" the officer wondered.

"Cleaned the insides," Au told him.

The significance of Au's answer hit the official immediately. The germ might have come from inside

164

the chicken. It might have been scratched from the earth, eaten, and lain dormant inside the fowl's stomach. The theory appeared so logical and much preferable to believing the germ had come from a public place.

"Have you or any members of your family been inoculated against cholera?" the officer asked methodically as he prepared to write the answer on his pad.

"No," Au replied, dipping his head humbly in recognition of the oversight.

"Goddam," the officer cursed quietly. He filled his lungs with the air he would need to begin an angry reprimand, then decided against saying anything. He settled for a contemptuous twist of his head. To calm his anger he walked into the hall and began surpervising the details of evacuating the first floor of the building. Each cholera case brought more fear, more knowledge, and more precaution. Yet none of these brought the water the city needed to end the threat of an epidemic. Chinese were dying, yet it was Chinese to the north who refused, for political reasons, to sell the colony more water.

Miss Bishop, watching her racial brothers prepare to leave, obediently prepared to leave with them. As they walked out the door and passed her without extending the appropriate invitation, she felt superfluous, a forgotten member sacrificed to a higher duty. When the officers were out of sight she went into the room to approach Au, but saw in how he hid his face inside his hands his preference for solitude. Telling herself she had nothing to say to him, and telling herself also that Po was blind and would not know she had come into the flat to find friendship, she left.

During the taxi ride home Miss Bishop relived every moment of the night, attempting to discover in each, or in all as a whole, a personal significance. Every move, every touch, every sensation recalled was studied. Po's rigid body had accepted her embrace, but had his acceptance been a concession to her authority, her silver dollars, or a natural reaction stemming from his beautiful shyness? The father was handsome. He had shown himself to be strong enough to stand up to the vaunted foreigners who wanted to dominate him. Some of the answers the father gave the officer might not have been true, but even in the dangerous circumstances he had the right to protect his personal life. Sometimes calloused government officials demanded more from the Chinese than they did from each other. Besides, she remembered, the father had given her a tender look of appreciation on seeing her care for the boy. The father knew his friends.

After the strangers had left his flat, Chung-kin's absence settled hard on Au. Without the sound of her scratching slippers and grumbling objections the room was bare. Half of it was missing. A woman, a wife, one who had given him a son, a home, and then held them together. All things had emanated from her, the family's center. Without her, and without the new child she still bore, the burden of perpetuating the family's name fell on Po.

As though surmising the burden Au's mind had just transferred to him, Po stood, his cot squeaking from releasing its burden, and walked to his father.

Au watched the child come closer, feeling his way across the disheveled room. He grabbed a damp towel, as Chung-kin might have done. But Po's face had no tear begging to be wiped away. Had the boy's life been so miserable that there was little difference between sorrow and joy?

"Is mother very sick?"

"Yes."

"Will she die?"

"I don't know."

Cholera was death and germs; cholera was one person touching another and both dying; cholera was a bug with a devil inside that crawled in the dirt; and cholera was the evil Chen had relegated to the hillside squatters. But cholera also came to the hillside squatters because they were refugees. How had cholera invaded this flat meant to be closed to strangers and squatters and devils and foreigners? "Here," Po called as he reached Au's cot. He extended a cupped hand filled with the coins collected that day.

Au took the coins but, like Po, he said nothing about the silver dollar. "Find your toothbrush and good clothes," he ordered as he dropped the change in his pocket. "Put them in one of the plastic bags. We have to go to a place where the doctors will prove we don't have the disease."

Sounds of commotion came from the hallways to tell Au it was time for them to leave also. People grumbled as police shouted angry instructions down the stairway. Only the children screamed gleefully in the new excitement. Au pointed Po toward the door so they would be ready when the signal came.

The first floor residents used disorderly behavior as a means to object to the militancy of the police. Orderliness indicated subordination, and subordination was loss of face. The children raced back and forth, darting in and out, and laughed, oblivious to the impending danger. Their exaggerated actions dared anyone to forbid them from getting a favorite toy or a book for reading. Doors along the hall slammed harmfully under the impetuous, youthful attack until the police put a stop to it. Wives growled unanswerable questions at their husbands, hoping their anger would stimulate the husbands into doing something about the impossible authorities. And older people, spoiled by the respect granted them for their age, grumbled aloud at the pain of having to leave so unceremoniously. The Chinese policeman at the top of the steps, while secretly condemning the government for not having the staircase cleaned, silently tolerated the odor in preference to irritating his elders.

By the time the tenants had navigated the narrow stairway they were formed in the orderly single line the police wanted. They were kept in line while walking the narrow passage through the crowd of onlookers, and were herded into the back of a waiting truck. The straight line, marching through the police guard, implied guilt, that the innocent tenants had done something wrong, and this further embarrassed them. They took it upon themselves to blame in loud laments the government so their neighbors might hear, might understand, and might exonerate them.

Au heard the disparaging remarks and felt guilty. The disaster striking him had involved his innocent neighbors. To keep Po from sensing the guilt, he said, "We're going for a ride in an open lorry. You'll enjoy it."

Au's voice, strong and unafraid, helped Po shut out the unwelcome groans of the others. He concentrated on the ride. Side movement, forward movement, and movement without effort on his part. It was like a bus ride in Canton, yet a ride in a windstorm since the lorry had neither sides nor windows. He concentrated on the relationship between the sound of the engine and the speed of the wind hitting his face.

The lorry raced down the hill, braking hard at intersections, and headed into town where traffic increased. Outside the residential area the wind brought such rapid changes in odors that Po's sensitive nostrils could not identify them singly. Emerging from the commercial section the ride continued to the wharf where the smell of debris at the water's edge explained all. A waiting Medical Department water ferry was the last island-side stop.

Au held Po on the bench until the other passengers got out. He then half lifted the boy by one arm to hurry him over the unfamiliar terrain. The launch attendant reached to lift Po onto the floating craft as though he had been told ahead of time that the boy was blind. The last off the truck, Au and Po were the last onto the launch. People's need for the security of their families, and separation from strangers, had left open several single seats, but no doubles. Au stood in front of Po until the boat was safely underway.

He kneeled to be heard. "Do you remember the last time we crossed?"

Po grunted his objection to Au's disturbing voice. He wanted no help in discovering the new sounds. Besides, it had been two years since he had crossed the channel. Two years, with so many changes in his life, was a very long time.

"The boat is small," Au went on, his voice urging Po to listen so between them they might shut out further thoughts of their loss. "The water makes this one move. The whole boat is no larger than the cabbage truck," he added with a laugh. "We're going back to the Mainland side. The bay is filled with large ships from all parts of the world," he went on, describing what he saw. Lights, strung decoratively around the military craft disguising their purpose, dotted a scene so novel Au could not accurately describe it.

Po yielded to the diversion. "What do the ships look like?" he wondered.

"They're big," Au emphasized. His desire to impress Po pushed him to make the ships still bigger. "As long as a block. As far as from the flat to the barbershop. But thin. No wider than our building. They float like your cup on a bucket of water."

"What color are they?"

"A little brighter than the water."

"What color is the water?"

"At night the water's black. So black that I can't see it."

Po's eyes, forgetting for the moment that others might be trying to look into them, flashed open in astonishment. Au could not see black. If Au could not see black, then no man could see it.

At the Kowloon wharf two small Medical Department vans flashed their headlights out over the water as a signal, and Po's head turned so noticeably that Au was impelled to ask, "Did you see that?"

"Yes."

"It was the white light from two autombiles on shore."

Po felt numb with surprise. He could see white! White was also the color the sun made when he stared directly at it. But then, the foreign woman was white also. Why could he not see her? The puzzle teased as the small boat docked.

The older passengers stumbled in their struggle to get on solid ground while the young children raced back and forth on deck pleading for a longer ride. To stretch the minutes, the children straggled until being forced into the rear of the two vans. Separated from their parents who had been hustled into the first van, the children spent their journey on the Kowloon side mournfully watching ahead, fearing their parents might disappear and make them alone in the world. The two vehicles stayed close, however, as they wound their way down Chatham Road, across the railroad tracks, and onto a back lane where speed was reduced in respect to narrowness.

The passengers examined skeptically what the lights of the city shining across the dark tracks had to show them of their new home. Paralleling the lane on the left was a solid brick wall. Barbed wire on the top of the wall curled in fearsome circles to keep people in, or keep them out. Beyond the wire stood a two-story building with barred windows. Lookout towers perched high on each of the building's four corners. A forbidden, landlocked island, a prison. Each quickly judged his future inside the place.

Apprehensions eased but slightly when the two vehicles turned into a gate and came to a halt at the far end of the compound where no armed guards or uniformed soldiers were seen. A medical officer sauntered leisurely from the building to escort the new victims to the lighted courtyard enclosed within a lower brick fence. He faced his charges to give them their instructions.

"This is the Chatham Road Isolation Center," he recited with a disinterest that explained how many times in the past the sentence had been used. "You'll be here for a week. The men are to go to the baths on the ground floor; the women to the baths on the first floor. Leave your clothes inside so we can collect them for cleaning and disinfecting. You'll be given new clothing to use until yours are returned. If any of you have valuables," he said, nodding at the shabby people to let them know he was wasting his voice, "you can leave them at the desk where they'll be kept safe for you until you are ready to leave again. After you have finished bathing go to the medical office for a physical examination. The attendant will show you where it is."

With the instructions given, the officer sucked in a patience-inducing breath. All the questions the newcomers would raise had been answered in the opening statement, yet the questions would nevertheless come. The people had been too excited to listen. He snatched the list of names from the driver and began counting heads, a way to be useful while the people wasted time.

The two vanloads stood in tight little family groups, each apart from the other and all apart from the officer, yet all close enough to hear everything being said so that nothing important would be missed. When the officer made it clear he would say no more, and all adjusted to the fact that nothing could be done to avoid internment, they marched slowly to the baths telling themselves that a bath anywhere, even in prison, would be a luxury during the water shortage.

A Red Cross worker approached Au and Po as though knowing beforehand that they would be arriving. The clean set of clothing she handed Au reminded him of Chung-kin's laundry still hanging to dry on the roof of the flat. He wondered how long it would stay there. The possible presence of cholera germs might guard the laundry better than a set of watching eyes. It was possible also that some brave thief might steal the clothes and sell them quickly, believing it could be done before the germ found him.

During his bath Au gave up worrying about the laundry with a fatalistic shrug. It would be gone long before he could return to claim it. A fool, a thief, cared nothing for danger. It could not be helped. After the bath he helped Po into his new, unfamiliar clothing and led the way to the medical office for the examination. The first to appear, they had to wait until the doctor found the forms the nurses had already put away thinking the day was over.

The examination was short. To determine if Au or Po were cholera carriers, the doctor took rectal swab tests. Po yelped in surprise when the swab invaded his privates, and remembered the woman who had done the same when his shoe had invaded hers. He forgave himself. His punishment was greater than what he had inflicted on that woman. Seven times greater. The doctor said such tests would be taken each day for seven days.

The day had been more than unlucky. It was a disaster. As he lay on the strange cot, in strange clothing, listening to strange sounds and voices, Po's thoughts gave no clue of what to expect in the future. The past was gone. Without Chung-kin to upset his plans, there were no plans. Au had once said a man had to return to his native village to die, and Chen had said that a son had to look after his father. Beyond these two requirements, what else was there?

CHAPTER EIGHT

In the early months of World War II soldiers in Hong Kong battled uselessly against being cut off by the enemy. Japanese troops fought not far to the north, while Japanese ships and submarines patrolled the sea to the south. Cargo ships that somehow managed to worm through the enemy's blockade were scarce. Thus, supplies inside the "Fragrant Harbor" were limited and had to be protected from theft and damage but also kept available for rationed distribution. The government constructed temporary godowns along the harbor's beleaguered edge for just such purposes. When the war ended, government rationing and army controls ended with it. The godowns fell into a disuse that lasted for years.

Then, in 1956, the cold war brought the colony a surprising series of political riots. Each side of the continuing Chinese revolution fought to convert the Hong Kong citizens. To end the uprisings, the police began jailing known members of the notorious and illegal Triad Society, the secret league behind organized crime in the colony. The jails bulged, yet still more suspects were listed for arrest. Additional space was needed to store this cargo, the human by-product of a divided country. The rice godowns along the wharf were enclosed with brick, barbed wire, watchtowers, barred windows, and renamed a prison. When the innocent were freed, the guilty deported, and the riots ended, the buildings again fell into disuse.

Now the colony's water shortage brought the buildings a cargo of suspected cholera carriers. If the disease was to be controlled, it was necessary to control suspected carriers. The former godown-prison was given a new name, a new purpose, and new inhabitants. It was converted into a detention center, and became the new home of Au, Po, their unfortunate neighbors, and many others.

The two larger outer godowns were made into living quarters to house single women in first floor dormitories, single men in ground floor dormitories, and family units in separate rooms whenever available. The building in the center of the quadrangle was converted into a dining-recreation hall.

The first morning Au awoke surprisingly refreshed. The luxury of the hot bath, clean clothes and bedding, and the knowledge that life's burdens were to be assumed by someone else, brought him a relaxation not found at home. He lay in bed staring at the gray ceiling, thinking about seven days without struggle. A week seemed forever. He wanted to refuse to get up but his conscience warned him to survey the camp and learn its routine. His obligations had to be posted somewhere, and the bulletin boards in the dining hall seemed a likely place to begin looking for them.

Clouds hanging low over the nearby bay soon displaced Au's contentment. The surrounding hills, which last night flicked their lights so cheerfully, were now dull and forboding. The morning sun was limited to diffused rays between the clouds and the sea. It too was caged. The damp, uncomfortable air was heavy with depression, and the empty watchtowers predicted the day's intentions. Open doors in the compound hinted at a truce as they were meant to, but their hints were overshadowed by barred windows and gate guards. The implied freedom was psychological. Pleased in knowing that what intimidated him would not be seen by Po, Au resolved to keep his premonitions from influencing his son. Under proper leadership the week could be a vacation for Po. With that hope, Au went back to the dormitory to see if the boy was awake.

Following breakfast, the camp's new members were singled out and given anti-cholera inoculations. The sting had no sooner left their arms when they were assembled in the dining hall for lectures and demonstrations. The cholera germ, it was explained, hibernated under dirty fingernails and dirty toenails. Thus, each of them owned a home for the bug. When the lecturer calculated that his threats had sufficiently frightened his audience he demonstrated the proper method of cleaning these homes.

It was shortly after lunch that the sun finally cut through the low clouds and began flooding the camp with its warmth. A half hour later the loudspeaker penetrated the noise of many conversations with the sound of Au's name, calling him to the front office. Foreseen by the ominous morning, the message was a formality. Chung-kin was dead. She had died in the hospital—a fact he had accepted the previous night. Knowing it would happen minimized the pain, yet the belief was now a reality. Confirmation did nothing to fill the void he had already entered the night before.

Au came from the office to lean against the building's wall, staring at the freedom of the open front gate. A man's place was with his family. Everything a man possessed was possessed by and for his family. The world had nothing more useless than a man alone, a man without a family, and all things in the world were useless when there was no family to share them.

Confinement would prevent Au from participating in Chung-kin's funeral, a duty prescribed by family. Since it was a contagious disease that had killed her, it was unlikely that the hospital would release her body. Family rituals would have to be altered. Perhaps Cousin Liu would do something. Perhaps it was best to do nothing. Under the circumstances, it might be best to stay away.

Au turned away from the gate and his thoughts. The death, now official, had to be explained to Po. He looked across the courtyard to see Po sitting on the bench where he had been when the loudspeaker's summons came. Surely Po had prepared himself, surely he had surmised Chung-kin's death when he had asked about it the previous night.

Au sat down, touched his knee against Po's, and lit a cigarette. "The message came," he opened the subject calmly. "Your mother died of the disease this morning in the hospital." Although weakening, the calmness begged the boy to accept fate.

Other than pinching his lips together in determination, Po gave no outward sign of emotion.

After a period of silence Au asked, "You knew?"

"Yes."

"How?"

"My friend told me cholera kills you."

"Which one?" Au prodded. "The white woman?"

"She's not a friend."

Au smiled. His son had friends. "Then who?"

"Another one."

The news pleased Au. By working, the boy had found another life. Begging had permitted him to escape the restricted confines of being blind, and with friends outside his home he had others to lean on, others to relieve the responsibilities of his father. "Let's go for a walk," Au suggested, hoping to get closer to his son now that he knew the boy was capable of living away from his parents.

As they walked the courtyard Au worried about Po being able to accept the death without help. He watched the young face for a sign of tears, a signal of surrender, or an indication of bravery being forced. But nothing came. Au struggled with conflicting desires. He wanted the boy to be dependent because dependence would give him a reason to live, but he wanted also to see his son advance into manhood. From Po's reaction Au knew the boy could be a man when he had to be. When he was with his mother he was still a child.

Po continued walking silently, sullenly, yet alert to extraneous noises near enough to involve him if he

179

got careless or too close. All the while he kept the feel of Au's hand in his.

They walked in slow, pensive circles for the balance of the afternoon.

In his desire to return to the familiar bench that had given him solitude in the morning, Po barely touched his dinner. He went out to the bench to think, yet refused to share his thoughts with his father.

Au sat alongside quietly, respecting the privacy of his son's mind, for such periods were the beginning of manhood. Each had to reflect on the consequences of Chung-kin's death in his own way, yet in granting Po this right Au discovered that his sorrow multiplied for not being shared. Chung-kin was already lost. Now Po was being taken away by early maturity. Recalling how his own youth was shortened by the war, Au grieved over his inability to stop the cruelties of life from doing the same to his only son.

After dinner volunteer workers from outside brought newspapers into the camp and dropped them quickly to avoid being mauled by the news-hungry internees. The crowds stood in small circles, bickering and snuggling closer to those who had successfully retrieved a paper. Only a small item appeared that night. World affairs and the prolonged water shortage had cheated cholera of its newsworthiness.

CHOLERA

Another Death

Four new cholera cases, including one death, were reported over the weekend. Total deaths to date number 3, total cases reported, 81.

Au Chung-kin, the 38-year-old wife of an unemployed laborer from Central District, died at Infectious Diseases Hospital this morning. The victim had been sick for three days. A 4-year-old boy and a 56-year-old man were found suffering from mild cases in Wanchai District. Neither had received inoculations. A 30-year-old woman from Western District was also found suffering from a mild case. She had been inoculated earlier this year.

Six cholera contacts and a cured carrier were discharged this weekend. One carrier and 228 contacts remain at the Chatham Road Isolation Center.

The first time Au ever saw Chung-kin's name in print had to be a death notice. And as full and active as he believed his life was, the newspaper summarized it all with "unemployed laborer." The small news article, like life itself, ridiculed him. Masked by its coldness was the destruction of a good woman who had held together an injured family. There was no hint of the repercussions of the tragedy. If there was relief in the article it could only be that the impersonal print kept Chung-kin's life a private affair. The disease and her death, unlike her life, belonged to everyone. Au returned to the bench, electing to keep from Po the family's insignificant moment of notoriety.

The minutes of dusk dragged in their hollow bitterness. From the bench Au watched the people roam the yard. Untouched by death and disease, most were free to enjoy the change forced on them. Someone's misfortune had awakened them, had cracked their family shells just as his misfortune had awakened his neighbors. Strangers were made temporary friends by the power of confinement. Yet, one by one, as the evening waned, they slipped surely back to their families so nothing there might escape their notice.

In an attempt to pull Po's mind from lingering too long in the seclusion it wanted, Au began counting the rooms and mentally distributing the 228 contacts the newspaper had mentioned. A weak effort to determine how crowded they were, it nevertheless achieved its purpose. Po became engrossed in the arithmetic. When the courtyard loudspeaker again called for Au to come to the front office, he hoped Po would continue the calculations.

On the way to the office Au hesitated, needing moments to anticipate what would be asked of him. Nothing had been said about money, either for his stay in the camp or for Chung-kin's hospitalization and burial. Deep in his hidden fears also was the belief that the government had uncovered the family's illegal entry into the colony. Guilt grabbed him. Had he not feared government reprisal he might have taken Chung-kin to the inoculation center or to the hospital a day sooner. The newspaper said cholera had claimed only three lives in spite of the camp's large crowd. The disease was not as deadly as fear and rumor made it.

Resigned to fate, Au shrugged. Let them ask for money, he had none to give, and let them search their records, his reasons for entering Hong Kong had died along with his wife. In his need for strength to defy the authorities, he told himself it was time to walk north, to prepare himself for his own death so he might be buried with his ancestors.

By the time he reached the attendant at the gate Au had worked defiance into his attitude. "I am Au," he declared. "I was called."

The uniformed Chinese attendant leaned his head inside the small cubicle guarding the gate. "Yes," he acknowledged on bringing the head out again. "You have a visitor." As he spoke his eyes appraised Au. "You can talk," he instructed, pausing for emphasis, "in the examination room. Don't get too close to your visitor," he admonished with a sly laugh and compounded the mystery with an evil wink. "Don't pass germs."

Befuddled by the attendant's peculiar hints Au eagerly entered the room to learn what awaited him. Inside he stopped short, surprised by what he saw. Snuggled comfortably in the doctor's chair was the English woman, the woman who had come to the apartment. Seeing her made him blush. Her presence had put ideas into the attendant's head.

Au stared at his visitor, waiting for her to explain why she had come. Feeling uncomfortable when she failed to speak as quickly as he wished, he asked, "How do you feel? You didn't look too well the other night."

Au's concern erased the edges of Miss Bishop's loneliness. "Fine," she smiled. "Fine today. I'm sorry for having acted so miserably last night. I've . . . I've been away from direct client contact too long," she explained weakly, apologetically. "I forgot for the moment what to do." This man was different. He listened attentively, appeared interested, yet, without effort, he had assumed the supposed authority of his sex. "I'm sorry. Truly I am."

To elaborate the apology was unnecessary, and Au ignored it. "What brought you to the flat last night?" he asked politely, curiously, taking the seat opposite her. "I don't know what might have happened if you hadn't come when you did. Did Po ask you to come because his mother was sick?"

The question, by implying she and Po were already friends, warmed her. Apparently Po had said nothing to his father about their confrontation. Dear, blind, begging Po. "No," she decided to answer. She wasted seconds by nervously rifling her purse for a stick of gum. Au lit a cigarette. She pulled a few more useless papers from the purse so time might establish her unwillingness to answer. "How is Po?" she asked finally, skirting the subject on her mind until after testing his attitude.

"Fine," Au answered obediently and saw her eyes light with pleasure. "He asks about you," he lied appropriately. His guess was endorsed by the pride in her smile.

Pretending weakly to hide the pleasure she knew was obvious to him, she tossed her head to throw the hair back from the sides of her face, then looked down to her lap. "Did you get the news about your wife?" she asked, trying to return the conversation to him.

It became his turn to dip his face. "Yes," he answered. "This afternoon. It was expected. I've seen cholera before. During the war. So had my wife." He shrugged, an attempt to explain fate must be accepted. "She was weak from overwork and from carrying a baby."

As he talked she studied him for signals of the depth of his sorrow. Experience had leaned her toward viewing all Chinese marriages as unions of convenience; arranged affairs consummated to appease family and history rather than to fulfill love. Knowing he had been trained not to show his emotions, she watched each move, each expression for an

184

indication that with him it had been different. The Chinese knew how to end desire, but not how to nurse it. They often rejected as useless the love life had denied her. Pulling herself out of the thoughtful trance before it had a chance to embitter her, she saw Au studying her as hard as she had been studying him. She looked to her lap to keep him from reading her mind.

Embarrassed by the reaction his staring had caused in her, Au said, "I'm sorry. You've come to see me for a reason. I haven't given you the chance to say what it is."

"How is Po?" she asked again.

"Fine," he recited. She wanted to talk about Po.

"What will Po do now?" she asked, proving his thoughts correct.

"I don't know," he answered obediently. She must have plans for Po. "I've been looking for work for two years with no luck. Now I have no wife, no money, no work. And a son to look after." He laughed easily, attempting to tell her he was willing to allow fate to take a hand in his affairs—if she had come as fate's representative. "The most important project is for me to find work."

For a moment she reveled in his troubled admission. "I've just had a marvelous thought," she declared pretentiously. "I know of a school for blind children. They just might have an opening for another boy. I know the superintendent personally. There's no charge. The government will pay for you. Would it help you if Po went there?"

Au frowned in his failure to impress her with his lack of work. Po had work. Po's income had also been steady, needed. Still, to live off Po's income would be worse than the two years he had spent living off Chung-kin's income. Po's begging would become dishonorable when its only purpose was getting money. "It's a difficult time for decisions," he told her finally. "I'm sorry," she agreed. "I should have known." "Some schools," he remarked weakly, "are workhouses for the blind. If Po wants to work I'd rather he stay home with me and work."

To avoid staring at him, she turned toward the windows as though responding to a noise outside. An urge to leave, to get away before he led her away from her purpose surged as it often did when the Chinese tried to use her. Her planning had not included the possibility of the boy's father wanting to lead her in another direction. Chinese parents, historically, sacrificed everything to send their sons to school. Perhaps this man thought he could get both a job for himself and school for his son if he handled her properly. "He won't work at this school," she said. "I can assure you of that!"

"What can they teach a blind boy?" he asked skeptically.

Perhaps he was ignorant rather than negative. "Reading, writing . . ." she answered, then paused. Other than these two, she did not know what the school taught. "He'll get a good education," she guessed.

She could see in Au's eyes that now it was her ignorance that was exposed, and surmising herself on the receiving end of his distrust irritated her. "It's a Christian school," she added, submerging in the short explanation the fact that Christian schools were operated by white people and, therefore, had to be good. After a moment in which he failed to respond with enthusiasm, her thoughts discovered another possible objection. "He'll be told about the Christian religion," she admitted, "but he doesn't have to listen . . . or . . . or believe. He can stay in the school even if you don't want him to join the church."

Au got up from the chair slowly. "I'll have to think about it," he said. As he inched his way closer to the door he smiled at her. "First I have to find work for myself," he explained, submerging in the short explanation the belief that the color of her skin entitled her to know hundreds of people who might employ him.

She opened herself to the warmth of his smile. "I'll come back tomorrow night if it's all right with you. My evenings are my own. I'm alone." She stood up and stepped near him to judge his height. She was inches shorter. "I'd like an answer about the school tomorrow . . . if you can give one. Openings are hard to find, but I have a few friends." She turned her back on him to walk toward the door. "Too many refugees, you know," she explained casually over her shoulder.

"Of course," he agreed. Refugees. The refugees were blamed for all of the foreign government's failures. Except for the government, Hong Kong was pure Chinese. A man living among his own people was not a refugee. "I'll let you know tomorrow."

They walked together out of the building and to the front gate. Ignoring the open-mouthed guards studying the biracial friendship, they nevertheless overheard one guard comment proudly, "She speaks good Chinese!" Halfway to the taxi waiting in the compound Miss Bishop turned to wave a quick, friendly farewell.

While returning to Po, Au tried to subdue his

suspicions of foreigners. The woman had not belittled him for his poverty as he feared she might, and since she hadn't he needed time to consider her possible motives. The courteous treatment given her by the camp's officials was not wasted on him. It alerted him to her authority and her ability to get whatever it was that she wanted.

Po had left the bench, so Au walked on to the dormitory. It was dark, the white woman's visit had extended beyond the normal bed hour. Inside the dormitory he saw that a Red Cross girl had taken it upon herself to help Po.

"He doesn't remember which cot is his," she smiled, shyly in Au's stern presence.

By the second day of isolation all apprehensions over being interned in a former prison had been replaced by a spirit of vacation. Life for many had never been so good or so easy. They were awakened, fed, schooled, organized, occupied throughout the day. Rectal swab tests became the source of numerous jokes, to the annoyance of the medics who had tired of hearing each new group discover for itself the same old stories. Day after day the tests proved that no one connected with the Lyndhurst tragedy showed signs of being a carrier. The germ in Chungkin had come from the chicken in the poultry house as suspected.

The Red Cross girl continued looking for opportunities to entertain Po. The boy had no mother, no friends in the camp, and his father, she correctly assumed, was incapable of keeping him busy all day. The other children played roughhouse games, games that excluded the blind. But Po stayed unresponsive to the girl's questions and suggestions. The camp, the girl, the games, all were temporary. They neither proved nor solved a thing.

At the same time as had happened the night before, Au was again called to the front office. This night, however, the message was delivered personally, reflecting the quiet respect befitting the white woman's position. Au put Po on his cot before leaving in answer to Po's request. The boy had tired of the Red Cross girl's benevolence.

Miss Bishop waited until Au was comfortably seated in the chair opposite the desk before she began. "How was the second day in camp?" she asked, opening the discussion safely, and with a friendly smile.

"We are well cared for," he told her.

"Does it bother Po to live among the boat people?" she asked, hinting at what she had learned about the camp during the day.

Au laughed freely, surprised. Her knowledge eased the tension. Yet, the boat people with their bad habits were Chinese—his people, not hers. "They spend their lives on boats," he offered as an excuse. "They're simple," he admitted, "but good people."

"I'm sure they are," she agreed amiably. "But sometimes they forget they're not on their boats any longer. They use the floor for a toilet."

"The camp puts lime on the floor," Au excused them calmly.

"Pity the volunteer girls," she moaned quietly her concern, asking him to accept her knowledge about the Chinese as a reason to be honest. "They have to clean the place."

"They're Chinese," he answered curtly. "They understand."

"So do I," she confessed. Proud of her ability to get him to fight back rather than kowtow as he might have to a foreigner, she explained, "Does it bother Po? I mean, he can't see where he's walking."

"No," Au answered quickly. Her concern and favors would demand repayment. He had nothing to give and no right to incur a debt.

"Would you like a room to yourself?" she persisted. "Po's blind. I could arrange a single room because of his handicap."

"No," he insisted cautiously. "I think it's better for us to stay with a group." Feeling it wise to temper what appeared to be stubbornness, he added, "This will end soon. Po thinks too much when he's alone. It isn't good for him to think too much."

His rejection of her several offers brought a period of silence, a time during which she might look for an expression of understanding, a hint that the impasse had strengthened the acquaintance by giving them the ability to survive it.

Au needed the silence to wonder why she was so concerned about him, or Po, or both of them. During the night he had concluded he must do whatever possible to get an education for Po, but now, since she still had not reintroduced the subject, he worried that his stalling might have cost him the opportunity offered the night before. This woman was white, English, in government, wealthy. She would be justified in doing whatever necessary to protect and increase what she had rather than concern herself with getting something for someone else.

"I opened a case file on Po today," she admitted sheepishly, an effort to end the awkward silence. "By opening a case file I can assign it a number. A bit of

Welfare officialism. We need a number to hold the opening at the school until you have time to make up your mind." She paused, giving him an opportunity to interrupt if he desired, but he said nothing. "Po is now an official government case. Government now shares his problems." Again she waited, expecting him to express an attitude. But again he offered nothing. Letting his apathy aggravate her, she decided Po's problems had to be settled whether Au liked it or not. "Harsh as it may sound," she continued defiantly, "he has no mother and his father is unemployed. Government has the right to do something. Do you mind?"

Au went through the motions of lighting a cigarette to hide his pleasure. His refusing to cooperate had induced her to reveal everything without his having to beg. "I'm sure you're doing what is best," he answered.

"Heavens!" she barked, blushed, and stifled a humble laugh meant to cool the seriousness of his acceptance. "I wish I shared your confidence in my efforts. After the past couple of days, considering my horrible behavior of the other night . . . well, I'm not so sure of myself any longer. As a matter of fact, I wanted to tell you also that I can destroy the file on Po if you want me to. I only opened it to allow you more time to think . . . under the circumstances. I had to do something to keep the school opening reserved."

Au stared, blinking at the darkness outside the window.

Then she scolded herself for giving him too much of an option. "You must have strong reasons for not wanting Po in school," she guessed, trying to encourage him into explaining his position.

"I thought about the school last night," he admitted finally. "After you left. The more I thought, the more I knew there was nothing to think about. Of course the boy must go. It would be unfair of me to let my unemployment keep him from getting an education." He paused to emphasize that his need was also serious. "I don't know what they can do to help him," he added, "but they should be given the opportunity to do what they can." After stating his decision he saw her wide smile telling him he had taken the course she wanted. "What do we do now?" he wondered.

She nervously patted her hand on the chair's arm, anticipating the project's next move. "Tomorrow," she decided, "I'll telephone the school and tell them Po is definitely coming. We'll have to select a date so they can prepare for him. Have they told you when you'll be getting out of here?"

"Neither of us have shown signs of being carriers. I think we'll be discharged either next Monday or Tuesday."

She pursed her lips, subconsciously strengthening herself for a delay. "Would you want some time with Po at your flat before sending him off to school?"

"No," he spoke slowly. "I think it would be better if he went directly from here, if that's possible. He'll miss his mother if we go back to the flat."

"Yes," she agreed reluctantly. "It's better not to remind him of his mother so soon." She smiled, the case was keeping step with her hopes. "Is Po excited about going to school?" she asked expectantly.

"I haven't told him about it," he admitted.

"You haven't told him?" she asked disbelievingly. In her imagination an excited Po loved her for making it possible.

"To tell him before it happened would give him time to fight going," he reasoned, resenting the pleasure she was getting at his expense. "He mustn't be given the chance to form an opinion. I'll tell him about it either when he brings the subject up or when time runs out. Soon he'll ask what we are going to do when we get discharged from here," he smiled from knowing his son so well, "and then I'll tell him. He won't like the idea. He doesn't want to give up begging."

"He *wants* to beg?" she asked, her voice giving Au the chance to say he was joking.

The break in their worlds loomed ominously. He knew no way to explain to one so rich how begging had made Po an adult, a man who had earned respect. He evaded the truth rather than disappoint her. "I'm grateful for your help and consideration. I don't know how to repay you. I have no money, you know."

Prolonging the righteousness he made her feel, she scanned the desk for misplaced objects that might have come from her purse. "You don't owe me anything," she admitted. "It's my job." To keep her eyes from revealing a concern she wanted to keep from him, she got up and left.

Instead of walking with her to the front gate as he had the night before, Au stayed in the office to review everything said between them, hoping to understand her. He stayed until silent pressure from the guards, braver in the white woman's absence, forced him to leave.

The lights in the dormitory were still lit when Au returned. Po, sitting alone on the cot, appeared to be anticipating his return.

"It was the white woman again?" Po asked.
"Yes."
Po shifted uneasily. "Am I going to school?"
"Yes," Au answered and took advantage of his

son's blindness to stare in astonishment. "Is that what she wanted to talk about that night when she came to the flat with you?"

"Yes."

During the remaining days in the camp the women sat in large circles noisily discussing their husbands, their children, their homes, their problems, and their neighbors, and proudly watched their children play the games organized by the volunteer girls. And nothing prevented the adults from enjoying a game of Mah-Jongg, although to gamble, the games had to be held in semiprivacy to excuse the Chinese guards from enforcing the white man's rules. Those wishing to participate in group activities did so in a spirit of union. Union was enjoyed since the friendships would be temporary. Small family cliques remained, but were strong mostly in the seclusion of hearts and nights.

Au kibitzed a Mah-Jongg game, one that had begun before his arrival in camp, until he was invited to join. As though shy and reluctant, he joined and then proceeded to win. Beaming with false excitement over his luck, he kept his skill concealed by praising the ability of the losers. Money was essential to starting life anew as a widower. Chung-kin's death made the flat a luxury.

After dinner, in the cool twilight, small groups formed to discuss seriously and deeply matters of no consequence. The constant turnover allowed the talkative to tell and retell their favorite stories to people who had not come to listen but had come to feel the security of being with a crowd. The leaders made no demands on the shy because it was the shy who made them leaders.

194

Po obstinately fought the affection given him by the volunteer girls who singled him out with a passion. They loved him, he liked them, but for him to continue to use their assistance was to continue the acceptance of his own inability. He followed their suggestions grudgingly because he was afraid of what Au might do to him if he angered them. He considered his behavior a gift to their happiness.

When Au and Po got together after dinner they had little to give each other in the way of news, but much to give in the way of family and silent unity. Their need to belong to each other had to be strengthened to survive the threat of separation in the near future.

CHAPTER NINE

Thursday and Friday Victoria Bishop stayed in the office to catch up with the work invisible hands had stacked on her desk during her preoccupation with the Au case. The case, now an official problem as well as a source of inner pleasure, had been opened to all the tentacles of assistance the administration offered. And Victoria Bishop secretly allowed her love for the little beggar to nourish on the plans she had for him. Although the procedures were routine, since the boy's assignment to the school-home was sanctioned by the sole remaining parent, she nevertheless kept the case folder at hand with all its starkly pathetic details. Each mark, each line, each checked box made the boy that much more familiar and that much more in need of her. She told herself she was developing an ideal case for administrators who needed perfect examples to display at budget time. The father of the client was unemployed, had been unemployed for two years, had actively searched for work during those years, and in spite of it had not abandoned the blind child. Add to this the fact that the boy was without a mother and the synopsis was ready to be submitted as a classic. Everyone would agree she had proceeded properly. Everyone except the client, the blind beggar.

By handling the case personally Miss Bishop was assured that questions pertaining to its origin could be discreetly submerged. Only on rare occasions did a worker stumble across a need as positive as the Au case. But since most of Welfare was more than busy in keeping up with cases coming through normal channels she feared that her looking for more work might be considered strange. The Au case must be considered preventive. Early discovery had brought it to the department's attention before coming through the jurisdiction of the courts. Sooner or later all begging children were dragged before the magistrates on some minor offense, and then their records were marred for life. Often, as a result, the children developed a distrust of government and of governmental authority instead of welcoming the intervention. This boy, Po, had been spared the court's drama and its aftereffects. She was delighted.

Saturday morning she first telephoned the Isolation Center to confirm the Monday release of the Aus, then she called the Protestant Home to inform Mrs. Hoff that Po would be coming. Monday, she promised Mrs. Hoff, she would deliver the blind boy and the necessary documents authorizing government payment for his keep. Mrs. Hoff expressed her satisfaction that the reserved cot was at last to be filled and her happiness that it would be filled by a government-sponsored child. "We need the money," she explained honestly.

With the district details completed, Miss Bishop dropped the forms in the mail for headquarters' approval. This done, she left her office. Remembering how both Harry Leong and Mrs. Hoff had caught her unprepared, she decided to get as much information as possible on the Au family before going on with the case. She left for the Records Division of the Registration of Persons office where refugees were listed—oftentimes unknown to the refugees themselves since the information came from irritated landlords or suspicious employers.

Weekends were the loneliest periods in Victoria Bishop's life. On Saturday afternoons and Sundays her office was closed, freeing the workers to wander to club swimming pools, bars, homes of friends and relatives, beaches and restaurants where they could spend the energy they had saved during the week. To maintain her façade of overwork, Miss Bishop usually avoided such places. If she went she had to appear unescorted, and she preferred not to lead others into suspecting her morals or into thinking she starved for companionship. Loneliness was pathetic, but it was worse still to be an object of pathos. To keep free of those capable of suspecting her plight, she avoided them. To fill the empty hours, she often went to headquarters on quiet Saturday afternoons with the hope of being discovered working so her colleagues might be released from the burden of worrying about her absence from social events. She put out of her mind the thought that those she saw at headquarters wanted to be seen there for the same reasons.

This afternoon, however, as much as she wanted to be seen, she hoped desperately not to be seen by Harry Leong. The beggar boy case had been made too much of an issue for Harry to forget so soon. Normal, polite conversation with Harry would call for a review of their last talk, and Harry would confirm what he had suspected all along; that helping the boy was more necessary for her than for the boy. But since his last promotion, which took him as high as he could go, Harry didn't hang around the office on Saturday. He usually drove his family out to Deep Water Bay for swimming whenever the weather permitted.

Since the chance of meeting someone at head-quarters at lunchtime was remote, Miss Bishop stopped first at her favorite restaurant for a snack. Actually, the Moscow Palace was more of a conveni-ent habit than a favorite eating house. Nevertheless, one needed an acceptable excuse for doing anything, and habit was as good an excuse as society needed. She climbed the steps to the first floor dining hall and took her usual bench in the corner where she could observe without being observed. When the waiter handed her the menu she had long since memorized she pushed it aside and ordered cabbage soup with dark bread, as famous in Hong Kong as were the girls of Wanchai. She smiled dutifully back at Mr. Wong, the proprietor, who, as usual, bowed his head in re-spect to her presence.

Lunch completed, she walked briskly to the Star Ferry, boarded the Meridian Star, and proceeded to the island side. Following the usual path up the tunnel and through the lane leading to the North Point tram, she sighed in the lane's deserted bareness. The path was as lonely without its beggar as she was. She slowed to allow her imagination to produce a picture of him. He belonged to her now. No longer would he be the victim of inquisitive eyes. She would make him an honorable member of Chinese society, a member equal to those who lorded themselves over him by giving him coins.

It was not until seeing the newsstand that Victoria Bishop realized the past week had been so busy that she had not taken time to keep abreast of the world's other problems. Catching the old newsman by surprise she greeted him with a mechanical "Good afternoon," quickly checked his stand, helped herself to the only English paper visible, a copy of the *South China Morning Post*, and held out her change. The newsman, busy shuffling through his papers, ignored the offering. She dropped the thirty cents on the stand, missing the coin box by inches, and continued on to the tram.

Chen popped up smiling and waving a magazine, but the white woman was gone. He looked around to see if anyone had watched his foolishness. No one had. The culture magazine was another waste. He cursed the unpredictable foreigner.

From the Registration of Persons files Miss Bishop withdrew the three cards on the Au family. On Po's card she crossed out the old Lyndhurst address, then after a dreamy moment inserted the address of the Protestant Home. On the wife's card she scribbled the morbid details of death. Writing the small note re-created the tragedy she had witnessed, threatened to sicken her, and hurried her on to Au's card. Irresistibly her eyes noted his age, 45; then she corrected the information under "marital status." After finishing,

200

she stared out the window, concentrating on what more her heart hoped to extract from the card. Their lives had crossed, and, unlike her encounters with Po, her acquaintance with Au was not known, even to Harry Leong. Suddenly her conscience twinged with the guilt that accompanies being caught reading some-one else's mail. She returned the cards to the file and left.

The following morning she awoke pleased by how her dreams had survived in fantasy through the night. As the rays of the bright sun slanted through the bedroom window, their cheerfulness lulling her into semiconsciousness, she smiled until the shock of being late for work crashed through her half sleep. She grabbed the clock angrily, mentally scolding it for not awakening her, and then saw the alarm had not been set. Sunday. Of course, Sunday. Returning the clock to its stand, she slid leisurely between the sheets, beg-ging their comfort to sustain her a while longer. But it was too late. Her heart still beat from the fear of being late for work and it could not be calmed.

Days in Hong Kong began beautifully if one were of a mind to appreciate them. The early red rays of the sun reflected from the bay to diffuse the fog with a peculiar orange haze. The color sprayed the distant hills and sleeping buildings. The air was fresh, washed by having traveled the thousands of miles of ocean to the south. Gently blowing during the night, the tender breezes covered the city and in its millions of crevices formed a feathery wand of magic that sparkled all the wonders of the exotic East. Although the mysteries of darkness vanished as millions of small breakfast fires polluted the freshness with their red tongues, excitement was generated in the knowledge that night would restore it all. The intrigue was submerged but temporarily.

That was years ago. That was when Miss Bishop still believed she would be rewarded for following the rules, for obeying the laws, for servicing justice, for spending herself unselfishly, and for voicing her ideals. Since she now felt none of these were rewarded, she experienced bitterness and selfishness. She blamed her spirit's decline on the Chinese who felt no obligations to each other, on the Chinese who did much too little to help themselves. As though living temporarily away from home, the Chinese valued only monetary or personal gains.

The unfriendliness that age was teaching her to see in the Chinese she also observed in the colony's Britons. The English soldiers and sailors who once whistled suggestively and teased her into joining them were gone. They were being replaced by young boys who resented her presence among them as though they feared she might write to their mothers about their behavior.

The English who had spent years in Hong Kong were equally bad. Most of them were married and had little time for anyone or anything beyond their families. They preferred living in seclusion so their complaints against their jobs, their fellow workers, and their hardships would not be overheard and used as an excuse to send them home. Many became drunks, afraid to go home except for the occasional furlough taken mostly to prove that home was no longer what it had been. Expatriates, entrenched, they refused to help each other. Their dinner invitations to Miss

Bishop were born of a need to feel superior; they judged her loneliness greater than theirs. She refused these offers regularly without caring if the refusal might make them more bitter. Invitations were condescensions.

Fully awake now, Miss Bishop sat on the edge of the bed. The next conscious thought brought cold shudders. Age and now the water shortage made a cold cloth-rinse bath impossible. For breakfast she fixed a small bowl of porridge, a pot of tea, some toast, and ate while listening to the news on Rediffusion. When the news ended the station slipped unannounced into a religious service, one taped from London for replay, and she jumped to shut it off before getting homesick. Sunday was a bad day. There was too little to do. A day hardly worth the effort.

Habit directed that the morning be spent in cleaning the flat. Chinese *amahs* were cheap, but they left the rooms disheveled, often worse on leaving than on entering. The ivory-carved statue was off center on its doily, the pictures askew, the chairs unequally spaced around the table. The rooms looked as though the cleaning woman had moved everything intentionally, either to annoy her employer or to prove they had been touched. Chinese were strange that way.

Hong Kong's glamour was diminishing while its price was increasing.

When the flat was precisely to Miss Bishop's exacting requirements, she felt free to go outside for some window-shopping. Her search for a nice cloisonné vase in Ming green continued leisurely. To end the search would be to end Sundays. Each time she saw something she liked, the price was too high.

Chinese merchants, who celebrated their ability to rob all their customers, were adrenalined to even greater heights whenever a foreigner entered. She kept trying, however, because the search had become a Sunday habit. It stimulated her because it angered her.

Sunday evenings she usually went to the Moscow Palace for dinner. The feast preceded the ritual of attending the nondenominational church nearby. She walked into the Palace's small first-floor bakery and aimed herself toward the steps. Noticing how the carpeted steps were strewn with bread crumbs, she walked carefully to avoid driving the crumbs deeper where they might never be picked up. Perched in the comfort of her customary booth, her Sunday mood was more critical than usual.

The waiter, slower than she wished to pay attention to her, tossed the menu instead of handing it when he finally did arrive. She fumed at his back as he walked away. She had become such a positive Sunday night fixture her tip was counted before given. The waiter's jacket was spotted with food stains. Leniency classified it as dirty. Actually, she decided, it was more than dirty.

In a mood to be aggravated still further, she accepted the waiter's help. The man dropped the silverware as carelessly in front of her as he had dropped the menu. The pieces just lay there demanding to be arranged properly. Then he brought a glass of water—an advertisement to everyone watching that she was an American tourist! His thumb was partly submerged in the sloshing soup. Then he held the cream pitcher dangerously over her cup of tea as though intuition would tell him precisely how much she wanted.

By the time Mr. Wong walked over to give his customary Sunday night greeting, Victoria Bishop had enticed herself into a near rage.

"How's everything tonight?" Wong asked, his painted smile grinning down at her while his eyes roamed, checking the premises and keeping watch on the waiters. He remained dutifully at her side, awaiting her traditional answer.

The calloused, perfunctory behavior only served to goad her anger. She leaned back to look straight up at her persecutor. "Mr. Wong," she sang emphatically, trailing the name slowly to indicate more was coming after she finished glaring at him, "Your restaurant is filthy! The filth is horrible. The waiters," she said, waving both hands, hung loosely at the wrists, toward the waiters, "are dirty! Impossibly dirty! Irresponsibly dirty! They treat their customers with absolutely no respect. As a matter of fact," she corrected, "with utter disrespect!" She shook her head at nothing to underscore her anger.

Wong, startled by the unusual outburst, stayed nailed to the spot. For years this woman had answered him with the same polite, meaningless smile and the same polite, meaningless words that he had given her in the same polite, meaningless way. It was habit, like the bread crumbs on the steps, the food stains on the jackets, the mice in the kitchen. A safe habit. He stared, confused, searching her face for the reason for the change.

"You need someone to bring a little organization, discipline, and business atmosphere in here," she continued, knowing the Chinese looked to the English for advice and leadership. "If you don't get someone," she warned, shaking a finger at him, "You'll lose your reputation." Having vented her feelings she felt better. She nodded silently at the truth of her statements, looked down at her food to tell him he could go away now, and settled herself to enjoy the meal.

Wong, however, refused to budge until the reason for her rage became clear to him. The outburst had a definable Oriental flavor. First he had to discover what she wanted, then she could put a price on it. "Who do you have in mind?" he asked, trying to entice her attention from a biscuit. The small roll, a day old, had lost its moistness. It was dropping crumbs on her lap.

"Who do I have in mind for what?" she muttered, irritated by his lingering.

"For the job of organizing the place and giving it a business atmosphere," he recited accurately. He laughed, proud of how Chinese culture had invaded this woman's Western ways.

Exasperated at his stupid persistence, she roughly pulled the spoon from the teacup, splashing little brown spots on the cloth. She smiled as he winced. The tea spots soaking through the cloth would keep him from reversing it. Revenge made her feel still better. She leaned back and sighed. Each time she thought she was beginning to understand these peculiar people something strange like this happened to confuse her again. She put the spoon back in the tea and stirred gently, wasting time, hoping he would leave.

But then—of course! Au's name, prominent in her work all week and her dreams of last night, came once more to her mind. "As a matter of fact," she smiled coyly, "I happen to know someone who could do wonders for this . . . this filthy place. A marvelous man." The match, in imagination, was perfect. "A very presentable, older chap who could control these . . . these young scamps. He's a proud sort, a handsome man. He keeps himself clean, too. He'd make an excellent waiter," she concluded, allowing her mind to picture Au as her heart wanted him to be.

Wong stroked the back of his head pensively. This woman had been a steady customer for many years. Europeans were peculiar people. Confusing at times. A single, accidental abuse and they took their business elsewhere, and they bruised easily. He had no need for another waiter, but if he had to hire one then he wouldn't have to replace the next young boy who quit. The boys left him fast and often—whenever they'd saved enough money to go back to school or learned enough English to get a better job in one of the newer hotels. In a week this woman could spend more money for food than he paid a waiter for a month's work. Keeping this woman happy was more important than being temporarily overstaffed.

"Bring your friend around," Wong said pretentiously. "Perhaps I can use him."

"I just might do that," she promised. Her stomach revolted nervously in victory.

That night, in church, she offered up a special prayer of thanks.

The next morning Miss Bishop awoke feeling groggy, yet relieved that Monday had arrived at last. In preparing to attack the pleasant duties, she recapped the entire restaurant episode. The more she reconstructed the job offer in the light of morning, the more her apprehension grew. The Chinese were tricky. They had fooled her often enough in the past. Wong's offer might not have been honest. Wong might have been fooling her, trying to pacify her, trying to tell her what he thought she wanted to hear from him. The offer could have been a typically Chinese excuse meant to tide her over the unhappiness of the moment.

During breakfast, in a mood of pessimism, it occurred to her that even if Wong's offer were serious, Au might not take it! Au and Po would certainly be on edge on the day they were being separated. Both of them had the right to be against everything today. She debated holding off telling Au about the job, yet she knew she could not. Details were always handled as they arose.

While doing the breakfast dishes she fretted over the uncontrollable factors. Yesterday's confidence was gone. The value of social work was as nebulous as was the worth of Mrs. Hoff's religious work at the blind home and Wong's job offer. One had to believe all things happened for the best, else decisions would remain forever inside those who made them. Certainly religious workers suffered depressions just as she did. Missionaries used their faith to end depressions, and Au claimed thinking too much was the cause of depressions. She decided to follow Au's wisdom. Doing as he dictated gave him power over her, and this she liked.

Of course Wong's job offer was real. It had better be. Wong was aware she knew people in Health Inspection who could close his place. And Au, after all, had lived two years without work. He would jump at any offer. At the camp he had argued his main concern was employment for himself. Work for him was as imperative as school was for Po.

Dedicated and anxious, she left for the office earlier than usual.

Seated at her desk in the quiet reward of being early, Miss Bishop took several minutes to shake off the lingering effects of the shoulder-to-shoulder crowds and the crush of getting through Hong Kong's streets. She sobered slowly, sadly. It had been years since she had arrived at work angry over someone's touching her purposely in the crowds. The young men once felt her stealthily, as though her race would make her body different somehow beneath its dress. She brushed aside the remorse and dialed the Isolation Center. After the center confirmed that Au and Po were to be released, she asked that a message be given to Au telling him to wait until she arrived.

That settled, she looked at the clock before dialing the garage. It was too early. Armsrong got drunk regularly on weekends and his helpers knew they could be late for work on Mondays. Worrying that the government cars might all be assigned before Armstrong got in, she busied her mind with the details lying in front of her.

Preparations for the new week successfully consumed most of the morning. It was not until the papers authorizing Po's admittance to the Protestant Home came in the mail that she began excitedly anticipating the afternoon. "Au Po-tong," she read the name that so much needed her attention. Dear Po. The name was quaint. His father must have put a lot of love in its selection. Could the boy, or his father, possibly be thinking of her now just as she was thinking of them?

Her thoughts nagged her into making another telephone call to the Isolation Center. She had forgotten to let Au know she would be there to pick him up shortly after lunch, and asking him to wait without giving a clue as to how long was cruel. Better still, she decided, her secretary should make the call. The camp's officials would be impressed by learning she was high enough in government to warrant having her own secretary. The knowledge might win special favors for Au and Po.

On the other hand, her secretary was a typical Chinese giggling gossip, the type who would get a great deal of pleasure from spreading false rumors about her boss, and her boss's boyfriend, a Chinese at the camp. The Chinese loved rumors that involved their white superiors. Reluctantly Miss Bishop made the call herself.

In spite of Armstrong's notorious Monday inefficiency, the beige public vehicle waited obediently outside the office when Miss Bishop stepped out. She gave the driver his instructions and then settled in the rear seat. Her composure held until the car turned into the camp's front yard where Au and Po waited, but then it gave way to churning agitations. Although the two appeared somewhat melancholy, she thought they also appeared anxious and primed for the new adventures she brought.

Au watched the driver carefully as he left one side of the car to walk around and open the door on the opposite side for his passenger. The man had the face of a coolie, flat and round, and his gait had the rhythmic bounce that betrayed years of carrying heavy stick-hung loads across his shoulders. Somewhere the man had learned to drive, and somehow he had won a good job with the government. He might have been an early, cooperative protégé of the white passenger.

To prevent her feelings from flooding out to Au, Victoria Bishop looked down at Po, hoping to decipher from his expression an attitude toward her presence. But the face revealed nothing. She put her hand on his shoulder, but then removed it quickly as the touch moved the boy closer to his father. "I don't think Po likes me," she teased, attempting to disguise the hurt.

"He's shy," Au apologized.

She sighed. "I suppose we're ready to leave?"

Au nodded and pushed Po to the car, into the center of the rear seat where he could act as a buffer between the two adults. When the car got underway Au watched the driver as though the man needed his help in negotiating the narrow lane. The subterfuge replaced conversation until the vehicle reached the open streets.

Leaning forward, Miss Bishop instructed the driver, "We'll go first to the school." She nodded meaningfully to Au, but then sharing secrets through visible signals in front of a blind person seemed deceitful. "I think you'll like the school," she told Po, patting his leg. "You'll have many young friends to play with and many things to learn. You'll enjoy it," she instructed.

The silence following her declaration forced Po into answering. "Yes, Ma'm," he acknowledged.

The car whipped and twisted angrily through the crowded business sections of Kowloon. The driver, no longer a humble coolie, frightened holes in the streams of pedestrians until the car finally emerged on the fringe of the New Territories.

The Protestant Home was a flat-roofed, two-storied brick building, an island in the middle of a playground. The whole compound was surrounded by a cyclone-wire fence that separated it from its taller and larger neighbors, a new series of Resettlement Centers. By contrast, the noise emanating from the overcrowded Resettlement Centers made the school grounds seem a secluded retreat. The car inched along carefully as though frightened by the noise and the rambunctious children who popped like firecrackers out of the huge buildings.

Once safely inside the school's office, Mrs. Hoff and Miss Bishop exchanged pleasantries while Au, on guard, watched both of them silently. Po, transfixed by the sounds of so many children coming to him through the open door, kept an ear aimed in the direction that would tell him the most.

When all the small talk had been accounted for, Mrs. Hoff announced perfunctorily to everyone, "We're happy to have the new boy with us." Getting Po's attention, she proceeded to question him briefly about his age, his prior schooling, and what name he would prefer the other children to use when speaking to him. The last question was offered as a reward for having answered the first group correctly.

Po was stunned by the woman's expertise. She had pulled answers from him without his realizing, and had accomplished it all without touching him— and from her name and accent he knew she was white.

Turning her attention next to Au, Mrs. Hoff asked about Po so that she might verify what Po had told her. She cleverly proved she had many ways to get the information she needed, and would do so if necessary. When she handed Au documents needing his signature she explained that the school was sponsored by a religious organization, adding that she hoped Au would have no objections in such a way that Au knew his objections would be meaningless.

Au said what was expected of him. He claimed no objections to the Western religion, and directed this statement down to Po's ear so the boy would know how to answer such questions in the future. He claimed also that he was both proud and happy that his son had this opportunity to attend school. There were many things the boy had yet to learn, he added, but avoided asking just what the school intended to teach.

Po, listening attentively, drew his own conclusions. From the inflections in Au's voice he extracted the answers meant for him, and separated them from the answers meant for politeness. Once Au's direct message was established he let his mind drift back to the outside sounds still filtering through the open front door. Somewhere in those sounds there had to be a clue as to what the other children were learning.

When Po's mind returned to the conversation he heard Mrs. Hoff saying " . . . the classrooms are on the ground floor. We sleep on the first floor. Your son will have his hair cut. Some of the children come to us with bugs, you know. We take care to make them uniform in dress and appearance. Laundry is easier that way. The new members are allowed to keep their canes until they gain the confidence to give them up voluntarily." She touched Po's head without looking down at him. "Most give up their canes inside the first month. Some consider the cane a form of security," she explained to Au. "Giving it up is difficult at first. But to keep the cane would make them different, and they hate being different more than they love the cane. In our gymnasium we have both the instructors and the equipment for building young minds and bodies." Two more quick pats on Po's head told him to be patient, that she was still with him. "You'll like it here," she instructed, this time looking down at Po.

Po understood the first of what she said, but the last part had come too fast for him to retain all of it. He stood mute, waiting for instructions instead of general information. As sure as this woman was that he would like the place, he knew he would not.

Au felt uneasy with the two foreign women discussing so openly what, until now, had been a part of his family's secrets. He and Chung-kin had accepted Po's blindness as they accepted fate. Ignoring it over the years had almost made it disappear. Unsure of the value of discussing the blindness, he shifted uncomfortably from one foot to the other, nodding when it appeared correct to do so, and gradually let his mind drift, wondering why the women took such pains to convince themselves the school was good for Po. If the school was truly so good, it would need no explanation. Certainly both women knew he had no choice. He had no job, no wife, no means of caring for Po.

Mrs. Hoff ended her dissertation by emphasizing the rules granting parents the right to visit their children on weekends or to take them home. She then suggested, "Why don't you two go out into the yard and say your good-byes while Victoria and I work out the formalities?"

Happily dipping his head in relief, Au was as humble as one must be when getting something for nothing. He touched Po on the shoulder and led him into the open yard. They stood side by side at the fence, touching, for a long time before either dared venture a departing word.

"The school is better than your work," Au decided. "Here you'll learn things. You'll learn the things all boys should know, and you won't have to work while doing it." Not knowing how to say what he felt, he said what was expected of him. "Be good in your studies. It's important that you learn to read and write." He spoke slowly so Po would absorb the instructions, the parental commands meant to be taken without question.

The silence holding them extended until Miss Bishop came out of the office signaling to Au that it was time for them to go. She stopped in front of Po, put her hands on his shoulders and squeezed gently, begging him to understand and accept her love. Not knowing how to say what she felt, she said, "You'll like it here, Po. I know you will. I'll come visit you whenever I can." With this promise she left hurriedly, before either Au or Mrs. Hoff could see the tears forming.

Au grabbed both of Po's arms firmly for a time long enough to convey his silent message, yet short enough not to embarrass Po. A final signal, he shook the boy gently and then followed Miss Bishop to the car. As the vehicle pulled away, he unashamedly watched through its rear window.

Po stood by the wire fence, holding himself close to it by hooking his fingers through its mesh, and listened to the dying sound that was taking away his father. A school bell rang, but he gave it no attention.

When the sound of the car had completely gone, Po's mind was awakened, alerted to the rapid scuffing of shoes against the pavement. Running feet. Children. Children running and laughing. He stood stone still to let his ears determine from which side of the fence the sounds were coming.

CHAPTER TEN

W-e-e-e-i-n-g! The wire fence sang from being hit.

Po jerked his hand from the wire and rubbed his fingers. His knuckles smarted as thick, warm blood seeped from a cut. He pulled some clean toilet paper from his pocket that he had taken from the Isolation Camp and used it to wipe away the blood. Gravel rustled behind him as he wiped.

"Does it hurt much?"

It sounded like a girl's voice. "No!" he lied angrily.

"Are you a boy?"

"Yes." His mind stayed with the sting in the cut.

"We must learn not to put our fingers through the fence," she recited, imitating her teacher's tone and voice. "The boys from the Resettlement Center on the other side wait for us with sticks. Hear them laughing?" she asked. The laughs, already fading, were leaving with the sound of running feet. "I'm a girl." After this informative tidbit she stopped talking. The fact was meant to have significance. She waved arches with her small arms across the void until one arm hit Po on the shoulder. Her hand crawled down until able to grasp his hand. She hung on so he would not escape her or her conversation.

Po was not in a mood for talking. Especially to a girl. His fingers hurt, he stood alone without family, in a place unknown and unwanted, and, above all, he was about to give up all prior habits by starting a new life. School. All things were foreign, as foreign as the white woman, and there was no way to run from them. Still, a friend in the absence of everything else might be useful. "What's your name?" he demanded.

"Bee-Noi-what's-yours?" she answered and asked, running the so-often-used words together.

"Po," he answered tersely. "Why do the boys in the Resettlements want to hit my fingers?"

"I don't know," she said casually. "I guess they have nothing else to do. They're refugees. They don't go to school. All they do is play on the street. Mrs. Hoff put me in primary four. Are you in primary four?"

"I don't know. I just got here," he said, willing to surrender a bit of his anonymity in exchange for her answers. "Do you like it here?"

"Oh, yes," she exclaimed, filling the air with a puff of girlish enthusiasm. "I like to study. I'm learning to read. Do you know how to read? I can only read a little, but my teacher says I'll learn fast. We learn to read in primary four. Miss Chow is my teacher. She also teaches us how to sing. I hope they put you in my class. Do you like to sing? I'm just learning. Miss

Chow says I sing good already. Do your fingers still hurt?" She stopped for breath.

Po's mind struggled to keep abreast of the changing subjects, the torrent of questions, the tirade of enthusiasm. Unable to follow it all, he answered the last question. "They hurt only a little. Are you blind?" he wondered.

"Of course," she answered and sighed that tiny breath of exasperation little girls save to punctuate their answers to foolish questions coming from foolish boys. "All of us are blind."

"Even the teachers?" Po asked, astonished.

"Of course not," she blew a sigh of disgust at his ignorance.

The debasing wounded his pride, and he had to justify what she found so ridiculous. "Well, then," he asked slowly, "how can they teach you to read?"

"We learn to read the bumps they put on the paper," she sighed. "You certainly don't know much about . . ."

"Hah!" So that was it! That was the secret both he and Au sought. Au could put bumps on the paper at the tea shop, and only a blind person could read them! The pleasure of the discovery waned in afterthought. Chung-kin was gone, Au had no work, and he had been stolen away by the school. Still this Mrs. Hoff indeed was a wise woman. "How long does it take to . . ."

The ringing school bell interrrupted him.

"I have to go now," Bee Noi told him. "I'm never late for class. Some of the students take a long time to get to class, but I never do. Miss Chow is proud of me. We can talk again after class if you like," she offered benevolently, a hurried concession to his letting her go. She scratched her feet noisily, skipping away unafraid across the loose gravel.

The day had been arduous. Nervous tension had drained Po's mind and muscles, and now, alone in the hot afternoon, the sun beat through his oversized coat to burn away all desires other than to rest. He pulled from vague memories Mrs. Hoff's instructions about sleeping on the first floor. Feeling his way back to the building and along the ground floor porch, he tapped his cane until finding a stairway. On the first floor he felt his way along the corridor until coming to a door, and this he entered. Inside the room he stretched across the cement floor, letting the floor's coolness lull him into sleep.

The heat of the afternoon sustained the sleep until a dream, a crazy dream, one in which cholera germs flicked into and out of his sides, brought a nervous end to the nap. After awakening he instinctively stayed curled and motionless to fool the cholera germs in case the dream had not been a dream at all.

The germs that had bothered his dreams were not germs. He reached out to touch one. They were toes. Toes punching gently at his sides, feeling, trying to prod him into doing something. With full awareness, he discovered himself surrounded by the sounds of giggling girls. Not knowing what to do, he feigned sleep still longer. A hand touched his leg and moved quickly to his crotch.

"It's a boy!"

Po slapped downward viciously to punish the inquisitive hand for what it had touched, but the hand was gone. Missing the opportunity for revenge frustrated him. He wiggled to sit up, using his arms to pull his legs to his chest.

"It must be the new boy. He smells different. He hasn't had his bath yet," the small voice ranted, again imitating her teacher's infallibility. "Po? Po, is that you?"

It was Bee Noi. "Yes," Po was obliged to moan.

"You're sleeping in the girls' room!" she scolded. "Mrs. Hoff thought you might have tried to run away. We were all looking for you."

The information helped confirm Po's growing belief that Mrs. Hoff possessed some form of supernatural intelligence. First she knew how to read bumps on paper, and now she knew how to read his mind. "I was tired," he complained bravely. "I knew this was the girls' room but I didn't care." He got up masterfully, but struggled ashamedly out of the room.

In the corridor he turned the opposite direction from which he had come and tapped his path further. There were sounds all around of rapidly moving feet, but he made the only sound of a cane's clicking and prodding. Miracles were commonplace. Perhaps Mrs. Hoff also knew how the blind could walk without using a cane. Just as he accepted that only she would know such things, another woman's voice spoke in his ear, and he felt the strong hold of a hand on his arm.

"There you are. We were wondering where you had gone." The woman held him firmly as she steered him to where she wanted him to go. "Come with me. I'll take you to your cot. You must learn to count six doors from the stairway to your dormitory room. Four doors from the stairway is the boys' toilet."

Inside the dormitory Po counted in unison with the strange woman. Three cots, a left turn, then two more cots. His outstretched hand slapped against beds as the beds went by. On the cot assigned to him his hands floated freely over the sheets, the pillow, and the bedstead, seeing everything they touched.

"This is your cot," the woman said. "I'm Mrs. Ling. I'm the amah for this dormitory. I stay in the corner to your right. I'm here all the time in case you need me or want me. Now I'd better go and tell Mrs. Hoff we've found you."

When the intermittent whistles from the amah's leather slippers sliding across the floor died from the room the sound was replaced by the hum of many feet coming closer. A bed or two squeaked and bare feet slapped on the cement. An occasional thump came from someone softly hitting the bedstead. Po rubbed his eyes and waited. Then, as in the cholera dream, he felt a tender touch. Quickly the one touch became a dozen. The hands descended down his arms until touching his hands. When skin touched skin the hands pulled away. Po reached instinctively for his coin pocket, but did nothing to stop the invasion which was too massive to fight.

When the initial contact provoked no angry reaction the hands came back. They lingered mostly on Po's head.

"He has long hair!" a voice announced.

The discovery buzzed in repetition. It brought more hands. "Why don't you use the sweet smelling oil?" someone asked. "If I had long hair I'd use the sweet oil."

"They didn't have any at the Isolation Center," Po lied. Their envying his hair made him feel superior. He felt a brave body move closer to sit alongside him.

"What's an Isolation Center?"

"The place where they put people who might have the cholera germ to prove they don't have it."

That produced a few startled exclamations, a few appreciative sounds, and a number of fearful withdrawals. "What's the germ like?"

"It has legs and lives in the dirt," Po remembered rapidly. Pleased that his authoritative answer held their respect, he smiled with it until their silence worried him. They had been to school. They could read and write. They might know more about cholera than he. As he had with Bee Noi, he might again be making a fool of himself. Still, they also might be feeling the bug crawl up their legs as he had when first hearing about it. "It can't hurt you if you catch it in time," he added, believing their silence begged this much of him.

"I'm Peter," the body touching close at his side said. "I have the cot next to you."

"Peter?" Po repeated, taken back by the strange sounding name.

"It's from the Bible," Peter apologized. "It isn't my real name."

Curious, Po reached out shyly and touched a short-sleeved shirt. He worked his hand up to short, bristly hair and felt it until shame overcame him for touching another human being. He pulled his hand down again to a safe place where it could touch Peter's hand without holding it. "I'm Po. I just came in today."

"I know," Peter answered. "The amah told us someone was coming in today. This has been an extra cot for a long time. We're ten in the room now.

Faint sighs, breaths, coughs, and sounds of movements came from all angles to tell Po he was the center

222

of attention. "Do you like it here?" he asked, not aiming his question at anyone in particular.

"Some of us do," Peter answered quickly to keep his status. "Some of us have been here so long we don't know anything else. Everyone says school is good," he confessed. "I don't have anything to do at home. My parents don't take me home on weekends because there's nothing to do. They have no place for me to sleep," he complained. He paused, waiting for Po to agree that a home should offer more than his did. When Po let the opportunity slip by, he went on, "We learn a lot in school. I know more than my older brother!"

Peter's bragging about his knowledge put Po on the defensive. "I have a cot at home," he remembered, "and work to do." He tried to sound worldly, older, superior.

And he did. The statement produced exclamations of surprise.

"What work?" Peter asked, quickly singling out the most significant part of what Po had said.

Po gloated in his advantage. Work was power, money, respect, prestige, even among the sighted. Possessing the advantage gave Po the right to reach out and touch everyone and everything. All the boys were dressed alike. Their conformity said they were a group, excluding him because of his hair, his clothing, his newness. Like he, they were blind, but they had been to school. They must have been told of their futures, they must have shared their knowledge. Combined, they knew more than he. He began to worry.

"What work?" Peter persisted after Po's movements had settled. "What work did you do?"

"People gave me money," Po answered quietly,

his confidence weakened. "It makes them happy to give me money," he added, cloaking as best he could his former occupation, hiding it in fear of their learning more about him than he cared for them to know. And they did know more. "You were a beggar?" Peter asked disappointedly.

"I didn't beg," Po insisted mechanically, his weakness releasing them from his hold. To compensate for the loss he let his anger overflow. "It makes people happy to give away their money. They get something for it. They get whatever they want. I make them happy. If they didn't give the money to me they would have to waste it on someone else!"

Peter scoffed, saying he wasn't convinced. "There's a boy in the other dormitory who was a beggar before he came to school. The dirt kept his sores from healing . . . and . . . and once the Triad threw him in the sea . . . at the battery!" The thought of being tossed into the water without being able to see which way to swim for safety exaggerated his excitement. "Did you ever get thrown into the sea?" he asked hopefully.

Po, sensing Peter's desire, grew angry at his inability to accommodate. "No," he barked contemptuously. "He lied to you! Even with the water shortage it isn't difficult to keep clean . . . and . . . and I worked for two years without ever being bothered by the Triad. He lies," he repeated, in an attempt to regain his supremacy. "I made enough to pay the rent on my father's flat every month. Sometimes I made more than enough to pay the rent!"

During the group's favorable reaction to Po's earnings the amah came into the room. She shooed the gathering away from the new boy and announced bedtime. The sharpness of the announcement was tempered with the suggestion that the meeting continue the following day. Knowing Po had slept through the dinner period, the amah had stopped by the kitchen for an extra rice cake. She slipped it secretly into his hand.

Po listened to the sounds retreat as the boys worked their way back to their own cots and used the privacy to eat the cake, his face tilted slightly downward out of habit. When the cake was half eaten he stored the remaining half in his pocket, snuggling it next to the paper he had used on his bleeding hand. The feel of the paper reminded him of the injury, and the thought reproduced the ache. The hand was swollen slightly.

The amah sat on her cot to slip into her nightclothes. As she did, she kept her eyes on Po, trying to read his mind, trying to learn his fears, as though sharing might ease his pain of the first night away from home. It was her habit to study her charges, and her hope to pick up where some mother had left off. When Po began to undress she turned off the lights. Darkness had a settling effect on those with partial vision. Moonlight coming through the open hallway door brightened Po's cot once her eyes adjusted to it.

Po undressed, and, as he would at home, laid his clothes across the end of the bed beyond where his feet reached. He slid between the cool sheets and let them engulf him in sleep.

Sometime during the night the amah tossed, inwardly disturbed, and forced her chubby body slowly into a sitting position. She scanned the room in the dim light for the peculiarity that had awakened her. The new boy was having a nightmare. Moaning and tossing, he almost fell out of his cot. As she watched she wondered what forms his dreams took since he had never seen anything in his waking life. As she was about to get up to go to him with consolation, his dream stopped. He lurched and sat upright just as she had done a moment before.

Realization came slowly. The cot was different from the one in the flat and the one at the Isolation Center. The horrible fear of being lost and abandoned in blackness, alone, struck Po cold. It took him a couple of minutes to break the stark dream, to remember where he was, and to begin to sweat. Needing to fight back against the new sounds, the new people, the new habits, the new life, he began scheming. Au? He listened for Au's breathing, knowing it would not be heard yet wanting his ears to bring a miracle. Instead he heard Peter mumbling in his dreams.

The old life was gone. It had been a good life, why was it gone? He had made people happy. What was wrong with making people happy? No one had ever ridiculed him for his work, and no one, other than the foreign white woman, had ever told him his work was wrong. Why was it gone?

Desire to return to the old life nagged Po. It became essential that he get away, return to the familiar sounds and habits, get back to Au. After forcing the decision he coddled it until he had a plan and the courage to match it. To determine the time, he concentrated on the sounds around him. Several of the boys made soft, unintelligible noises and a solitary motor purred past on the street outside. It had to be

226

the middle of the night. He reached for his clothes, slipped quietly into them, and pulled his shoes out from under the cot. Carrying the shoes, he was cautious in lowering his bare feet to the cement so no one would hear their sound.

Po stealthily slid his hand along the edge of his cot to establish a straight line, let Peter's cot glide by, and then he turned for the door. As the amah had instructed, he counted three more bedsteads before braving the void to the wall or door, whichever his hand touched first. It all came back. Six doorways to the stairway, then the front yard. His mind was clicking, his bravery growing. He smiled confidently at touching the wall and slid along it, feeling for the door.

The line, so accurate it was maneuvered without a flaw, brought him into the doorway where he struck something unexpected, something big, something soft, something breathing, something human. The surprise shocked him dead in his tracks and held him shaking uncontrollably.

The huge unknown touched his arm. "Do you want to go to the toilet?"

Sweat oozed freely from Po's forehead at the sound of the amah's voice. He breathed long and deep, until time worked its calming magic. Unable to think of what she wanted him to say, he said nothing.

The amah smiled down at the runaway, and pulled him close and tight for comfort. His strong young body still shook, but it had the courage to remain rigid to her tenderness. "I can show you the way to the toilet if you have to go," she offered, asking him to take the opportunity to avoid the truth honorably.

Po tightened in stubbornness, his anger growing as his fear subsided. He felt her hands run over his face, over his dry eyes.

"Cry," she begged. "It will make you feel better." Feeling compelled by her concern to react, Po grumbled, "I thought I smelled a fire." He fought her off, turned around, and floundered his way back to the cot, striking madly at everything coming into his touch. By the time he reached his cot he was too angry to sleep so he sat there, hanging his legs over the cot's edge. Au had said he should work hard and learn well. Remembering Au's instructions took the pain out of the failure. While waiting to get tired he ate the remaining half of the rice cake. The school, the lessons, the strangers—they meant nothing. Au was all that mattered in the world. Po decided to do exactly as Au had instructed—he could do nothing else.

That afternoon when Miss Bishop and Au had driven away from the school she was so anxious to tell him about the restaurant job that she could hardly wait for the right moment to begin. The news, along with the afternoon, made her feel young and girlish. Happiness was having good news and having someone to share it. In spite of her happiness, however, she was reluctant to bring up the subject in the presence of the long-eared Chinese driver. Her age denied her the right to be seen with a man, any man, without someone translating the scene into marriage rumors. Young girls shopped. Older women bought. Life would have it no other way.

"I'd like to have a talk with you," she suggested to Au. "Could we go to my office before the driver takes you home?"

"This is the seventh day of my wife's death," Au reminded her. "Will it take long?"

"I'm sorry," she said, piqued at having forgotten the seventh-day funeral rites. "I'm afraid I forgot to count the days." She had encouraged herself to think of him as a single man. The memory of the wife was best locked away where it could do no damage to either of them. The wife was unreal, cold, blue, statistical, an official record. "Could you come to see me tomorrow?" Her dreams had to be kept alive. "Here's my card. It tells where you can find me."

Sensing she wanted something in exchange for all she had done, Au promised, "I'll be there early. Tomorrow I have to leave the flat. The rent is due on Wednesday."

"Where do you intend to stay," she asked.

"I think my wife's cousin will let me stay with them," he answered carefully to keep from hinting she had a right to know the address.

Victoria Bishop turned sideways on the seat to look bravely at his coldness. There was much to admire in Au, as her imagination had so often told her. He had deep brown eyes and heavy black eyebrows that gave his face character. The face was placid, troubled yet controlled, and deeply alive. He was mastering what might have destroyed a weaker man. His hair, being dry rather than slickly groomed, made him look Oriental but not slyly Chinese. Above all, nothing about him reminded her of any of the many despicable characters in her past. Her thoughts tickled the cavern of secrets she had stored away from her prying English fellow workers.

Aware of the examination, Au ignored it as best he could by staring ahead to where the driver was taking them. Her scrutiny explained she liked him more than circumstances required. It came to him as warmth. To be apathetic in return would be cruel. He glanced over and smiled into her waiting eyes.

When the driver dropped Au off at his flat it was early evening. The sidewalk traffic slowed, the idly curious wanted time to see who in their neighborhood had the use of a chauffeured car. Au, hardened by all that had happened to him in the past week, walked casually through them and into the building.

The flat was in disorder. Government cleaners had dumped all loose items into one huge pile in its center. Surprisingly, nothing was missing. He raked disinterestedly through the stack, salvaging what might be useful, and pushed the rest into a corner. On the roof deck he found Chung-kin's laundry, but it had been picked over and only her clothing remained. He took what was left and dropped it on the pile in the room.

Backing through the doorway to leave he suddenly became still. The scene had happened before, a last check of a room holding memories best forgotten. And now, staring at how little remained, he half expected the moment repeated from the past might predict what would come next. But there was no clue, no message. Other than the stark realization that this time the scene would be enacted alone.

On the darkened street the night's cool air was beginning to blow in from the bay to wash away the city's daily remorse. It refreshed Au. It reminded him of the advantages of being alone with sorrow. The outdoors held no family memories. The outdoors suggested the freedom and hope of tomorrow.

After eating some cooked vegetables purchased

from the food pushcart on the corner Au went to Cousin Liu's and made arrangements to live with them. In exchange for some space in their home he offered Chung-kin's clothing and kitchen utensils. Cousin Liu's wife, reluctant to accept death-stained articles, consented when she realized her choice was as Au offered or nothing at all.

The three sat around the small table reliving the events since Chung-kin's death. During the discussion Liu confessed he had done nothing about the burial since it was impossible to proceed without having the body. Both he and his wife had telephoned the hospital in an attempt to convince the authorities that Chung-kin was several years older than the hospital's records might show—an effort to increase Chung-kin's importance in the next world—but as convincing as they tried to be the officials put them off. The man on the other end of the line sounded Chinese but Liu preferred to believe he was a foreigner. In a helpless state that begged for understanding, Cousin Liu apologized for not taking a pail of fresh water, as ritual demanded, to wash the spot where Chung-kin had died. "They wouldn't let us inside the hospital," he complained weakly.

Subtly emerging from the confessions was the fear of cholera dominating the fear of improper action at a time of family death. The cousins were too shy to invade a strange hospital run by government white people, and were turned from trying by the disease. Both had lost days of work when it was discovered the germ came from the poultry shop where they worked, and both thought they had suffered sufficiently. They exonerated themselves.

And they were right. Nothing could be done, their

fear was justified. Au convinced them of his gratitude for their strong efforts on his behalf, although fruitless, and assured them a closer set of relatives would not have done as much. They not only believed, they also welcomed him to their home, as before, until other arrangements could be made.

Back in the solitude of the street, his head buzzing from the reunion wine, Au prepared for the funeral rites. He bought a new earthenware pot, then went to his friend's stationery shop. He peeked through the cracks in the boarded front to see light creeping out from under the curtains that separated the shop from the living quarters. Alternating between beating on the door and looking through the crack he kept up the assault until a light flashed between the wide parting curtains. It was Hop, dressed in nightclothes. Au backed from the door to let the lights of the street identify him as he waved at his friend.

"I stayed away from the Mah-Jongg game tonight," Hop explained as he let Au in. "I thought you would come," he said, talking while pulling the string hanging from the single bulb in the shop's center, "but not so late! I had given up waiting."

"We were late in getting released from the Isolation Center," Au lied, a false apology. "Then I had to take the boy to a school in the New Territories."

"A school?" Hop repeated, surprised. "What can they teach him?"

"I don't know."

"Where are you living?"

"I made arrangements to live with my wife's cousins."

The trouble on Au's face demanded Hop's sym-

232

pathy. "I hoped you would come early enough for me to make up a few new pieces," he complained. "Now you had better take the store samples. I'll replace them in the morning."

Au fingered through the pile of small paper dresses trimmed with gold and lace and selected the two he liked the most. Chung-kin was never much for fancy clothes. She admired good clothes only for her family. Next he fondled a small cardboard house, his eyes lighting with the pleasure of knowing Chung-kin would love it. It had room extensions on both sides, large enough to accommodate three generations. He bundled the toy with the paper clothing while Hop added wads of imitation money and paper gold bars.

Scanning the small cubicle for still more, Au's eyes went up to a large horse, so large it had to be hung from the ceiling.

Hop quickly fashioned an extra large cardboard bar of gold and pushed it in front of Au.

"She rode a horse like that during the war," Au said, attempting to explain his lust. "We stole it from a rich farmer. She loved it. It made her laugh. She was a good rider too!" he exaggerated to ward off the hand-sized automobile Hop was now offering as a substitute. "She wouldn't know what to do with an automobile," he pleaded.

Hop sighed helplessly. "Never mind," he told himself. He moved the stool under the horse and brought it down. The showpiece of his wares, it represented many hours of tedious labor. It hung heavenward to bolster his ego whenever the ego sagged. As he got older the horse told him he might never again be so perfect. The ordeal was too much. "You'll pay me just as soon as you can?" he demanded, attempting to stop sentiment from ruining his business.

"Just as soon as I can," Au answered as obliged.

Holding the horse upside down Au used its hollow interior as a basket for the dresses, the money, the gold bars, the house, the camera, and the few incidentals. It was more than Chung-kin would need for her voyage to the next world. With misty, grateful eyes he nodded thanks to his friend and left.

The eyes of Hop were equally sad. As he watched his Mah-Jongg partner leave with an armload of his best work he decided there had to be a better business, a more profitable business. In Hong Kong it seemed only the poor died. Either that, or only the poor came to his shop. He whistled softly at remembering how many would have been unable to make the journey to the next world if it had not been for his gracious credit. His wife complained, but he also complained he had no choice. He was too old to develop the hard heart one needed to get rich in business. He could neither change his heart nor change his occupation.

Hop watched through the door crack until Au was out of sight. Tomorrow. Tomorrow business would get better. The gods would favor him in reward for his kindness. Tomorrow he would begin work on a new and better horse, one without the mistakes he had made on this one. He smiled the satisfaction his thoughts brought. The market owner three doors away was a friend, rich and old. Very old.

Au bought fresh food at the night cart by the wharf, and then, to be alone, he walked over the rough piles of debris the city trucks had been dumping to enlarge the harbor until he reached the water's edge.

The protruding, jagged edges of bricks and broken cement assured him only those with special purposes would venture so far. One by one he pulled the replicas from their container, bending, folding, and smoothing them until their shape was restored. Then he put the pot and food in place before starting the fire.

Slowly and colorfully Hop's masterful creations burned their way into the great void between worlds. The seventh day of Chung-kin's death, the first of the seven weeks that she would need his assistance to complete her journey. As he threw in the simulated money and gold he thought of how little she would need all he was giving. She had managed a whole life without them. Still, next week he would have to bring more. She needed money to buy her way past the Demon Barrier Gate. Next week, he reminded himself, he would have to bring nightclothes. She was always so shy about nakedness.

Facing the bay, Au squatted comfortably while the flowing waves of orange fire brought back the early days of his marriage. Like youth, early marriage is always happy. Happy also were the days shortly after the war was won and when age had prepared them to accept the obligations and purposes of their marriage. The war had destroyed old traditions, giving young couples the right to stroll hand-in-hand unashamedly. During her pregnancy with Po, Chung-kin's eyes had sparkled.

But then came the fever that produced the infant's blindness.

His sorrow growing in recollection, Au wanted to get away from the rites that brought the sadness. He stretched his tired, cramped legs and dipped his bare feet in the water to refresh them. The fire had long since gone out, the early breeze blew at the paper's ashes to separate them from this world. He took a last look at the pot with its food, bowed respectfully to the stirring ashes, and turned to go back.

With a sigh, Au looked skyward to brush away the pangs of guilt. It was near morning. Junks were beginning to back their wooden hulks to the quay. The wharf was creaking to life. He stopped short with a premonition that Po needed his help. He sensed Po trying to come to him. After a few moments he tried to shake off the nonsense by telling himself Po was safely in school, tucked in bed, resting, preparing himself for the new life. The boy was sleeping, getting the strength he would need to learn whatever it was the school thought it could teach the blind.

CHAPTER ELEVEN

His first morning in the school Po was jarred awake by the sound of a male voice warning the boys to get up before they missed their breakfast. After his restless night and taxing failure to escape, he was in a mood to sense overtones of prisonlike threats in what he heard. But there was none. The dormitory exploded with shouts coming from bodies anxious to put excitement in the new day.

Almost immediately Peter was brushing next to Po, filled with the heat of his youth and the authority of his chosen assignment. "An older boy is supposed to look after each new arrival," he explained quickly. "Can I look after you?" His fingers roamed the bed sheets searching for Po's hand.

Suspicious of friendliness, Po remained silent.

But Peter's hand found Po's. He pulled, directing

Po's hand to the far end of the cot. "Feel that?" he asked foolishly. "That's a metal box! It's only for you!" he added, his delight getting out of control. "If you have anything valuable to put in it the school will give you a lock and key!"

Po felt what had been put before him for a second then pulled away. He reached for his coat and jammed his hand inside its coin pocket. The pocket was empty. "I have nothing valuable," he remembered abruptly.

"Neither have I," Peter exclaimed so naturally that it said to have nothing was average. "Do you have a toothbrush?"

"Yes," Po answered proudly. The Isolation Center had given him a new one.

"Throw it away," Peter hissed coolly.

"What?"

"Throw it away," Peter insisted and fairly bubbled with suggested mischief. "If you don't have a toothbrush," he explained in a whisper, "they'll give you a new one!"

Not about to be enticed into making a mistake, Po slipped the brush into his coat's inner pocket. Peter might be wrong. He fought against Peter's interfering frenzy long enough to get dressed, and then yielded to the tugging that pulled him into the hall and two doors down. He smiled when Peter told the attendant that Po didn't have a toothbrush. Peter believed he had thrown it away, and the attendant believed he was without one. He smiled victoriously as the new brush and paste came into his touch.

The noise in the toilet was deafening. The boys knew the hard walls mercilessly echoed their shouts, so they shouted. They screeched and yelled and laughed, believing someone somewhere would be annoyed and would think they were both naughty and normal. And they had more than an ample supply of noise to release; noise accumulated inside them during the night's quiet. In the din they enjoyed the power that came from hearing they were part of a crowd.

For Po the toilet was like the morning marketplace where farmers came to buy and sell cabbages. His head spun. Peter was at his side shouting louder than all the others. But he was shouting unnecessary instructions, unnecessary news. Peter was publicizing the school's new arrival and his exclusive claim to it. His shouts brought the desired respect when the boys realized someone was talking instead of making senseless sounds. They listened. Peter's information made the other boys think Po was a simple-minded coolie. Everyone learned the new boy's name was Po, that he was a former beggar who got enough money to pay the rent, that he had long hair, and that he had lived in the cholera Isolation Center. Secrets, Po learned, were quick to vanish in this place.

As he washed, Po concentrated on the accidental touches hitting him on both sides. The boys were both larger and smaller than he, their voices both higher and deeper, and they moved much more quickly than he. The only cane to be heard tapping on the hard floor was his own. Rather than concede their ability, he reminded himself that he didn't use the cane in his own home either.

At the completion of his toilet Po followed Peter to the ground floor dining hall. Peter explained the tables were set for four and were lined up for easy counting. Again the air bulged, packed with voices as a hundred vociferous children were determined to be heard in spite of it all. Po shook his head at the confusion and clung sheepishly to Peter's shirt as he was led through the constantly shifting mob. By now self-conscious about it, he held his cane close to his body, beneath his jacket, to keep it from being accidentally discovered. When Peter led him to his chair, Po hung the cane over the chair's back and leaned against it.

Peter's table introductions were subtle, hidden as an accidental part of the morning's conversation. The voices explained Po shared the table with Peter, Chen, and David. Shyness all around stopped the conversation. Po toyed with the idea of bragging about his friendship with a newsman also named Chen, but decided not to. The name was too common, the city was filled with Chens. If newsman Chen had had a blind relative something would have been said about it months ago. The mention of a friend to this new acquaintance might be a mistake, one that might bring embarrassing laughter. Yet, the fact that the table had a Chen was reassuring. Po warmed automatically to the new Chen's voice. Chen was a Chinese name, understandable, acceptable—unlike the names of Peter and David. One day, he decided, he must test Peter and David by suggesting casually that they might not be pure Chinese. In the meantime he settled on believing they had strange ancestors to get such names.

Afraid of not having enough time to eat, Po finished his breakfast quickly. While waiting for instructions he listened to the clacking beats of soup spoons rattling against rice bowls, and of chairs chatting their tattoos against the cement as their occupants used unending reasons for coming and going, for getting up or sitting down, and altogether acting as though silence were a crime. Suddenly he felt an unexpected touch on his shoulder.

"Do you want more?" an amah asked as she held cooked vegetables close so his nose could identify them.

The surprise flipped his stomach into revolt. He had no ready answer. It was difficult to refuse free food, but he worried that his turbulent stomach might reject it. Thinking it might be a mistake to take more, he waited for the voice to ask someone else first. He sat still, pretending he had not heard, pretending he did not know it was he the amah had spoken to.

"If you take more," the amah went on, correcting his behavior, "you'll have to eat fast. The bell will ring soon."

The woman was right. Within seconds a bell screeched, louder than the noise of the hall. The volatile exodus that followed made Po's entrance appear leisurely. Peter hung on tightly, dragging Po through the stumbling, feeling, sliding, laughing, pushing, excited crowd until they reached the door to Mrs. Hoff's office.

"I have to go to class," Peter explained sadly, separating himself reluctantly from the pleasure of helping the new arrival. "You wait here for Mrs. Hoff. I'll come and get you tonight."

Po sidestepped to get away from the strangeness of the passing students. He went into the familiar office where the quiet encouraged him to think. Walking deeper into the office until bumping the desk, he waited until hearing sure, quick footsteps approaching. He turned one ear to the source of the noise. "Good morning, Po. How are you this morning? I hear you got lost last night."

It was Mrs. Hoff, moving closer to the desk as she spoke. "I thought I heard a fire," Po replied sharply, implying dissatisfaction with the subject. The dormitory amah was an informer; he listed her among his new enemies. Varying sounds said Mrs. Hoff had been too occupied with other things either to hear his reply or to comment on it. His unfriendly attitude had also gone unnoticed.

"Mr. Chung here is our caretaker and barber," Mrs. Hoff said, an introduction and hint thrown together. "He'll take you to the yard. Take the chair on your right with you when you go."

Po listened to papers rustling on the desk and interpreted the sound as a signal that his instructions had ended. He felt for the chair, found it, and carried it out, following the departing footsteps of Chung. In the safety of the yard he asked, "Why must I have a haircut?" Chung was Chinese, a man, an ally.

"You might have lice."

Fear of cholera germs brought rectal swab tests, and now fear of lice brought short hair. Po submitted silently to the haircut until enough hair had fallen to indicate how drastic the operation was. The wind cut close to his unprotected scalp and the heat of the morning sun burned through the stubs of hair.

"Do I have lice?" he challenged Chung sarcastically.

Chung moved his searching fingers through the small uncut patches. "No," he concluded happily.

"Now you can't put it back!" Po scolded angrily.

He swung his arm around the chair to strike at the man.

Chung dodged the swinging arm and laughed at the game. "You're one of the lucky ones," he offered as appeasement. "You look much better with short hair. Not many of the boys do," he lied, Po's silence driving him into justifying the butchering. "Some of them look funny." He swept away the long fallen hairs clinging to Po's shoulders. "How old are you?"

The compliment, by coming as an unwanted consolation prize, was rejected. "Thirteen," Po mumbled, anticipating his next birthday.

"Thirteen already?" Chung exaggerated. "The short hair makes you look even older! Now you look like a man!"

Po flinched. Manhood would take away his profession. It was a plot. The school was scheming to speed away his days of begging. "I want long hair," he demanded. "My father has long hair!"

"Take the chair back to Mrs. Hoff's office," Chung instructed, his job on the unhappy victim finished. As he watched the chair get dragged through the loose gravel he smiled, proud of the boy for the independence he displayed. The boy's hand was moving inquisitively over the damaged head.

"You didn't use the sweet-smelling oil," Po muttered from a safe distance since he was not sure if Chung's patience could be pushed further. The soft complaint pleased him. It dared him to feel like a man.

"My, don't we look much better," Mrs. Hoff decided on seeing Po's angry expression. She watched the bumps beneath the lowered eyelids move, independent of each other, and knew his mind was appraising her decision. "All the new arrivals are assigned to the kindergarten for a couple of months," she went on professionally, "until they become familiar with schoolwork. I'll take you there," she added, taking his hand. "Tonight the amah will have your new school uniform ready."

Too upset to react in any other way, and resigned to his inability to alter conditions, Po trudged wearily along until a door opened and he was led inside another new room.

"This is Po," Mrs. Hoff said. "The new boy." She bent to bring her mouth close to Po's ear. "Po, this is Miss Lim. Miss Lim is your kindergarten teacher."

Po acknowledged the teacher's presence with a shy grunt.

Translating the negative signs she saw in the young face, Miss Lim acted quickly. She led Po to a small chair, pushed him down on it, and then raised his hands so he could feel the top of the table in front. She waited until the hands finished their search, finding nothing, and then placed in their grasp a flat disk with a pole sticking up from its center. As the hands saw what they felt she handed over a box of plastic rings, each with a center hole and each a size different from the others.

"Put the circles on the stick with the largest one on the bottom and the second largest on top of that. Keep going until you finish," she ordered, then quickly left him before his unhappiness won her sympathy.

The stool's size was in the uncomfortable middle of being too low for him to sit on yet too high to squat on. The strain, however, was momentarily overcome by the challenge of the puzzle. Po began by taking the rings out of the box and determining which among them was the largest. He dropped it over the peg and began the search for the next largest. When he finished, his hands examined what he had constructed. A single error was rectified before its discovery could damage his pride. Finishing had given him the satisfaction of doing something right, and that helped him forget the misfortunes of the morning haircut. He sat patiently waiting for Miss Lim to notice his good work and praise him for it.

While waiting, his mind was freed to focus on the other sounds coming from the room. There were tiny voices. Many of them. Mumbling, quiet voices. The insensible sounds of banging and gurgling mystified him. To end the confusion he reached across the void to the next chair until his hand fell on something small, something human. Disturbed in thinking he knew what it was, he left the chair to walk farther down the row. Another child, then another. Each infant he touched stabbed his pride and increased his distress.

When the disgrace of his discovery had been proven and he could tolerate it no longer, he shouted his indignation. "I'm in a room filled with babies!"

The sudden outburst startled Miss Lim and frightened some youngsters into crying. "Po!" Miss Lim shouted in a voice offering no option, "get back to your chair. Get back there immediately! We don't leave our chairs until exercise time!"

Red-eared with fury, Po spat defiantly to the floor and refused to move without the teacher's help.

The first week of school ended as miserably as it had begun. Po's only means of objection was a negative attitude, so he relentlessly maintained this attitude to the dismay of those whose duty it was to keep him in line. The only one to stay loyal through Po's nightly attacks on everything and everyone who obstructed his return to the old life was Peter, but Peter's motives were selfish. He enjoyed the superiority of his position and the exciting danger of associating with such a rebel. Peter knew Po would calm down as they all did and then the excitement would end.

As Po ranted to those willing to listen, he gradually granted himself the right to exaggerate the good of his past life. The stories made his past what it had to be to justify the way he was acting in school, and from the repetition he began believing himself what he exaggerated to the others. Hidden in his forest of discontent was the constant thought of running away, of salvaging what was left of his dreams before they escaped him forever. People on the street had accepted him in his work because he was a young boy. In the school he was one of the older boys.

His ideas of escape, however, were undermined by two memories. One was Au's command to learn reading and writing; the other was the failure of the first runaway attempt—and his fear. He tried to believe that when he had succeeded in learning to read and write he would then be able to conquer the fear.

At night, alone in bed, he imagined many ways to get away. The dreams came boldly; his feats would draw gasps from those who mocked him, yet he kept them to himself. Surrounded by informants and controlled by Mrs. Hoff's inhuman wisdom, he planned in hatred a scheme to walk away, find a bus, ride to Cousin Liu's flat, and then live in the triumph of a family reunion. In reconstruction the voices of the two cousins were manufactured since he had not heard them in many months. Yet the voices were what they had to be—happy voices filled with the pleasure of seeing a lost family member. Everyone would understand his desire to get away from the horrible injustices of kindergarten; just as everyone understood why the Chinese ran away from the hunger of their homeland. Both escapes were made with the intention of returning. Au especially would understand.

The childish plan skipped easily over the money Po did not have for the bus ride, over his not knowing where to catch the bus or what number bus to take, and over the fact that his family would berate him for giving up his chance for an education. In his ignorance the city was no larger than that part he cared to remember.

When the boys less patient than Peter heard Po extol the profits of begging they laughed at him. Luke, the other beggar, had also described his life as a beggar and had told them what they wanted to believe: begging was bad. And, since they were locked in school, it was better to enjoy the school than to dream of a life they would never have.

Po's response to the dormitory's badgering was to scream, "He lies!" each time Luke's conflicting recollections of begging were thrown back at him. The anticipation of a confrontation between the school's two former beggars raced messengers into Luke's dormitory carrying Po's accusations. A meeting between the two was inevitable, and not long in coming.

It happened on a Sunday afternoon. Although it seemed to Po that he had been living in the school for months, it was actually only the second Sunday he had spent there. Between thirty and forty of the students, the number varied with the week, spent their weekends with their parents at home. A few of those remaining were visited by parents or other relatives, and this took them away from their classmates. Many of those who had been abandoned by their parents when their blindness became evident had given up waiting for something special to happen to them on weekends and contented themselves with what was available.

Po had not yet abandoned his hopes of having a visitor or a surprise. He sulked around the yard beating his cane against the wire fence waiting for something, anything, without thinking too much about what it might be. He waited, and he waited in a place where he knew others could see him if they came, near the front gate. The thought of someone coming and then going again because he couldn't be found worried him into the vigil. All visitors had to pass through the one gate.

He stopped rattling his cane against the wire fence—a move calculated to draw sighted eyes to the noise and its maker—to listen to the approaching sound of footsteps scratching across the gravel. From the sound he could not identify the maker. The steps came closer, then stopped.

Whoever it was he had come directly to Po.

Luke had heard the cane rattling against the fence and walked bravely forward. As he neared, the sound of the cane stopped. So he also stopped. There were no other sounds, other footsteps, the cane's owner had not moved. Luke ventured closer, reaching out yet feeling nothing. Cautiously, he stopped a moment, then decided to gamble on his instincts. "If you say that I tell lies once more . . . just once more . . . I'll . . . I'll beat you to death!"

Although the sound of the voice was new, what it had said identified its owner. The message was given earnestly from a very deep and mature throat. Po backed against the fence to expose only the front half of his body to the threat. The sound had also come from up high. Luke was big. The fence wires moving in and out against his back explained that Luke was not afraid to put his fingers through the wires and pull them for exercise.

"If you try," Po responded, preparing himself, "I'll hit you with my cane a hundred times!"

Until hearing this, the cane had been Luke's accomplice. It had pinpointed Po's location and had exaggerated the younger boy's weakness. Its value as a weapon had been overlooked. Although the sound of Po came from below, the voice was lifted by the threat of the cane. "I don't lie," Luke insisted. "Begging is a dirty business!" As he spoke he moved back a few prudent inches to be certain he was out of the cane's reach. He waited in the silence for a change in Po's attitude. It did not come. "I have scars on my legs," he remembered. "Do you want to feel them?" He tilted his head, trying to pick from the quiet some hint as to what Po was planning on doing. "I was kicked so many times the cuts wouldn't heal. I tried hard to make money. I followed the sailors for blocks! I even rented a baby once. Did you ever rent a baby? It cost me fifty cents a night to rent her. I carried her on my back for three nights and I didn't make any more money than usual." He moaned, the recollection reproduced the old wounds. "That dirty *saoi jai* pissed down my back and into my shorts every hour. When I took her off at night my shoulders ached," he added, his bitterness encouraged by Po's silence. "All I got for my fifty cents was the feel of a girl."

Po weakened when the sound of agony invaded Luke's memories. He let his eyebrows rise to open his eyes. He wanted to ask about the difference in a girl, but did not dare. Luke was no friend, he had a right to lie. As a matter of fact, Luke had to be lying. Their begging days could not have been so different.

The silence encouraged Luke to think he was winning. "When I had a bad night begging, my father made me sleep on the side of the hill. If I rolled over I'd slide onto the rocks. I tore my shorts on those rocks. The only clothes I had, and I tore them. I had to sit in a bucket to wash them." Self-pity turned into anger when, after all the confessions, Po offered nothing in return. The anger reminded him of his mission. "I don't lie," he insisted. "If you keep telling the others that I lie . . . " he paused in respect to the sound of the cane rattling the fence, "they might make me leave the school," he said, moderating the original threat, reducing himself to begging again.

The embarrassing begging by coming from someone as big as Luke built shame in Po. Luke had been a beggar, he was begging now, and beggars did not lie. "My parents wouldn't allow me to work at night," Po argued calmly. "But in the daytime . . . I was given enough money to pay the rent on our flat. I don't lie either. I think working like that is better than staying here in school," he insisted, wanting Luke to understand he was attacking the school rather than another beggar. "I gave my father sixty dollars each month to pay our rent. That's the truth!"

"Never mind," Luke scolded. "When you begged you paid the rent. But here you don't have to beg and you don't have to pay any rent. The rent is free, the school is free, the food is free, the clothes are free." He inched carefully closer, out of habit, his arm reaching out to touch the one to whom he was talking. "Po, the other students like you. You make them laugh. You make them think school is good. They want you to stay. But it's different with me. When I came here no one would talk to me. Mrs. Hoff almost asked the government to take me away because I used the language of the battery. It was the only language I knew. I didn't know it was bad until I got here. Some of my words were so bad the teacher screamed at me so the others wouldn't hear what I said. I had to learn to talk all over again. Half of what I said came out before I knew it was bad."

Both boys breathed heavily in relief, the danger leaving their encounter.

Luke was the first to tire of the impasse. Po was young and stubborn, he had to be led. "Po, leave the school if you think begging is better," he suggested. "I'll even help you run away if that's what you want. But don't tell everyone that I lie. I don't lie."

The compromising offer relaxed Po. It let him make peace without having to sacrifice his pride. He knew he could not run away, could not leave the school. Au would never permit it. Luke obviously was a former refugee who had taken to the hillside huts. Without the protection of a good family, Luke had learned to live with and associate with others his own age, and perhaps lived in fear of his parents abandoning him if he fought back.

The more Po thought about their differences in spite of blindness and begging in common, the more he knew he had to forget the differences. Luke had said the other boys liked him, liked him in spite of what he had been saying to them. "How did you get a name like Luke?" he asked pleasantly, hoping to change the subject and thereby salve some of the injury he had unwittingly brought to Luke. After Luke's tales of his past it was inconceivable that he could be anything other than pure Chinese.

"My real name is Liu-kee," Luke told Po. "But the teachers like to call us names from the Christian books. It makes them feel good. They decided to call me Luke." He paused, wondering if the similarity was evident. "The white people find it hard to remember so many Chinese names. I think that's the real reason they give us new ones. Never mind. If they give you a Bible name that you don't like, then don't use it . . . when they aren't around."

Po felt Luke's hand touch his arm and the fingers walk down until they entwined with his. They stayed gently together. It was Sunday, a day of peace, and after the discussion they had little, if anything, to fight about. The school had expected its two former beggars would one day get together, bound to friendship by their common backgrounds and common experiences.

"Do you ever get visitors?" Po asked, the reprieve warming the friendship so his mind might be freed to its original desire.

"No," Luke answered as he bumped his chest against Po's shoulder, a subtle attempt to learn the actual differences in their size. "It costs thirty cents each way on the bus. My father has no money. If he had money I don't think he would spend it on a bus." He tested the armistice by swinging Po's arm back and forth. "Most of us who don't get visitors spend Sunday

252

in the yard by the gymnasium. Are you getting any visitors?"

"My father will come just as soon as he finds a job and gets some money," Po promised himself. "The white woman from the government said she would come to see me too," he remembered proudly.

"When visitors come," Luke explained, "they usually come in the morning. Before it gets too hot. Would you like to go to the gymnasium with me?"

Reluctant to leave his front yard vigil even though it was already afternoon and hot, Po weakened in his need for a friend. When he heard Luke's feet positioning themselves in the direction of the school buildings he decided to go along. In the first few steps Po learned that his movements were slower, more laborious, even with the cane's help, than those of Luke. He concentrated on what Luke was doing and tried to imitate it.

When they got alongside the door of the front office, Po stopped stiffly at hearing an approaching sound.

"Hello, Mr. Po."

Po stopped and instinctively pinched Luke's hand in his to secure it. His skin prickled, his hair perked as though trying to pull itself out of his head. It had been weeks since last hearing that voice, but not long enough to forget. It was Chen, the old newsman. The sorrow of loneliness bloomed in Po until self-pity misted his eyes. The voice offered hope for sympathy.

Po danced a small, excited step. "Good morning, Mr. Chen!" the words coming happily from the old routine. When he recognized his mistake he laughed freely.

"I think it's afternoon," Chen corrected needlessly so that he might laugh also.

Luke's shyness insisted he get away.

Po's mind awakened to Luke's tugs. He held on more firmly than before. "This is my friend," he told Chen, wiggling Luke's arm so that Chen might recognize him. "His name is Liu-kee."

Chen looked at the larger, ugly boy. He smiled, then flushed for smiling silently at someone who could not see the smile. The boy's puffy features, nevertheless, smiled back as if they knew they had been given something. "Mr. Liu-kee," Chen acknowledged politely. He watched the boy sashaying sideways in his desire to get away.

And Po found himself surprisingly proud to be able to introduce one of his friends to another. He let go of Luke's hand, releasing the newer friend, and listened as Luke walked away.

When they stood alone Chen was filled with embarrassment over the sentiment that only coming to the school could subdue. It made him feel uncomfortable. The other children, those scattered over the yard playing, were blind. A few of them turned their heads and stopped their games as though knowing a stranger was among them. He pulled Po toward the shade and seclusion of the front steps.

With short hair and a uniform that fit, Po looked a bit peculiar. He looked more like a young man than like the boy who had stood begging in the wooden lane. Even Po's face had been made to look older. Po was growing before Chen's eyes, his experiences did much to equalize them. But Po might also be clever enough to fear growing. Chen decided to say nothing about what he saw in his friend.

To Po, Chen's voice had not changed and nothing

had happened to alter their friendship. Unaware of being scrutinized, he relaxed, knowing they did not have to talk to enjoy the security of being together. At last he asked, "How's the newspaper business?"

"Not as good as before," Chen answered. He shrugged helplessly. It was true. Sales had dropped to where they were before the beggar came to crowd the lane. He was still saddened by how quickly his customers could slip out of the habits forced on them by the beggar.

"Is it because of the cholera bug?" Po asked innocently.

"No," Chen complained. "I think it's because there's so little news. Many people stop to ask what happened to you, but they don't buy any newspapers for the information I give them. I tell them you left because they didn't give you enough money," he lied.

"Good!" Po exclaimed, and giggled at the deception. It was better than telling his customers the truth. "When I go back," he laughed, "they'll feel bad. They'll give me more to keep me from going away again!"

Chen turned sideways to look in surprise directly at Po. "You're coming back?" he asked, and watched for an indication that Po was joking.

"Yes," Po answered, leaning over to keep his whisper confidential. "I plan on leaving just as soon as I can. They put me in a room filled with babies because I haven't been to school before." He smiled his secret and the joy of having Chen's attentive ear once again. "You know," he began again, "I suspect they cook the rice twice to make it bigger. They don't want us to eat so much."

The childish logic made Chen laugh. "I don't think the school would do that," he scoffed. "Most of us can't get enough water to cook the rice once!"

Po cringed. Chen had not changed. "The school is owned by foreigners," he explained, knowing how Chen distrusted foreigners. He paused a moment to test the safety of the subject, then decided to leave it. "Who's taking care of the newsstand for you?"

"My wife."

"Your wife?" Po asked in disappointment. Sharing Chen's friendship brought a twinge of jealousy. "Do you think she can handle it?"

"She once had her own stand across the road from mine," Chen related. "That was many years ago. Neither of us made enough money. I married her to have the business to myself," he laughed.

The clever logic made Po laugh, too. Apparently Chen had used this as an excuse to marry the woman. Now he used it as a joke. Po kept his smile because it relieved some of the strain their weeks apart had brought to the reunion.

"There isn't much business on Sunday afternoons," Chen said to rationalize his decision. "My wife likes to take the stand once in a while. It gives her a chance to read the magazines."

Quiet reflection followed. Chen wanted the time to adjust to the changes he saw in Po, and Po wanted the time to let his nerves rest in the calm of being with someone he trusted. Neither struggled for more to say. Po wore a smile of contentment and kept his face tilted downward as if resting his mind also.

Finally Chen felt obliged to speak. "I don't understand why you want to leave the school. I thought you would be happy here." He looked around for evidence that Po should be happy. The school was clean, pleasant, and away from the crowded city. The boys walked the front yard happily in pairs, locked together by the hundreds of little secrets boys share only with their closest of friends. The girls skipped gaily in staggering lines with arms hooked together, and enjoyed pretending they were having more fun than the boys. It was a scene of happy youth, days gone for Chen yet days available for Po.

"The opportunity to go to school is very precious," Chen remembered his grandfather's words. "You must know that. Many parents have no money to send their children to school," he scolded mildly. "I don't understand why you want to leave."

"I don't need schooling to find work like the others do," Po answered after deciding Chen's argument applied only to normal children. "Besides, what can they teach me to make me better in the work I already know so well?"

Chen bristled at the counterargument coming in disrespect to his age. But had he not, over the months of their relationship, tried to disguise his age? It might have been his attitude that contributed to Po's thinking. Perhaps by accepting Po as he had he had also accepted the honor of begging, leading Po to believe the future demanded only better begging. Now he worried if it was his duty to destroy the illusion. He waited, hoping Po did not want or expect an answer.

Anxious that his question would be forgotten in Chen's aged silence, Po repeated it. "What can they teach me?" he asked, renewing the challenge.

Feeling compelled to continue with the distasteful subject he had mistakenly opened, Chen reached beyond his knowledge for an answer. "People with schooling get better jobs," he answered, casually hoping to shame Po for not knowing it. "They make more money," he recited. "Your work is fine, but in school you might learn to do something that takes less effort and makes more money."

"What?" Po quickly wondered. "What kind of work?" he demanded to know, hoping Chen had a satisfactory answer to the question that had stayed fruitless in his mind for so long.

"I don't know," Chen barked back. "I don't know what they teach in these schools." The growing pressure pained him. The discussion had passed being a game, passed being sentimental. The only answer to come to him was honest. "I've seen grown beggars working at night," he confessed quietly. "They sit on the crowded corners playing the *yee woo* and singing to the people. Sometimes they bring their wives and children to show how poor they are. Sometimes," he recalled since it happened to him too, "they get stepped on. People don't see them. They have scars on their legs. You don't want that to happen to you, do you?" he asked, then sighed, exhausted by emotion. "There must be something else."

"But what?" Po begged to know. "What can they teach me?"

The frantic tone of Po's voice made Chen hate himself for undertaking the visit. Sunday was a happy day at home, a day with his whole family, a day of freedom from the newsstand that came too seldom. Why had he come to visit Po? Had he come to bring more misery to both Po and himself? Po's problems were large, too large. Po's desperation made Chen feel inadequate; it was turning the happy visit sour by demanding honesty. "What are they teaching you now?" he asked, pleading for a release.

Po breathed deep in resignation. Chen had nothing new to offer. If Chen did not know what, other than begging, the blind could do then no one would know. Chen read the newspapers everyday. He should know everything. "Nothing," he answered finally. "They teach me nothing. I sit in a classroom filled with babies and put puzzles together."

"What will they teach you after you have all the puzzles put together?" Chen persisted stubbornly, determined now not to let the subject end with no answer.

"I don't know," Po mumbled as he let his mind slip back into dejection. "What can they teach a . . . a . . . a blind beggar?"

Definitely, the boy had grown. Chen began to feel aged, yet relieved at not having to play a youthful game any longer. Po's question did not want an answer. The question was a farewell to a distasteful subject. Chen slipped an arm around his young friend's shoulder. "I'll fight off anyone who tries to take your spot by my stand," he promised, and hoped that hidden somewhere in the promise was the answer Po truly wanted.

Po quietly appraised the promise for what it did to his dreams.

And in Po's silence Chen suspected the reunion had been ruined by their openly sharing confidences. The visit, he decided belatedly, was a mistake. By staying longer he might turn the mistake into a disaster. Friendship with someone possessed by unmanageable problems was always a mistake, especially when the friendship progressed where they could no longer pretend the problem didn't exist. In getting up to leave, Chen had to excuse himself since Po was blind. "I must go," he said, asking for forgiveness. "I told my wife I wouldn't stay long."

"Yes," Po agreed sadly. He had decided the reunion was both good and useful. He was sorry it had to end. From Chen he learned the price he was paying for going to school was the sacrifice of his good, young begging years. Begging for the aged was not good, not profitable. It would be for him as it was for Luke. He had also learned that the only thing of value the school could teach him was how to play the yee woo. He walked alongside the old man as they went to the front gate. "You can visit me again," he pleaded, "if you like."

Chen reached down for Po's hand.

Po moved in quick, small, nervous circles, hanging onto Chen's hand, anxiously searching for something to say that might prolong the visit. "How did you find me?" he wondered finally. "How did you know I was here?"

"When you didn't come to work on Tuesday I wondered about you," Chen said. "You never missed a day before. Then on Wednesday I saw a woman's name in the newspaper and guessed it might be your mother. I waited a week, then I had my wife telephone the Isolation Center. They told me you had come here to school."

"That's good," Po confessed quietly. "You can visit me again if you like," he repeated.

Out of Po's sincerity Chen tried to pull the belief that the honesty of their conversation had not left damaging scars. "What happened to the white foreign woman?" he asked. "I never saw her again," he lied.

"Oh-h-h!" Po gasped. "She's the one who brought me here. She made me do it! She works for the foreign government."

"She liked you," Chen remembered, still a bit jealous of the money going only to the beggar. "She didn't want to like you," he sneered, "but I guess she couldn't help herself. Maybe she can help you."

"Hah!" Po remarked crudely. "She hasn't even come to visit me!"

Chen hummed his concern. "The white people will never understand us."

"The white people will never understand us," Po repeated automatically. A twinge of satisfaction crept through his body. His secrets were safe from all foreigners.

"Good-bye," Chen offered, squeezing the hand still in his.

"Good-bye," Po answered.

Chen walked toward the bus stop aware that Po was listening to his footsteps. He looked back to see the boy prancing slightly, as he often did in the wooden lane whenever he felt happy. Chen allowed the first bus to pass to give himself more time to watch Po. Po left the gate as soon as the bus pulled away. Guilt crawled into Chen's conscience; he was a thief stealing pictures from an unsuspecting victim. He turned his back on the school while waiting for another bus.

For the first night in weeks Po went to bed a happy student. The visit with Chen refreshed and restored the beautiful but fading memories of a year he wanted to preserve. It also brought him knowledge of what to do to protect his future. He recalled carefully every word that had been said. The prize among them was the yee woo. The one thing he must force the school to do, to repay him for the time he was to give them, was teach him how to play the yee woo.

In pleasant afterthought he once again heard Chen call him "Mr. Po." Po felt honored by the respect regardless of what the others thought of him as a beggar and regardless of how old the salutation indicated he had become. He was a businessman who had earned the right to be greeted formally by such an old man. Better still, Luke had heard Chen's greeting. Luke would tell everyone about it.

The whole school would know of the respect bestowed on Po by the old man, for Luke neither lied nor put false values on begging.

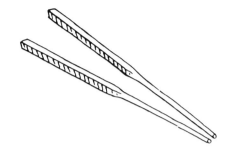

CHAPTER TWELVE

The day following his release from the Isolation Center Au met Miss Bishop as he had promised. Inside her office he watched her move pieces of paper around until several neat stacks decorated the perimeter of the desk. The clear pleasure in her face released some of the tension tightening his body. He kept his hand inside his blouse, clutching the age-yellowed documents of family history he had brought along. Some of the details the papers sought to prove might be hard for her, a foreigner, to believe, yet there was no other way. There were many in Hong Kong who openly expressed anti-communist sympathies for one reason or another, mostly to impress the foreigners in government, but he had not been among them. So, expecting her to attack him on this issue, he had used the morning preparing to defend himself for the years he had spent in the northern army.

The minutes Miss Bishop wasted on rearranging the desk papers did little to offset the effect Au's presence had on her. When apart from him she wished to be with him, and when with him she wished to subdue the power his presence had over her. She moved restlessly in her chair, as though something not pertinent to his visit had been overlooked, and struggled to keep the lost composure from being obvious. Avoiding his eyes, she began the conversation by waltzing into and out of various insignificant subjects until her nerves calmed. She successfully guided her meaningless comments into the story of her restaurant incident with Mr. Wong, and let the surprise of the job offer appear realistically as she told him about it.

Her exuberance, contagious for being natural, forced Au to smile. "Luck often comes that way," he schooled her. The job was what he wanted and needed. In silence he tried to read in her face what she wanted and needed in return for the favor, all the while steeling himself against what she might ask of him.

Victoria Bishop saw Au look back at her just as the merchant had yesterday when he let her walk out of his shop without accepting her generous offer for his Ming vase. The merchant had seemed not to want her money, and Au seemed not to want the job. She let her tongue flick wetting her lips, and tried to retreat. "I'm sorry to have acted so foolishly," she apologized without meaning it. "The way I heard about the job opening made it look like the work of Providence. In welfare we often seek such things, but rarely find them. When we get them we often get excited about it.

Your people," she said, underlining the difference his stare seemed to want to express, "prefer giving work to their relatives." She sighed, feeling that his culture now demanded she give him a face-saving way to reject the job. "What you do with the opportunity is entirely up to you. My job is your welfare. I'm not here to force you into taking something you may not want. I'm sure there are many others on our books who would be glad for the work," she added, pressuring him by looking down at the open case folders on her desk, "should you decide against it."

Beneath his stoical display Au's body tingled. He began to worry that she would misunderstand his reticence and perhaps withdraw the offer before a display of humble dignity would allow him to accept. She had talked of tablecoths and silverware and of a proprietor who spoke openly and freely to foreigners. She had money, and she frequently ate in this place. It had to be more than a simple tea shop. It had to be something more than he had ever encountered.

"I'm not sure I can do the work," he offered humbly, asking her with his look to change his mind. "I know nothing about being a waiter." He saw then a touch of confidence in her smile. If she was not already a friend, she wanted to become one. Again he tensed. Foreigners were quick to offer help and equally quick to withdraw the offer when something embittered them. She had still left unsaid whatever it was she expected from him in return.

"Do you want the job?" she asked cautiously, sensing the tension and guessing he feared embarrassing her by failing at the work.

Au's worried mind weighed what came as an

ultimatum. If he took the job and failed in front of her it would shame both of them. He crossed his legs and shifted in the chair. All too often life was what one got rather than what one wanted. She was positive, a foreigner unwilling to yield to Chinese practices. Without an option, he gave the answer she wanted to hear. "Yes," he admitted weakly.

His response, by being forced, rekindled her doubts. The job might not be right for him. "It's an opportunity," she said, urging him to believe her, "and you should take it. If you fail . . . " She stopped when she saw him flinch, and silently berated herself for introducing the possibility of failure. Nevertheless, as though it had not happened, she continued, "If you fail we'll both be proud that you at least tried. It's important to try first and worry later."

Her own failure in handling the conversation brought her eyes to his in search of strength. He would not fail, as she just had. Waiting table was a relatively simple task. Au was straight, handsome, the type of man any woman would enjoy seeing come to her table. A peculiar combination of intelligence and humility glimmered in his dark eyes and defied failure. Since hearing of the job she had envisioned him waiting on her, showing to all the restaurant's curious eyes the depth of their friendship.

When she looked at him again, he quickly turned and gazed out the window. Another mistake. She had cornered him with her desire. She had asked him to give up his suspicions of foreigners in a moment, while she had taken a whole week to surrender her suspicions of him. She directed her thoughts to Wong, the proprietor. Many times, in one sneaky way or another,

Wong had managed to cheat her. Au's welfare was more important than Wong's ill-gained profits. If Wong suffered financially from Au's mistakes all the better.

Curling her nose spitefully at the absent Wong, she told Au, "Come back at noon. We'll go to the place for lunch. I'll introduce you to Mr. Wong the owner, and a man you might have to guard yourself against," she added, winking at him.

The prospect of having lunch with a white foreigner, in a restaurant for tourists, and in a place where he might end up working was too much for Au's reserve. "I must have lunch with my cousin," he lied apologetically.

The answer, implying he was tenaciously keeping the distance race put between them, piqued Miss Bishop. Family. With the Chinese it was always family. This was not the time to put family obligations above duty to self and duty to people outside of family. Then, as the hurt had time to subside, it occured to her that he had no money. And, if she had judged him correctly, he would be too proud to let a woman pay for his food. Her luncheon suggestion, under the envisioned circumstances, had been cruelly inconsiderate and selfish. "Of course," she agreed amiably. "It's better that we go right now. No need to prolong this thing. Come to think of it, I have an engagement for lunch myself."

As they left the office Miss Bishop's secretary, her head bent dutifully over a typewriter, nevertheless watched the sway of the departing Western dress. Over the past two weeks the sway had become a revealing habit. The walk had those tiny, forced movements meant for eyes wanting to see something special in the body. The girl smiled. Miss Bishop was leaving without giving a detailed itinerary of her whereabouts. The man looked poor. He wore the kind of clothing sold by street vendors. And—most interesting of all— he was Chinese.

Long before Miss Bishop brought her protégé to his restaurant Wong had made his decision. Only the appearance of a ghoul would cause him to change his mind. But he reasoned that Miss Bishop had been in Hong Kong long enough to identify and thus avoid ghouls. Hiring her choice would obligate her to continue eating at his place, and she might bring along some friends to see and share her discovery. She understood foreigners better than he did. Hiring the new man would be buying more of her helpful tips.

On meeting Au, Wong's mind spun with ways to get rid of Miss Bishop so he could negotiate wages without letting her know how little he paid his help. Meanwhile, springing up in Miss Bishop's head were excuses to get away so the waiters would not begin to speculate about this friendship. And Au searched for a means to get Miss Bishop out of the shop so she would not embarrass him with sentimentalities during money negotiations.

"I must go," Miss Bishop apologized. "I have a luncheon engagement," she explained, attempting to prove the truth of the earlier lie.

"Of course," Au agreed. He walked to the door with her, watched her cross the street, and then returned to face Wong feeling strong enough now to exaggerate his friendship with the good customer.

For the first month inexperience caused Au to make mistakes, but the mistakes troubled him more than they did Wong. He learned from the mistakes, was careful not to repeat them, and both he and Wong saw how this attitude separated him from the younger men. To beg forgiveness for his errors Au was overly humble with his customers. Toward his fellow workers he maintained a polite attitude of friendly aloofness. His fatherly age gave him permission to act as he did and proximity forced the younger men to accept him as a fellow worker. With a pretense of self-sacrifice, he took on the 7 A.M. to 7 P.M. shift seven days a week, the shift the younger men hated since it took them from their chance for afternoon school. The day shift gave Au two free meals and allowed him evening Mah-Jongg games with his friends.

After three months Wong was looking with hidden pride and satisfaction at his new employee. As predicted, one of the younger men left to take work elsewhere and staff size was back to normal. The new member was a prize. Once, after Wong had methodically finished tongue-whipping a waiter for failing to supply the table with its total requirements, it was Au who came up with the face-saving solution. To sooth the erring waiter's pride, Au confessed that he too had trouble remembering all the utensils. He suggested that the knives, forks, spoons, napkins, spices, and all other necessary equipment be arranged on a single table so that the waiters could simply pick up one of everything. The scheme was foolproof. Wong blessed Au with a small, secret pay increase, hoping the reward would foster more such thoughts.

Since the restaurant catered to tourists and English-speaking Chinese who wanted either to practice or to show off their knowledge of Western ways, Au's inability in the foreign tongue handicapped him. He decided to let his customers become his teachers. The menu was printed with the English words directly above those in Chinese. The customers not only pointed to their choice, they also spoke it. Associating the new sounds with the sight of both languages was simple. And whenever a customer failed to point at his choice Au faked a slight deafness and waited until the finger hit its target. The method guarded against mistakes by either of them.

In an effort to avoid English conversations with his customers that went beyond the menu Au presented condiments and sweets stacked on a tray, offering the customers everything the restaurant had available. The short cut stimulated sales, especially among those who did not know that each additional condiment bore an additional price. Wong beamed. His regular customers knew better and the trapped tourists would not come back anyway.

Noted also in Wong's tally of Au's virtues was the regular appearance of Miss Bishop. A new Miss Bishop, one pleasant beyond being polite. She had given up her usual bench to sit in the area serviced by the new waiter, and she passed several tests Wong made by moving the new man's area to see if this also moved the new Miss Bishop.

Au himself was more than satisfied by the many ways the new job served his purposes. In the three months he had been working, Wong had given him two small wage increases. He knew, however, there would be a limit and so began scheming for more money without Wong's knowledge. The cook was approximately Au's age, and Au encouraged friendship that was natural in the crowd of younger men. Instead of eating a reheated, canceled order of Western food as the others did, Au ate fresh Chinese food with the cook. Deep in the kitchen's shadowy web of hanging pots and pans and choppers Au ate better than Wong did.

Conversation with the cook also brought confidential information: Au's efficiency was increasing the size of the customers' tips. Although Au shrugged benevolently at hearing this news, he nevertheless set out quietly to change the imbalance. Every ten days, when the tip box was unlocked and distributed, the other waiters collected an unfair share of his wealth.

His next pay increase, Au decided, would have to come sometime after his customers placed their tip on the silver tray and before the contents of the tray were delivered to the locked box. None of the waiters were fools when it came to money. Even the deepest and most argumentative discussion slowed when another waiter was in the process of walking tips from table to box. The movement demanded attention until the coins were safely out of sight. Purity and honesty were exercised best when witnessed.

Practicing alone in the Liu flat at night Au saw that by pressing down with his thumb he could almost cover a fifty-cent coin. From a distance the thumb succeeded since the coin and the tray were the same color. Covering the coin in one quick move took practice, but dumping the smaller coins in the box with the big one anchored was easy. The thumb could also casually cover the "10% added" notices on bills flashed in front of hasty tourists.

In that three months Victoria Bishop, too, was practicing schemes. To get away from the office, she sacrificed the prestige of supervisory work to handle personally the cases demanding outside attention. To ease her conscience, she reminded herself of the trauma and mistakes that had accompanied the near mishandling of Po's case. Had she not been out of touch with casework those mistakes might not have happened.

Whenever she went to the Moscow Palace she would slow on nearing the top step and delay until finding Au's territory. There was nothing so wasteful as eating at the wrong table, and nothing so embarrassing as having some impertinent young waiter take it upon himself to point out Au's area whenever she headed in the wrong direction. The cost of seeing Au more often was not as expensive as Wong's greedy smile indicated. Au gave her free food whenever he could, and as often as he did they both enjoyed the humor in robbing someone as closefisted as Wong. Both cultures, it seemed, made merchants fair targets.

Although her small affair was kept secret and restricted to the restaurant, it nevertheless was strong enough to change Victoria Bishop's habits. Several times she caught her secretary sneaking out of the office early, and, strangely enough, instead of being piqued she was pleased. She and the younger girl had something in common. The guilt of sneaking out early, by being shared, was lessened. For the first time in years Miss Bishop was eating her dinners before seven, before Au got off work, and for the first time since she had been with Welfare few cases were sufficiently important to keep her late at her desk. It was impossible for her to freshen away the tired look of overwork she wore at the office and still be at the Palace by six. Most of all, for the first time since being in Hong Kong her heart felt the joy of believing it shared part of another human's life.

The problem of eating an early dinner came after the dinner was finished. At home, alone, the evenings threatened to go on forever. Often, to fill the time, Miss Bishop would pretend Au was with her, talking through the rooms to her while she worked in the kitchen. It was difficult to envision him sitting stiffly in the living room doing nothing, so he would be scanning a newspaper. They would talk back and forth, discussing subjects that went beyond the petty problems with food, customers, and proper behavior that they discussed at the Palace. She would ask him many questions about Po, questions that focused on his parental interest in the boy and thus hid her earlier need. The fantasies were satisfying. They allowed her the right to share. In them Au cared about her and she cared about him. They made her feel like a girl again and renewed the need to share even these foolish dreams with someone else as schoolgirls always did.

Most satisfying of all, her dreams and brief meetings with Au lessened her need for Po. Po's presence had pleaded to her motherly instincts. Au's presence was pleading to her femininity. Her earlier desire to visit Po was being reduced to a nagging obligation. Au would be suspicious of her being possessive with his son. It was better for her to keep her contacts with Po in the line of work. She turned her mind away from memories of her bungled, shaming encounters with the boy. Au had reason to be suspicious.

In their short talks at the restaurant Au had politely told her Po was happy whenever she brought up the subject. But they both knew how Po felt about the school. She had separated him from his father. By now the boy might hate her.

As Au's confidence on the job grew, Miss Bishop's confidence grew also. Her hesitancy over reaching for friendship lessened. At first, remembering how quickly he had reminded her of his wife's seventh day funeral rites, she worried about how long a Chinese man would mourn his dead wife, how long he would remain uninterested. Perhaps the time would have to be extended because of her mistakes with him in the past. And perhaps it would always be longer with a foreigner. Miss Bishop had no way of knowing, but she sensed, after three months, the time was nearing. As busy as Au was, he always arranged to walk past her table and let his eyes touch her with a message of union, of partnership, a look that explained the friendship needed no words to be kept alive. Whenever a particular problem of work bothered him he waited until she came to solve it rather than go to Wong or one of the other waiters. Sometimes she suspected he created problems just so they might talk for a minute or two. And he always repaid her advice with free food.

To keep the scales balanced, or perhaps leaning slightly in his favor, Au decided he had enough money to give Miss Bishop a gift of appreciation for finding him the job. Time had taught him her habits, and this eased his fear of making an unintentional mistake. Everything she did for him increased the pressure for him to show his gratitude. The present he finally

274

selected and bought was a scarf of white silk, to imply purity, with a red junk embroidered on one end for good luck, and a phoenix on the other end to signify royalty. A practical gift, a safe purchase since the evenings were beginning to get chilly.

On the auspicious night, after allowing Miss Bishop time to finish her dinner undisturbed, he requested she wait for him.

Victoria Bishop was delighted. "Please don't hurry," she beamed, wanting time to check her makeup.

Block after block they strolled, window-shopping leisurely, filling the moments with insignificant comments. Both were aware that casual glances in their direction lingered to become the typical stare that both Chinese and whites direct at interracial couples. Both understood the need to ignore this commonplace conversation and purposefully unhurried progress. But when she studied too long the bargains arrayed in an Indian-owned store he gradually lengthened the space between them to draw her away. The window was filled with shawls. With one remark she could destroy the value of his gift. In response to her surprised expression he instructed, "You should always buy from a Chinese."

It was not until they reached the entrance to her building that he could bring himself to tell her what she had already guessed. "I have a gift for you," he explained, handing her the box he had been keeping half hidden behind his back.

Appropriately masquerading humble surprise, she hesitated to accept the offering. She clasped her hands and held them under her chin in contrived helplessness until seeing that her delight pleased him.

"Come upstairs while I open it," she suggested. "We'll have a cup of tea."

The turbaned Indian building guard, sprawled in his wicker chair in the exposed foyer, opened his eyes and stared at Au.

The invitation that had caught Au unprepared was more awkward for having been overheard. Hoping vainly that she might be joking, he held his smile until seeing that the offer was innocently serious on her part. He backed away shyly, worried about what the guard already thought, and what her neighbors might surmise if he and Miss Bishop were seen.

"Oh, come along now," she teased as she tugged at his arm, leading him down the hallway and into the elevator.

He kept silent. The elevator indicator consumed his attention. It stopped moving at number six. Walking to the door of her flat he stayed several yards behind, watching, as in their silence she examined the wrapping on the gift.

To Au's slight relief, Miss Bishop pulled a key from her purse to unlock the door. It appeared they might be alone, unwitnessed. He looked up and down the quiet corridor. All the doors appeared to be tightly closed. He entered her apartment and stood awkwardly next to the door while waiting for her to say what to do next.

"Close the door," she suggested, reading his mind without looking over her shoulder at him. She placed her purse in its overnight location on the buffet. "The box is beautifully wrapped," she purred. "What a pity to open it!"

He closed the door quietly, gently, twisting the knob to keep the latch from clicking as it caught.

While fondling the string on the bow she paused to wonder what the box might hold. It could be something strange, something so peculiarly Chinese as to make it difficult to express appreciation. Chinese gifts were often so steeped in Eastern culture that they held little appeal to the Westerner. She walked the box to the coffee table. "Please, sit down," she requested, on seeing him still standing by the door. He was in her apartment! The dream so often dwelled on was a reality, although he was not as pleased as she had imagined.

Au took the first chair, the one closest to the door. "You live alone?" he wondered aloud. The flat was big enough for two or three families. Certainly she had an amah or two.

"Yes," she sighed, offering the opportunity to share the oncoming complaints. "Servants are such pests. I had a live-in amah for a while, several years ago, but she wouldn't listen to me. The flat was the way she wanted it, not the way I told her I liked it." She laughed. "I'm sorry," she went on weakly, "instead of talking I should be making my guest something to drink. Let me put the water on for tea."

Her delaying the opening of the gift so that he might go worried him. The gift was meant to be taken and then forgotten. By the standards of her flat, his gift was meaningless, perhaps less than presentable. After she disappeared into the small kitchen he let his eyes scan the room freely. It was huge, too large for one person, yet it had no bed. Sleeping rooms had to be hidden behind one of the closed doors.

She peeked around the kitchen to see him sitting stiffly erect, perhaps nervous, not at all as she had envisioned. "I'm so excited," she called through the opening. "I can hardly wait to see what's inside the box."

"It's nothing," he worried quietly. "Just a token."

What more could he say? Growing still more uneasy in the Western surroundings he reached inside his blouse for a cigarette and matches, expecting the automatic actions to bring relief. After lighting the cigarette he looked for a place to put the burnt match but found none, and was about to drop it back into his pocket when he spied a small decorated dish in the middle of the coffee table. Just as the match touched the dish Miss Bishop came back into the room carrying a tray with cups and a pot of tea.

"Oh, my! That's an original Ming," she scolded mildly, at the same time feeling pleased that his accident had given her the chance to impress him with her collection. "I'll find you something else," she offered, lowering the tea tray. She picked up the match stick and held it as she would a live bug. She took a saucer from inside the buffet and placed it in front of him.

His first mistake. Or was it? There might have been others less in need of correction. The room obviously was not for smokers. He laid the burning cigarette in the saucer, intent on letting it go out, politely ignored. But the smoke curled to hang lazily in the still air before tracing a crooked path in her direction. Impossible to ignore. He reached down to snuff it out.

"This tea service hasn't had much use," she explained while brushing imaginary spots from the silver with the tip of her finger. "I'm afraid I've been neglecting it. Too many other things to worry about."

278

She poured the tea with a laborious flair, as though having practiced pouring for the queen. When the cup was full she pushed it across the small table toward him and then leaned back against the sofa.

He bent to touch the cup, but not to lift it. She had not lifted hers.

Feeling relaxed since the tea was served and out of the way, she returned her attention to the gift sitting in front of her. She untied the ribbon, laid it flat across her legs, smoothed out its wrinkles with the damp palm of her hand, and then warily lifted the lid from the box.

The scarf was elegant. It had the deep beauty of the sheen of pure, rich silk, and its little figures of scarlet were meticulously embroidered against the field of white. As she admired it she felt its coolness by sliding it across her cheek and letting it flow on the strength of its own weight over the bare skin of her arm. She wrapped it around her shoulders and looked down to adjust the ends so their symbols were even and prominent.

Au normally refused to drink tea at night since it kept him awake. This tea, this night he sipped politely, enjoying its soothing warmth. He allowed the tea to keep him occupied, to keep him from displaying the pride he felt in the pleasure she got from his gift. "Do you always drink Chinese tea?" he asked pleasantly, proudly thinking she might.

"Yes," she lied, knowing the answer he wanted. "The Chinese do so much more with their tea than we do. I drink it all the time. Our tea is excellent," she moderated, "but we just use the one kind."

As they sipped the tea they talked in the safety of

the subjects brought up in the restaurant. Au confessed his satisfaction with his job, and his pleasure over how Wong had accepted him although he said nothing of the raises he had been given. She smiled with the pleasure of hearing him say it. His expression implied growing confidence, and this helped her.

As always he assured her that Po was doing well, that she had found the best solution for him. But, in fact, his two visits with Po had been strained; they had sat mostly silent. After what had happened to them, they both had learned not to tease the gods and themselves by happily projecting the future. And now their lives had taken divergent paths, and there was little he could do for his son. But how could he explain these things to Miss Bishop? She had done so much for them. She deserved to hear that she had truly helped them.

Glancing away from her, he saw her cup was half empty. To display his gratitude to her, he got up to refill it, walking around the table to avoid having to pass her the full cup with nervous hands that might spill the tea, spoiling the politeness of the gesture. Once beside her, it seemed wrong to leave, and he sat next to her on the sofa.

She felt, for once, at ease, and success relaxed him.

"The Chinese don't think it right for a woman to live alone," he remarked.

She blushed. The calm in which they lived together in her imagination had skipped over the trials of an introduction. Marriage to the Chinese was a social obligation and an open subject. While trying to accept it as such, and to keep from looking at him, she reached for the teapot and reciprocated his good manners by pouring him more tea. "I've been too busy to worry about that," she stated. "I really haven't had time to think of much else than my work."

He smiled. She was a pretty woman. Her hair was golden and as fine as the strands of silk in the scarf she kept around her neck. His unfamiliarity with light hair and blue eyes gave her an exotic charm. As touched by and as concerned with the problems of others as she was, she would make an excellent wife for a man.

His closeness excited her. Her body began to react to the possibility of the dream coming to life. She rested her head on the sofa, attempting to be comfortable. This close he looked different. His starched black blouse with its stiff priest-like collar gave him dignity. No longer a poor refugee needing her help, he appeared capable of controlling her. The midnight sheen of the blouse matched the sheen of his jet-black hair. "I went to school where there were only girls," she felt obliged to explain into his considerate silence. "It was during the war. The boys were gone. After the war I came directly to Hong Kong."

"Didn't your parents help?" he wondered.

Concerned over his ability to unmask her, to draw from her all the secrets she had successfully kept from her fellow countrymen, she pretended innocence. "Help?" she asked. "Help with what?" His nearness bothered her.

"Help you find a husband," he explained simply.

"Oh!" she replied, with false surprise and giggling slightly. "Parents in England don't do that." She looked into her teacup a moment, wondering if she had to continue the awkward confession. Her inability to decide frustrated her. "I suppose I should think about marriage," she conceded, telling herself it was for his benefit, "but I . . . well, I just don't know." She braved a look directly into his eyes. He was smiling, interested. "What about you?" she asked. Her courage in bringing on the crucial moment frightened her. Her voice sounded unnatural. "Have you thought about remarrying?"

Au reached automatically for a cigarette as he sighed. Remembering what had happened earlier, he quickly put the cigarette back. The cook's daughter at the restaurant had indicated she might be interested in him, but their relationship was still too new to be discussed openly. The cook had not hinted at approval.

His failure to reply quickly to her questions as she had to his warned Victoria Bishop that she might have plunged too deeply too soon. "I don't mean marry again immediately, that is," she moderated in withdrawing. "One doesn't marry so soon after . . . " she paused, debating whether to take the mistake beyond where it might be retrieved. She pulled herself upright in the seat.

"Never mind," he smiled. "Of course. I must get married again. I must have a family. I need sons to look after me when I get old, sons to take me north when my time comes."

She thought a moment about his answer. It conceded nothing to the delicate moment. By establishing marriage as natural he could be accusing her of being unnatural. "I think being single has a lot of advantages," she fought back, her feelings hurt by his lack of consideration for her helpless lot. Interpreting his answer as abuse helped her build a protective wall against his growing power over her. She nourished the feeling. He wanted sons. Not a single blind son, but sons. Certainly he was capable of guessing her age. Was this his way of refusing her? Was he silently laughing at her plight? She glanced to see him smiling.

Alerted by her defensive attitude, Au complimented, "You have the qualities one looks for in a good wife."

"You wouldn't say that," she mocked politely, "if you knew me better."

He winced, his worries confirmed. She preferred to keep her affairs to herself just as he had hidden his own thoughts. Conceding to her her right to secrets, he turned his attention to the teacup on the edge of the coffee table.

His dropping of the subject made her feel more slighted. She had prepared herself to argue humbly her bad qualities against the good qualities he claimed to see. But he turned away, he was rejecting her. Anger brought control over her emotions and was welcome. Would he know she was a virgin? Would he laugh at learning it? Would he laugh at her inexperience? The Chinese were so difficult to understand.

Au waited in silence, uncertain as to whose turn it was to say something. Both had had the chance but neither took it. She was upset about something, perhaps his silence. Foreigners were so sensitive. The only known method of resolving a difference with a foreigner was to go away and wait until the foreigner came back pretending nothing had happened. But he could not leave the apartment without her consent. Frustration played on his nerves.

Miss Bishop avoided looking at Au while working her way back into the safety of her shell of correct British behavior. She reached to open the lid of the teapot and decided to shrug at the pot's contents before seeing what they actually were. She wondered whether to tell him the tea was cold, but he must know that for himself.

Au moved forward on the sofa as though preparing to get up. The action begged her to excuse him but she missed doing it.

His moving forward brought him more into her line of vision, and she could no longer ignore him. She looked directly into his embarrassed, forced smile.

God! He was Chinese! He was firecrackers and joss sticks, chopsticks and noodles. His breath was the smell of soy sauce and fire from the mouth of those hideous dragons that danced and snaked in the streets at festival time. He was the smell of tight little restaurants with coarse, loud people crowded into them. Where his lips should have been red, they were purple, and in profile the missing bridge to his nose made his eyes protrude as if they might jump out. He was that stiffening, sickly, smiling silence that stood alone in an English crowd and defied it. That cruel chuckle that came on hearing of someone else's misfortune. "I'm sorry," she announced, suddenly standing. "I have to be at work early tomorrow. So many things to do you know."

He, too, stood up, more anxious than she to have it over. "Yes," he agreed politely. He walked slowly to the door to disguise his willingness to leave. At the door he turned to bow in farewell only to see her putting the teacups on the service tray instead of watching him. He went back to help her carry the tray to the kitchen.

"We must do it again," she recited politely. Safe inside herself, and after seeing his back walking away from her, she felt remorse. "The scarf is beautiful," she remembered to tell him. "I love it. I appreciate it very much."

He turned away, confused by the sudden change. "I must also be at work early," he said, safely since his excuse for going was the same as she had used already.

She followed him to the door. "Good night," she offered as he walked out.

"Good night," he responded.

As he walked down the corridor his stubborn need to heal his pride made him recall each sequence of their conversation. It had not been his fault. It was she who had forced the friendship; it was she who had forced him into the uncompromising position. Westerners were foolish; they would never understand the Chinese.

Victoria Bishop leaned back against the closed door, holding it reluctantly against the man who had the power to turn wild the emotions she had contained successfully over the years. He had done nothing other than bring into her flat the gifts God had given his race. Instead of pretending to be offended to justify her clumsy inexperience, she should have been grateful that he honored her with such a beautiful gift. He was a refugee who had crossed the border looking to her government for help, not one looking for additional burdens.

285

If only Au were English! If only he could understand her needs! If only she could have a relationship that didn't sicken from what others thought of it. On impulse she opened the door. The hall was empty. She closed the door again. A frightened spinster still. A shame to Au, a shame to Po, a shame to her own people. Hong Kong no longer offered her a place to hide.

"I can't stand the loneliness!" she cried out.

CHAPTER THIRTEEN

The two longest months in Po's life were the first two he spent in school. Being placed in kindergarten came as a prison sentence to punish him for something he had not done. School was jail and he served his time with this in mind, searching for ways to shorten his term. His attitude remained dissident. He pouted angrily from morning until late afternoon when the class was dismissed, and then bled his discontent to Luke. Luke listened because doing so insured Po's friendship. Po was worth having around. Po neither scorned him for his improper language nor demeaned him for his working past.

Each time Po thought his uncooperative attitude was gaining ground on Miss Lim's patience she undermined his attack with a counterattack. "You don't seem to be able to get along with us here in kindergarten," she would observe correctly. "We might have to keep you until you do." The warning totally disarmed him. The old unhappy face, so useful at home with parents, brought nothing in school. Forced to relent he elected to play their childish games, but he did so with unyielding bitterness.

Whenever the plastic phonograph honked out the familiar locomotive record the children quickly laughed themselves into a noisy, bumping line and clutched each other's shirttails. They stamped their feet to the chugs while rolling on an imaginary, serpentine track around the chairs and tables. Po would wait until Miss Lim's voice faded as her face turned away, and then knocked loose the hands of the child holding him from behind. When Miss Lim's talking stopped the silence told him she had discovered there were two trains. He smiled and played an innocent caboose to the organized first train. The new, confused locomotive of the second train floundered, hands outstretched, and frantically searched to recouple the broken connection before crashing the entire line into a wall. After several such disruptions Po was made a heavyhearted caboose to the room's only train. The prestige of being a locomotive went to the largest child with partial vision. Po's pride kept him from trying to learn how large the largest child was.

Although he didn't know it, a friendlier attitude might have dismissed Po from the embarrassment of kindergarten within a few weeks. He had quickly memorized all the puzzles, had hooked together the beads in record time, and through determination had learned his part in the musical exercises after two lessons. It was the teacher's equally stubborn determination not to reward dissenters that kept Po where he was. Miss Lim and Mrs. Hoff discussed his actions, found them cute, but concluded he would do less damage by staying in kindergarten where the other children were too young to be influenced by his views. Nevertheless both women quietly enjoyed Po's ability to challenge them.

Over the weeks success in the field of music became an obsession with Po. Chen's frank disclosure, that older beggars relied on their music to get money, was engraved. So learning music, to Po, was second only to Au's command to learn reading and writing. Locked with the youngsters in kindergarten Po could do nothing about Au's instructions, but he could study music.

In every class of twenty there are those, the few, who have no ear for music. In his class Po headed the list. Music was no more in him than was sight. He had no ear for tones. He listened attentively, but managed in spite of his efforts to remain one beat off in timing. When the music reached the point where the children had to clap hands in rhythm, his clap was so noticeably late in starting that the class took extra time out to laugh at him.

The children particularly enjoyed performing their polished talents before honored visitors. For such special occasions each class prepared a routine and patiently practiced until it was executed to perfection. The kindergarten was divided into four sections. One clapped to the beat, another rang bells to the beat, the third made the beat by hitting drums, and the fourth sang a specially chosen verse of some song, preferably a song of the visitor's home country. Po was tried repeatedly with equal failure in each group. In each he displayed an unusual degree of no talent. His timing, so off, disrupted the class until they giggled and lost concentration. Miss Lim's solution was to eliminate him altogether. She relegated him the task of holding the flag in the corner while the others performed. The solution took from Po the music he so desperately wanted to learn and made him still more unhappy.

Night after night Po searched the school yard for Luke to ask, "What can they teach us?" and night after night Luke had no useful answer, other than to suggest they study geography so they might understand the land of their ancestors. Although their common background made it interesting to speculate on the future, Luke did not share Po's distaste for the present. Luke considered the school a happy interlude. Only clairvoyants could predict the future, but everyone could remember the past. Luke was as anxious to prolong his school days as Po was to end his.

While the other students earlier rejected Luke because of his harsh language and his selfish but honest stand in favor of the school, they accepted Po because of his brave rebellion against the little things they also disliked about the place. Po, in fighting his battle against the adults, was also fighting for them.

But Po stubbornly refused close friendship with anyone but Luke. Although Po was smaller and younger, his independence overcame the difference. They walked, arm-in-arm in mutual protection, around the yard, depriving others of their brotherliness. Through Po's persistence, Luke came to enjoy what they had exclusively to themselves. Although Luke had hated his begging days, he now enjoyed the exalted claims Po made for them. The price he paid for the friendship was to keep secret his desire to someday emerge from school as a teacher for the blind. To reveal such an exalted dream to Po might undermine their union.

When the other students became exasperated with the intensity of their studies they often asked, "Why must we learn so many things?" Many graduates left, only to return for visits during which they told stories of how the outside held nothing for them other than charitable families and institutions. Other students returned to tell of their successes, but they were less trusted. Braggards were liars. The handicap of blindness, in a city overpopulated with capable, sighted unemployed, was great. It was greater than Mrs. Hoff's gentle suggestions of employment goals. Mrs. Hoff was a white foreigner. It was much safer for the students to believe Po's exaggerations of the school's uselessness.

Nevertheless, many graduates did work as telephone operators, as machine operators, button makers, or wooden crate makers. There were still others, desiring to stay at home with their families, who created their own employment through the inventiveness the school had taught them. Many of the graduates became teachers to their unschooled but sighted brothers, sisters, and cousins. The school's struggle to place its graduates was more successful than the efforts of the colony's many employment agencies. Still, Mrs. Hoff's prudence, and the Chinese caution of the teachers, dictated that since future employment would not be available to all, it should not be promised.

Mrs. Hoff reluctantly promoted Po after two months. She gambled that he would be unable to contaminate primary four because Bee Noi was in that class and Bee Noi had a favorable, though provocative, influence on Po. Bee Noi consistently teased, and lorded over Po the fact that he knew less than she. She also thought she had certain rights over him because she was the first student to meet him. Her teasing penetrated his pride and drove him to new efforts in spite of his attitude. Whatever it might be, he was determined to do it better than Bee Noi. And Bee Noi, Mrs. Hoff noted, was one of the best students.

After four months in primary four Bee Noi continued to punch notes on her braille paper and slip them secretively back to Po. She felt permitted to do so since she was smarter than he and, therefore, had to give him special instructions. The maneuvering was observed but allowed to continue under the curious eyes of the instructor, Miss Chow. Po's irritation at Bee Noi's perseverence was visible, and his frustration was not entirely unpleasant to the teacher. Miss Chow noted Po often sat alone in the classroom on weekends to work, and it was possible that Bee Noi's prodding was responsible.

But the breaking point came. Bee Noi never ran short on instructions. Her hand reached back to scratch Po's knee with a note, and the note scratched until the only way Po could end the irritation was to accept it. Exasperated at her persistence, and at his inability to stop her, Po's face flushed hot. He jumped wildly to his feet. "I can't read!" he screamed at Bee Noi.

The students, startled by the sudden outburst in their dark world, slid their chairs excitedly and mumbled in the direction from which the commotion came. Questions flew back and forth as each tried to learn from the others what was happening.

The instructor, smiling now that the climax had at last arrived, calmed the class. Then, in a voice equal in volume to Po's, she screamed,"You won't learn by standing and shouting!"

The students chuckled their applause for the instructor's profound wisdom and then returned to their studies.

Humiliated, Po worked all the harder.

So it was not by chance that on a Sunday afternoon Po was in his usual seat, working alone, flipping his braille board back and forth as he tried to figure out the confusing difference between reading and writing. Writing required him to punch indentations in the paper from right to left while reading required that he feel the reverse of what he had written in the bumps from left to right. For weeks he had struggled to translate the bumps, and for weeks he had suffered the embarrassment of thinking his progress was slow according to Bee Noi's standards.

This day, submitting stubbornly but secretly to the teacher's suggestion, he tried to separate the two functions. First he wrote until he could do it without planning mentally beforehand each movement—the teacher had said writing had to be methodical. After having satisfied himself with writing, he concentrated on reading. Wiping his mind blank of the writing process he spent the afternoon memorizing the reading. Each word was practiced over and over again until it seemed safe to leave it without ever losing it. A touch tied together the symbols. His index finger developed a sensitivity that warned him not to toughen the tenderness by using the finger for any other purpose. It was only when a new word came under the curious touch that he ran small circles around the bumps while his mind categorized the whole.

Po learned quickly, and as he learned he swelled

in pride over his newly acquired skill. The challenge of the school, away from the disgrace of kindergarten, was pleasing. Yet he subdued his pleasure. The wall of hostility he had built was too well constructed with pride to be pulled down so easily. Whenever he thought it necessary he strengthened the wall by reminding himself that although the school might teach him many things, it could not teach him anything that would return his youth or change his future. The school taught nothing to improve his former profession.

Sitting confused over an abbreviated word, Po heard Bee Noi skipping her way toward his room along the corridor. He pushed his book aside to listen and prepare himself. He knew she would come. She always felt free to interrupt whatever he was doing, to join him whenever she could find him. Her petty, girlish questions and flippant replies to his insults amused him and fed his ego, yet he had to continue pretending that they annoyed him. Although he enjoyed her presence he still had to object to her tagging along. Luke once suggested rather crudely that neither he nor Po wanted to have her hanging around, but still big Luke had to bodily push her away before she would leave. She always went, but went skipping happily as though going had been her decision. Angry, he could do nothing to her in the way of revenge, but Po enjoyed wanting revenge because it was a reason for seeking her out. He felt superior when with Bee Noi.

Bee Noi slowed to locate the entrance to the classroom before skipping through its door. She skipped boldly down the correct aisle leading to Po's bench and crashed hard into a chair, a chair definitely out of place. She fell, got off the floor as though nothing unusual had happened, and said, "I'm pretty. Did you know that I'm pretty?" she bragged happily. She stopped all movement to listen. "Po, are you here?" A Braille board touched the wooden table. She faced the sound. "I'm pretty."

The trick had not gone the way Po planned. He had moved the chair, assuming her boldness would cause her to hit it and thus give him the opportunity to scold her for not being more careful. But she had ignored the chair and the fall, and he had lost his chance to scold. He sighed disgustedly at his failure.

"Po! I know you're here!" she warned with the quickness he lacked. She reached her arms in side circles looking for him. "I'm pretty," she sang out.

Determined not to give up on his original plan, Po barked, "If you wouldn't skip you wouldn't fall over chairs!"

Her hand rubbed her knee without her mind knowing about it. "The woman downstairs said I was pretty. Do you think I'm pretty?"

"No." The obvious answer.

"Why not!" The compliment had pleased her enough to fight the obstinacy that tried to make her think it untrue.

Rather than admit he did not know what it meant for a girl to be pretty, Po told her, "I just don't, that's all." The interruption had made him lose his place in the history lesson. He closed the book angrily. "What foolish woman told you that!"

"The woman downstairs," she remembered, happy again since he had reminded her of what the woman had said. She took a deep breath, one much too deep for the little sigh of false exasperation it produced. "The woman downstairs said to Mrs. Hoff, 'I wonder if this pretty little girl will go look for Po'," she told him.

"Stop skipping! What woman downstairs?" The changing location of her sounds made him impatient. Instead of hearing an answer he heard a giggle. Whenever he wanted something from her she teased him by not giving it. Whenever he wanted nothing she teased by giving everything except her absence. It demanded revenge. "There's a bee in this room," he warned. "It wouldn't leave me alone all afternoon. If you skip the bee will hear you and come and get you." He smiled as the skipping sounds ceased immediately.

Bee Noi listened in the silence for buzzing and kept her hands near her face for protection. There was nothing. Po was joking. "The . . . woman . . . downstairs," she repeated, spitting out each word as though he might be deaf. "I . . . told . . . you . . . that!" She sighed. Po was useless. "She came to visit you. She asked Mrs. Hoff if I could come up here and find you. She was the woman who said I was pretty." She sighed once more. "Do you think I'm pretty?"

"Visit me?" Po monotoned as he tried to think of who it might be. "Did she talk kind of funny?"

"Yes," Bee Noi remembered. "Why does she talk kind of funny?"

The white woman. She had said that she would visit. "Because she's from another country," he mumbled arrogantly. "She's a foreigner. She doesn't know what a pretty girl looks like. No foreigners know what a pretty girl looks like." Who else, he wondered, might be in the front yard. Who else might be impressed by learning he had a foreigner coming to visit him? Where was Luke? Never mind. He put the book back on the shelf. Bee Noi knew and Bee Noi would spread the word around to everyone, even to those who did not care to hear it.

"What country does she come from?" Bee Noi asked curiously.

He listened to the shuffling slide of her feet and decided not to answer. Another answer would provoke another question. With Bee Noi it never ended. He slipped the braille board into his pocket and hurried for the door. In his haste he stumbled in surprise over the chair he had used to trap Bee Noi. Fearing she would find out and laugh at him, he stopped to listen for what she was doing. She was closing the windows. Apparently she had cautiously decided to believe his story about the bee. "Don't close the windows," he ordered to keep her mind off the noise of his putting away the chair. Then, without waiting longer, he left for downstairs and the porch leading to Mrs. Hoff's office.

As Po came off the steps, around the corner, and along the open porch toward her, Victoria Bishop studied his every move, trying to re-create the love she had felt for him. After Au's tortuous visit she had appeared at the restaurant less often, and occasionally sat, as though by accident, outside his service area. Ashamed of her inability to get along with either the boy or his father, she tested her strength by trying to avoid both. The test proved Hong Kong to be still as empty as it was before they came along.

Po's short hair separated him from the picture she carried in her mind. The illusion of smallness that his oversized coat had given him was gone. His uniform fit perfectly, and six months in school seemed to have added inches to his height and changed his walk.

Where before he was an adorable, helpless child feeling with his whole body, he now walked toward her fast and confidently, as though knowing life had more hurts than bumping into unseen objects. He extended his hands for the information the cane formerly gave, yet he did so only occasionally. His feet raised flat with each step, ready to come down on obstacles rather than kick and stumble against them.

Po sensed Miss Bishop's presence, feeling a warm flush over his body. She was watching him. He slowed shyly as he neared. He tilted his head, jerked it slightly to aim at peculiar sounds, and waited for something to establish her exact location. His smile was hesitant, forced alternately into hiding and then into revealing his pleasure over her visit. The smile paused in fear that she might not be where instinct told him she stood.

The transformation in Po both delighted and frightened Miss Bishop. This was not the boy she had pulled tight to comfort in the flat when his mother was dying, and not the beggar who trembled in happiness when she had given him silver dollars. Her heart pounded—ached also. The changes she saw were so unexpected that they drove out the childish questions she had prepared herself to ask. He was a handsome young teen-ager, perhaps old enough now to realize the loneliness in her that brought her to him. The disguise of Welfare business that had cloaked her prior dollar donations was gone. As a result, she felt as naked to his mind as he was to her eyes.

"Hello, Po," she said finally, still unprepared to do anything more.

Po jumped in surprise at the nearness of her voice and then backed away a step. He had been right, she

298

had been there all along, watching him. "Hello," he answered, yielding the smile his tingling body wanted to give.

She shifted her feet and crossed her arms over her stomach. Nothing had been left unsaid at their last parting. She floundered under the burden of finding a new beginning. "How do you like school?" she asked rather mechanically.

Her voice came as from a friend, as gentle as it was when she gave him the first dollar. What she saw in him must have pleased her. She liked him, he could feel it. Feeling the warmth made him like her. "Fine, thank you Ma'm," he answered, remembering how she had disapproved of his begging.

"I thought you would," she said. She took a deep breath and let it out in a small sigh that said she knew she had done the right thing by putting him in school. She remained silent, observing, gratified, how nervously happy he was. But the silence developed into a burden. The obligation to sustain a conversation with someone unable to fill the seconds with sight flooded over her. "What do they teach you?" she asked, attempting to involve him.

"Many things we don't need to know," he spilled out. It was rote, the answer he gave to his fellow students.

The unexpected, honest complaint, so typical of the young boy she wanted him to be, produced a noisy laugh. "I suppose all the children feel that way about going to school," she consoled humorously.

Her laughter chipped his pride. It immediately said that his argument was invalid, that he was foolish, and developed into sounding as if she were laughing at his having to suffer without help in school. He waited, wondering if she was joking, and the longer he waited the more he resented her for referring to him as a child. His mouth twitched, fighting the decision to stay quiet despite her siding with the school against him.

The defensive look crossing his face warned her she had touched accidentally a delicate subject. But she could think of nothing else. She turned around, searching for help, hoping to see another child nearby that she could bring into the conversation as a safe third party. All the children, however, played away from them in the front yard. "I should have come to see you sooner. I didn't realize how difficult it would be for your father to get away . . . " She stopped. He would not appreciate her judging his father. "He'll visit you soon when he can get a holiday."

"He'll come again when it's important," Po explained.

"He hasn't had the job long enough to ask for special favors," she added.

Po was glad to speak of his father. "My father wants me to learn to read and write and I can do it!" he said proudly.

"How wonderful!" Miss Bishop exclaimed, flushing with the joy of sharing his enthusiasm, and eager to have Au disappear from the conversation. "All children should know how to read and write. Are you good at it?"

This second reference to being a child cautioned him. He considered challenging her to explain why reading and writing were so important, but decided he might lose the argument. "Not too well yet," he admitted, believing the tone of her voice and the quality of her questions said she wanted him to answer as a small child would.

The reunion she hoped would be warm and loving was becoming a wary tug of two minds—a challenge between strangers carefully weighing their words to disguise their true feelings. She wanted to embrace him with a show of love and honesty, but felt the opportunity to do so had already escaped in the crippled conversation. An embrace on their first meeting might have opened the conversation, freed it for honesty on both sides. Now Po, a proud and independent Chinese like his father, stood stiffly aloof, as in obedience to a strange authority.

After another clumsy moment of silence she confessed in desperation, "You look so nice in your new uniform. It makes you look like a young man. I'm not sure I'm prepared to stop thinking of you as a child."

He smiled, she was just like his mother.

And the waiting silence continued.

She wondered where she had made her mistakes. He would never know how he looked, or even how a man looked. Was it possible he shunned references to his appearance since he could not see? The compliment might have been hurtful. Disappointed again in herself Miss Bishop reached the decision she had known was inevitable. "I'm leaving Hong Kong," she told Po. "I'm going back to England."

"Do you have to go back and take care of your parents?" he asked.

From his expectant, anticipating smile she knew the answer he wanted. "Yes," she lied. "I have to go home and take care of my parents."

And her body filled with the pleasure of saying

something that pleased him. "I'm sorry that I haven't visited you long before this," she admitted.

"Never mind," he excused her as he must.

"It was nice being with you again, Po. I missed you. Truly I did. I shall tell your father that you are happy here."

"Tell him I can read and write," he suggested hastily.

"I will," she promised, gladdened by the opportunity to do something for him.

He backed to the building to give her room to pass.

The meeting, over, nevertheless hung together since neither took the initiative to end it completely.

His lingering saddened her. It burdened her. His problems tugged at her heart when she was with him, yet her heart was lonely without his problems. If he would only leave; if he would only reject her so that she would be free to reject him. She stepped bravely forward and threw her arms around him. "Good-bye."

His body tightened in surprise. "Good-bye."

She moved back and nervously tapped her fingers against her purse. Still he waited. She turned abruptly and walked away, toward Mrs. Hoff's office, looking back at him as she went.

The sound of her footsteps explained he could leave without offending her, even though the crippled beat of her heels let him know she was watching. She had said nice things to him. She had confessed he looked nice, that she missed him, and that she was happy to be with him. She proved it all with a motherly hug. She was both a good woman and a good friend. Now she was watching, and knowing she watched encouraged him to feel giddy and proud, and a little clumsy as he floated sideways to feel his exact location. Thinking she might not watch very long, he hurried to satisfy his yearning to show off. He wanted to show her the many things he had learned to do, things that made him normal and acceptable, even though blind. He went smiling into the yard searching for Luke and Bee Noi so she would see he had friends. Perhaps she was right. Perhaps the school was not so bad.

When Po left, Miss Bishop stopped to watch him walking like a dancer rather than anchoring his feet with each step. She saw him feel his way into the open playground, saw him stop, listen, change direction, walk, stop again, listen again, and repeat the sequence until he found a boy larger than himself. The two joined hands and ran in crazy circles while they laughed. They should not run so fast. It was too dangerous.

Mrs. Hoff was busily working over the papers on her desk so Miss Bishop used the opportunity to sit down by the window and contemplate quietly what had just happened to her. Po was obviously happy in school, happy at having his own friends, happy at having his own life and his own ways. The independence she saw in him made her jealous. What she had seen and heard was building a wall between them. She was still a foreigner, more so for having sight when Po had none. Her mind clouded with disappointment over the stilted reunion and how the school yard left no space in Po's life for her.

Within a few minutes, and without lifting her face from her work, Mrs. Hoff said, "You didn't get what you came after, did you, Victoria?"

The question shocked Miss Bishop. She looked to see if anyone else had come into the office while she

303

was dreaming. The question remained. Not sure of why she had come to the school, she cringed. True, there was this feeling of failure, but having the feeling so easily identified by the German woman irritated her. "That's a peculiar question," she complained, laughing falsely. "You knew this wasn't an official visit. I didn't come after anything."

Mrs. Hoff sat back, stretched, and pushed aside the papers on her desk. "Affection, Victoria, affection," she explained tiredly. "I've worked here for too many years not to see the need. The human heart is too small to gather in all the troubles of these children without breaking a little from the strain. And it's too big to ignore them altogether," she added. "It demands we do what we can. You might be wise in trying to sweep in the problems of just one instead of trying for them all." She looked up to smile and saw the worry still in Miss Bishop's eyes. "So many people come here to give the only thing they can, their love and concern, and then leave believing it isn't enough. They come to give and then think they've failed when they don't feel they've gotten something in return."

Victoria Bishop leaned to the window and concentrated on keeping her face from revealing still more— the truth—to Mrs. Hoff's experienced eyes. To subdue the fear that Mrs. Hoff had somehow learned that she had entertained thoughts about Po's father, she said in a complaining voice, "The boy's a terribly odd creature." It hurt, but it disguised her love with cruelty.

"Not at all," Mrs. Hoff maintained. "He's blind, that's all. He's blind. He can't see your smile, he has to hear it in your voice. He can't see the love in your eyes, he has to feel it in your touch. Communication in his world is a bit different from what it is in ours. He's blind."

"Oh, I know that," Miss Bishop replied as though offended by the childish explanation. "These Chinese," she moaned. "They're so tight-lipped and suspicious. I could hardly find a subject we could discuss! And I know him!" she added, exaggerating her surprise by raising her eyebrows. "I was the one who brought him here!"

Recognizing the complaint as one she might have made herself, Mrs. Hoff carefully chose the words that would indicate to Miss Bishop that religious workers avoided racial arguments. "You're an adult and he's still a child," she said. "Boys in school always have something to complain about. What did you ask him?" she prodded, determined to sway the discussion to safer territory. "Did you ask about him, or about the school? He doesn't like the school, you know. Not many of the boys do. That's the way God builds all boys," she added for her own benefit.

The successful, effortless pinpointing of her mistake irritated Miss Bishop. "I don't remember exactly just what we talked about," she lied. "It's useless. These people are so different, so difficult. They give nothing of themselves," she argued. "I've been with them, working with them for eighteen years. Eighteen years! And still not one of them is truly what I would call a friend, the type of friend I might have had I stayed in England. The Chinese absolutely refuse all cultures but their own, and the British in the colony, so help me, must be the dregs of London, sent here to get rid of them. If I met these people at home . . . I wouldn't have anything to do with them."

Mrs. Hoff studied cautiously the stiff reserve of the English woman in fear of seeing something others might also see in her if she let them. Her life had been equally friendless, equally afflicted. She had not had white friends when her husband was alive, but then she had no need for them. "I might not have the kind of friends you're talking about myself," she confessed. "My work . . . " she began, then stopped, hoping that stopping would explain that the work was the excuse. "The white friends I might have had seem to act . . . parts . . . not meant for them because I'm a missionary. Some of them . . . perhaps . . . think I'm acting a part also. I don't know. It isn't easy. When I'm with them their eyes shy from mine as though I were scrutinizing them from a religious standpoint. It's easier to avoid them, to set them free from me and what they think of me."

Victoria Bishop heard the confession, felt the pain extended for her touch, then withdrew by looking out the window again. Helping Mrs. Hoff was just as useless and trying as helping Po. Neither of them showed signs of wanting her help.

"Victoria," Mrs. Hoff called quietly, "we've both been in Hong Kong a long time. We have a lot in common, yet we hardly know each other. Maybe we've both allowed our work to keep us from being friends. Each time I see you," she remembered, "the only time I see you is when work brings us together."

Miss Bishop stared back a moment while searching for a virtuous excuse to reject the hinted offer. Mrs. Hoff was an older woman, a German, a woman whose superficial holiness reeked of condescension. What could they possibly have in common? She turned her attention again to the activities in the playground to keep Mrs. Hoff from drawing any conclusions from her face.

The indifferent stare told Mrs. Hoff her offer of friendship had been refused. To ease the conversation acceptably away from further danger she returned to the papers on her desk. "These children," she explained in a professional voice, "are the same as children everywhere. We have to tell them of God's love, and give a bit of our own love before they'll give of theirs." It was cruel, a calculated guess based on Miss Bishop's refusal to give a bit of friendship. "They're shy," she added, her conscience forcing her to try to remove some of the meanness in her accusation. "Most Chinese are shy. The children nevertheless are anxious for friends, but not for more adult teaching and adult discipline. Maybe you haven't tried hard enough," she added, still needing a little revenge.

"I'm not a mother. I haven't had much experience with children," Miss Bishop said in preference to either agreeing or disagreeing. She looked down at her purse to keep her face from showing she did not need a German woman coming into this British colony to tell her about her failures. "I think it might be too late for me to learn," she added and smiled nervously while unwrapping a stick of gum.

"Nonsense!" Mrs. Hoff laughed maternally. "Come back and see us again," she suggested, as a way to end the visit. "Once the word spreads among the children that you love them as God loves them, then they'll love you for it. They'll tell each other what a good woman you are. They like putting it that way. The next time you come," she went on as Miss Bishop remained seated, "they'll come to the gate to welcome you."

To escape Mrs. Hoff's patronizing, Miss Bishop got up and walked to the door. The children still played happily and apparently with no need to share their happiness with foreign strangers. It made no difference what Mrs. Hoff recited from her book, the children needed no one's love. "I don't know," she complained. "Sometimes I feel I've wasted a good part of my life helping people. Do you ever feel that way?" she asked, hoping the other woman did.

"We all do at times," Mrs. Hoff answered without hesitation. She got up to accompany her visitor to the door. "Even my husband did when he was alive, and there was no one closer to God than he." She patted Miss Bishop's arm. "Someday we'll have to have a good heart-to-heart talk about it."

"Yes, we must," Miss Bishop agreed sociably. Anxious to get away from the woman and the conversation before it opened her heart completely, she started for the front gate. Leaving the school was sad. Leaving emptied the rest of the day. She scanned the playground for another look at Po, but failed to find him. There were too many youngsters running wildly in all directions for her to search for Po without Mrs. Hoff guessing what she was doing.

"Oh! Victoria!" Mrs. Hoff called from the porch.

"Yes?"

"I forgot to mention it. We here, all of us, the children too, appreciate the contributions you've given since Po arrived."

Miss Bishop nodded to acknowledge hearing the message. She had hoped the foreign woman would have had enough sense to keep private contributions secret.

CHAPTER FOURTEEN

The momentum generated by Po's desire to catch up with Bee Noi and the rest of his class stayed with him during his second year in school. His discontent, however, had to stay with him also. After such a negative first year his pride allowed him no other choice. He continued to work diligently, needing to master Braille. The more he read the more he learned, and the more he learned the greater was his desire. His hunger increased his ability, and the ability earned him extra duties. When volunteers came to the school to read books and magazines so that they could be punched in Braille for all the students to enjoy, the exceptional students were those who helped with the translations. Po was among them, and his candid remarks made him a sentimental favorite of the outside readers. The few older students and teachers working with him were proud of Po's being selected for the prestigious assignment, but he still had to pretend it was punishment. It was what they expected of him. He kept his happiness hidden. The readers were visitors, potential friends, and he needed friends because Miss Bishop would never visit him again.

Now that his father's instructions had been followed Po opened his mind to subjects other than history, geography, and government. Numbers, he learned, went beyond reading and writing. They evolved into arithmetic and arithmetic was useful in any business. He searched for ways to use arithmetic as a means of protecting his begging future when school was over. There was much more to learn than just what the school taught.

The teacher, feeling Po's desire needed a reward, spent hours teaching him the many ways to calculate on an abacus.

Intriguing as this was, Po would allow no interest to take from him the hours when the music rooms were open. He would stand and listen to the music filtering through the open windows and hunt endlessly for the hidden beat. Each time he demanded the school teach him to play he ran headlong into the objections of the music teachers. He had failed music so miserably in kindergarten that his reputation had stayed with him. The teachers begged him to forget music.

Still Po's demands to learn music increased. Finally Mrs. Hoff called an emergency teacher's conference to study the problem. Since Po's approach was mechanical, they decided he should learn the piano. Piano lessons came written in Braille and the piano keys were sure. Thus, Po's fingers instead of his ears could be counted on to tell him his mistakes. And, to keep the exception from becoming a rule, the music teacher insisted on making a bargain. He wanted in exchange for the lessons a healthier attitude toward the school from Po.

Hints were dropped: stop poisoning the other students' minds in exchange for piano lessons. Weeks passed, weeks in which Po proved his pride was greater than that of the teachers. To end the confrontation and still save face, Mr. Leung, the music teacher, decided to give Po the music lessons as a reward for his continuing excellence in translating books into Braille.

Mr. Leung's scheme backfired. Po's demand was nurtured less by stubbornness than by what he considered a necessity. Older beggars used music to get money, and Po's mind reached into the future. Lean like his father, Po's body was beginning to inch him out of childhood and into manhood. The growth Miss Bishop had called to his attention frightened him. Children could bring people luck, but adults had little to offer. He could sell music or give music with the hope that consciences would insist the music be paid for.

So, when finally offered, Po rejected the piano lessons. A beggar could not carry a piano on the street —everyone knew that!

Mrs. Hoff's disappointment was equal to Po's. He needed music to replace his vanishing childhood, and she needed his desire for music to replace his desire to beg. As a compromise, she and Mr. Leung allowed Po to feel all the available instruments in the conservatory before making a selection.

Since, much to his dismay, the school had no yee

woo, Po chose the instrument most closely resembling a yee woo. He picked the violin.

After several months of savage sawing and fumble fingering the violin Po was still at the beginning of the lessons. In revenge, the music teacher used Po's lack of progress to encourage progress in the other students. Then the other students demanded that Po be given a room of his own so his torturing sounds would not be inflicted on them. In desperation Mr. Leung enlisted Luke as an ally. Luke's big-brother influence on Po, the instructor thought, might do what the whole school could not do. Luke was told that the rules would bend especially for him. He could visit his old friend Po during rehearsals. Mr. Leung was pleased to see Luke jump at the opportunity.

The next time the solitude of an afternoon overwhelmed Luke, he exercised his new privilege. Approaching the rear of the conservatory he walked the hallway listening for the horrible sound of a beginner. The sound was not hard to locate. He cautiously entered the room.

"Po?"

The music screeched, glad to die. "Yes?"

Luke felt his way around the walls and furniture to get acquainted with the new territory. "I wasn't sure it was you," he said teasingly. "I thought someone might be whipping a dog."

After a pause, Po chose to ignore the insult. The fiddle started squealing again.

"Why don't you play the yee woo?" Luke wondered. "It isn't so loud."

The penetrating whine of the strings again died as the sage advice filtered through Po's exhaustion. When it had settled, he again chose to ignore his friend's comment as he had ignored the insult.

Luke's roaming hands discovered a stack of music piled in a corner. He sat on the slippery top of the stack and calmly prepared himself to submit to the torture a little longer. The bad sounds ripped his tender ears. They might not be so bad in the open air where they could escape, but here, in the small room, their crudeness was multiplied until it cursed the ears several times. "If you play like that on the streets," he warned, "you'll give people a headache. The police will arrest you. They'll put you in jail."

The truth in Luke's prediction brought a helpless, desperate sigh. Po put down the instrument. "I can't carry a piano," he moaned, "and they don't have a yee woo."

"Maybe you'll get better with practice," Luke conceded, heartened by Po's honest confession. Fearing the friendship would weaken from more teasing, he suggested, "Let's go to the gym. It's open until five."

Po contemplated the offer a minute and then dejectedly put the violin back in its case. "All right," he agreed reluctantly as he hooked hands with his friend so they could find the yard and the gym together.

"With the yee woo you don't have to know music," Luke advised. "You can play whatever you like! I think you should insist they let you have a yee woo." Before reaching the gym, and fully aware of Po's ability to get what he wanted from the school, Luke added, "Try and get one for me too, will you?"

As always, the gymnasium was a reprieve. Lessons there resembled play. It was the only room never challenged as to why it taught what it did. Muscles growing stronger and bigger could be felt. When Po skipped rope he learned the floor would still be there when his feet returned, and when he bounced a ball he learned to make it come back to his touch. More than any of the other rooms, this one narrowed the difference between the sighted and the unsighted.

Having overcome his fear of jumping, Po continued to jump to develop his calves so he might walk with strength and sureness. He worked until he could jump harder, climb the rope higher, and bounce the ball longer and more accurately than Bee Noi could; objectives of importance because they gave him the superiority he needed before accepting her friendship. A girl, she had taunted him. But when he was superior the taunts became girlish teases.

Luke and Po entered the gym and began taking turns climbing the knotted rope. As one climbed the other stayed below to talk for it was the sound of their voices parting that gave them the sensation of height. Po went to the top of the rope and hung there, enjoying the sensation the strain of pulling brought to his genitals. When he heard footsteps coming into the room he tried to go still higher. The footsteps sounded like those of Bee Noi. He hung at the top waiting curiously, for the sound was strange; it might not be Bee Noi.

"Po?" she called out for him.

He laughed deep the pleasure he got from guessing correctly. "You sound like a baby," he teased. "Weak and far away."

"Po?" she repeated, ignoring his bragging over how high he had climbed. "Where are you going?"

The question came seriously through the space separating them. Po began to worry. Hoping the sound had changed in traveling a great distance, he pinched the rope frog-leg between the soles of his shoes and slid down. "What do you mean, 'where am I going?'" he asked.

"You're leaving school tomorrow," she told him doubtfully. "I heard Mrs. Hoff say so on the telephone. Where are you going? Are you coming back?" She fanned the air with her hands until touching him so they might hold on to each other. "Po?" she begged, "are you coming back?"

"Spying again!" he barked angrily, spitting out the reprimand. He knew nothing of leaving, which was bad, but worse, she knew something important about him that he did not know himself. "Always spying," he scolded disgustedly.

"Where are you going?" she persisted.

"What did you hear?" he asked. "How do I know where I'm going unless you tell me what you heard? How do you know Mrs. Hoff was talking about me?"

"I was practicing on the telephone switchboard," she explained. "I heard her. I know it was Mrs. Hoff. I checked. It was on the line going to her office. I didn't hear anyone else. Mrs. Hoff moved papers . . ."

"What did she say?" he shouted, exasperated by the length of her insignificant answer.

Bee Noi sucked in a breath of tolerance over his intolerance. "She said, 'All right then, you can take Po the first thing in the morning.' That's what I heard her say."

"Who was she talking to?" he asked. Miss Bishop had been gone for more than a year. Had she unexpectedly returned? "A foreign woman?" he wondered.

"I didn't listen any more," she said. "We're not supposed to listen like that. I only heard it by accident. I wasn't listening on purpose. Po," her voice cracked, "I'm scared. Why would anyone want to take you away? Have you done something bad?"

And the question resurrected in Po the memory of his many unpunished misdeeds. "Luke?" he called, the slits of his eyes opening in fright.

"Yes?"

"Do you know anything about this?"

"Mrs. Hoff never talks to me," Luke admitted worriedly.

Luke's worry and a sound that might be sniffles coming from Bee Noi reduced hopes that both of them were joking. "I don't know anything about this," Po confessed. "I think I'll walk past Mrs. Hoff's office. She might see me and call me in. She might have something to say. You stay away. She won't tell me anything if you're with me."

He no sooner left to walk the yard alone when he regretted not allowing Luke and Bee Noi to come along. In his solitude the walk was eerie. Several times he passed the office without anything happening to still his anxiety. He went closer, trying to test the possibility that Mrs. Hoff was working and had not seen him. He coughed. Still nothing happened. At last he braved his way to the door, and, after brushing his feet to draw attention uselessly, he tried the latch. The door was locked. Mrs. Hoff had already left for the day.

Po fretted his way through dinner doing not much more than playing with the food. Additional qualms came when Bee Noi and Luke searched him out to learn what had happened on his walk. He explained in hushed tones that he had learned nothing. Their concern, at first welcome, increased his worry. It kept him from trying to forget that something was to happen in the morning. He tried concentrating on the possibility of a mistake, most likely made by Bee Noi who might allow her imagination to twist the words going in her ear; but then he remembered the uncanny accuracy of her past rumors. She was a spy of the first order.

To be alone with his thoughts during the evening Po went into the front yard and stayed silent each time he heard the sounds of someone familiar. He stood facing the yard's wire fence until hearing the night bell ring. The students charged out of their favorite crevices and off the playground like ants into their nest. The sound of so much activity helped. Routine, for the moment, put the rumor out of focus.

Surrounded by the familiar noises of the dormitory he felt better. No one in the room knew of the rumor, so no one could question him. The only two who knew, Luke and Bee Noi, could not reach him. Their absence helped him ignore his worry. They had been afraid; he pretended he was not afraid. Knowing he was the center of their fear and attention made him feel important.

As he started to get undressed, busying himself with thoughts of the rumor's being false, of its being brushed aside by morning, of Bee Noi and Luke's concern for him, he heard the footsteps of the amah approaching. Instinct warned him. He stopped to concentrate on the sound. The shuffling peaked and then ended right where he feared it would, directly in front of him.

"Mrs. Hoff wants you in her office the first thing tomorrow," the amah whispered.

"Yes, I know," he whispered back.

"Do you know why?" she prodded.

"Yes," he lied, pushing at her to make her go away before she revealed his shame to the whole dormitory. As she slid away he breathed easier but deeper, conditioning himself to accept the mystery. By confirming Bee Noi's rumor, the amah's message made the night heavy with loneliness. Luke and Bee Noi were unreachable. The consolation and support he needed was forbidden by his past behavior.

Lying in bed, his mind fraught with bitter memories, Po realized his dissidence had finally caught up with him. Soon they would make him take back the life he once threatened to get back for himself. Now that it was promised, however, he doubted that he wanted it. And pride would not allow him to return to the school even for so much as a visit after being expelled. The nighttime dreams of escaping that had come so freely months ago were now gone. He could not bring them back. They had been childish wishes, and he had grown away from them.

His uncooperative antics in kindergarten; his unfriendliness in class; his obstinacy to the music lessons; his polluting the minds of happier students; his attempt to run away, and his superior attitude to all but Luke—all came in to haunt him since they could not be withdrawn, changed, revoked. The school was about to make him an outcast. The taste of rejection, coming to him instead of going out from him, was terribly bitter. He concentrated on ways to keep his disgrace from spreading to his family. Au's punishment would be severe, just.

Acknowledging nothing could undo what had been done, Po relived some of the past for what it had taught him. Crammed deep in the storage of his mind, shoved there to be overlooked momentarily, were thoughts of marriage, of children, of continuing the family name, and of providing great-grandchildren to worship Au's grave after taking Au north. The unspoken obligations passed from Au, and Au's father, and Au's father's father. Po accepted them with the realization that the blind married the blind. Bee Noi would be of limited use since she could neither play the yee woo nor sing as well as she thought she could, but she could produce children to help Au. More important, Bee Noi liked him as much as he liked her.

Proud of himself for not having stained the family's honor by begging at the school prior to now, he let the pride build until it supported his resolutions. He would not go to Mrs. Hoff to beg forgiveness, he would not beg for another chance. He had learned to read and write, and that was all Au asked of him. The challenge of tomorrow would be in showing those who rejected him that being out of school was better than being in. The school had cheated him of his young years; now it was his duty to prove he could survive in spite of it. When he walked out in the morning he would shout back to those who stayed. He would ask them why they stayed. He would make them wish they could go with him. They all knew the school taught useless things.

With a sensation of someone watching, Po came fully awake. The amah, perhaps, watching and trying to read his mind by what she saw on his face. He raised his head off the pillow. The dormitory was quiet. By the few subdued sounds he knew he had spent most of the night thinking. Soon it would be morning. Soon he would be living his disgrace for the whole school to enjoy. Resignation came out in a cold sweat and stayed to exhaust him, to drive him into tossing, half asleep, through the small balance of the last night.

The habit of waking at a regular hour brought Po sluggishly to his senses. He blinked and rubbed his eyes until the morning sounds dawned with stark foreboding. The hidden evil jabbed at his stomach until he felt sick. He washed and dressed with the hope that routine tasks would calm the nerves that gnawed at last night's confidence. Since he had put off the amah before she had a chance to tell him just when Mrs. Hoff wanted to see him, he debated whether to go before or after breakfast without reaching a decision. The thundering noise of toilets flushing and boys shouting kept him from separating the wise and clear thoughts from the unwise and unclear.

The ringing of the breakfast bell enticed Po to the open corridor. He stood alone against the wall until the clatter of feet running to the dining hall subsided. Although the footsteps had died, intuition said the corridor was still filled. There were ears all around listening for something to be revealed and enjoyed. If he called to the amah to ask when he should go to Mrs. Hoff's office the heads would huddle closer to listen and laugh and carry his shame to those who had not heard.

"Luke? Bee Noi?" he whispered desperately into the deceiving silence and having done it, regretted it. Should Luke and Bee Noi be there then he would be obliged to tell them. The others would hear also. The corridor would fill with those tiny sounds that speak to a dark world.

Apprehension increased as he trudged a pensive path to Mrs. Hoff's office. He walked as one walks into the unknown. With each step he paused, listened, hoped, heard, but everything he heard belonged to someone or something else. The deliberate walk he had hoped would calm him excited him instead. He hesitated in front of the office door to encourage his strength, and when strength permitted he turned quickly to go in. His body hit the closed door. He angrily tested the knob. The door was locked. Mrs. Hoff was still at breakfast. Why had he thought she would not be?

Noise from the street and the Resettlement Center filtered through Po's concentration and forced him into the old habit of backing against the wall for protection. Should he wait at the door or go to the dining hall? No answer came. He wanted time to think, yet with the time his anxiety grew and his courage weakened. Fear took away his ability to think. He froze, rigid against the wall, and let self-pity take command.

Suddenly footsteps easily identifiable as Mrs. Hoff's drew nearer. Everything inside Po stopped.

"Good morning, Po."

The sound of her voice was falsely casual. It acknowledged with insincerity the beginning of this day just as it had acknowledged with insincerity the beginning of all other days. It was followed by the click of the door key and then footsteps departing, fading inside the open office. Po waited outside with a last desperate hope that everything that had happened had been a mistake.

"Come in," Miss Hoff ordered. She waited until her student reached the front side of the desk. "You're leaving us this morning. I must say I'm sorry to have you go."

The voice was friendly. Disarmingly so. Po attempted to stand solid so he might hide his fear and disguise what was revolving his insides into sickness, but he failed. He shook, and he knew she could see him shaking. The sound of papers moving rapidly on her desk came through the void to tell him she might not be watching. She never watched. She never saw him. She cared no more about him than she cared for the others. She never came to them to ask their complaints, and she never reprimanded the teachers for their mistakes and injustices. What she had tried to do was superficial, an attempt to hide from him the fact that she could do nothing.

He tensed against the possibility that the lessons and the school had been useful, and that he had accepted them without paying by showing gratitude. He had nothing but gratitude to pay in return. To admit he had nothing was shameful. It was too late to withdraw and too late to repay. To retreat now would be as dishonorable as begging. The silence continued. Mrs. Hoff was writing and moving things on her desk. By ignoring him, she meant to scold him. And he was helpless to do anything about it.

Anger, at last, forced Po into attempting to justify his stand so he might not have to live with doubt for the rest of his life. He had to speak, or burst from inner fear.

"What can you teach a blind beggar?" he demanded quickly, trying to fill the question with scorn.

Startled by the sudden onslaught, Mrs. Hoff looked up at its source. The boy, the former beggar. He stood so erect, yet his lips quivered from the fear of knowing what they had let slip out. His head tilted to one side as though scanning the quiet office for something definable. She studied his features to find what sort of response this frightened figure wanted. She was ready to laugh, but common sense ruled. This one was braver than most, less frightened by life. Although his dissidence seemed sincere, it also seemed normal for a boy. His negative attitude had endeared him, had made him the pet of his instructors. He had challenged the wisdom of the staff and more than once his anger had shaken the school out of its complacency.

Mrs. Hoff tried to read the intentions on Po's face as the impact of what he had just said made itself felt. She began worrying that in the past he might not have been just childish and teasing as the teachers had chosen to believe. It was possible that he had been happy before coming to the school, and possible also that the school was responsible for the change. It might have been her indifference to his peculiar problems that put before her such an angry young man now. Guilt over her indifference nagged her. Many of the students resented the school for what it was—a charity directed at an uncurable handicap, a charity bringing a feeling of righteousness to its workers while pinpointing the handicap of others. Yet none of this could be helped.

Mrs. Hoff tried to subdue the pain of defeat Po's question brought out. The feeling was reminiscent of Victoria Bishop's final visit, a visit that grew vivid for its confessions. Like Victoria, she had given herself to government forms and statistics instead of enjoying the pleasures of friendship and human compassion.

Po. She stared across the desk at him. Had she loved him so little and from so far that he had failed to sense it? Had she encouraged him to believe that the school had time for him only when he complained? To salve her pride, she silently cursed the conditions that had put the school's enrollment beyond her ability. The refugee influx, she decided, had converted her into a machine; the desire to help everyone had taken from her the objective of Christian love.

Po grew weary of waiting for a reaction to his unanswerable question. Mrs. Hoff was still there, he could sense her presence. But she could no more solve the riddle than could Chen or Miss Bishop. Her silence explained he was right. "Who wants a grown, blind beggar?" he asked, fairly spitting out the secret that had poisoned his thoughts through the years.

She cringed under his anger as her heart cried out for help. Such a simple, understandable request. The need to be wanted. Had she never taken the time to let him know he was wanted?

But he was wrong! "I want you," she insisted angrily, determined to alter her past mistakes. "Many people want you. Your father wants you. Don't you know your father wants you, that he's coming to get you? Didn't anyone tell you? Didn't the amah say anything?"

Stubbornness refused to permit him to admit his error. The amah wanted to tell him, but he had refused to let her. Au had said nothing on his last visit, but why hadn't the coming change been sensed in Au's attitude? Had he allowed bitterness to flood out all hope?

"Miss Bishop wanted you when she was here," Mrs. Hoff continued. "Do you remember Miss Bishop? Did you know how much she helped you?"

He shrugged, his pride would allow no more.

"We want you to stay with us. We enjoy having you. I'm sure Bee Noi and Luke would want you to

324

stay." She paused, disgusted with herself for being so late in saying what should have been implied every day. "God wants you, Po," she added, retreating to familiar grounds. "God wants you. Beggar or no beggar!"

Po let the tension drain until his shoulders sagged. Feeling sick inside, he was too ashamed to return her attempts at kindness. Every defense he had prepared for the meeting was gone. He told himself not to believe what she had said, however much he wanted to believe it.

"Who wants a blind beggar?" he mumbled and closed his ears to any answers. "Why is begging bad only when the blind do it?"

Mrs. Hoff raised her eyebrows in surprise. She was begging, and he was smart enough to realize it. Everything she could think of, viewed from Po's blindness, was now so fruitless, so late, so inadequate. She stared at him, unarmed.

The opening of the front yard gate brought an end to the impasse. "Here comes your father," Mrs. Hoff told him. "Po, how we'll miss you! You don't understand. We'll miss you. Come back. Come and visit us whenever you like."

Po's head swam dizzily at the sound of buzzing voices until he felt the warm relief of knowing Au was standing at his side. The sound of Au's voice was at the same height as his ears. There was no question, he had grown out of his appeal as a child. He moaned, shook his head dejectedly, and said, "I can't play the yee woo," offering the excuse to Au if Au wanted it.

During the bus ride to the city Po moved to touch shoulders with Au so he might rest in the security the touch brought. His life at the school had changed many things, but the family remained unchanged.

He recalled fondly how Mrs. Hoff had gathered all the students in the front yard for a farewell, but remembered also the sadness of parting from Luke and Bee Noi. He remembered the old flat, his mother's death, the Isolation Camp, the unforgivable separation. Life for him had begun in Hong Kong. In Canton he was nothing, not even a beggar. He remembered Miss Bishop.

"The white woman went back to England," he told Au.

"She went back to her family?" Au asked.

"She was a good woman," Po remembered. "At school we have a globe. I could feel England. I also know all the provinces of China."

The bus twisted and cracked, honked and jerked until it got back into the city. Au let the touch of Po's shoulder tell him he had a son who could help. Po was larger, older, wiser. Au wondered if he would have to learn about his son for a third time.

"Was she pretty?" Po asked, remembering how delighted Bee Noi had been when Miss Bishop called her pretty.

"Who?" Au wondered.

"The white woman."

"She was a good woman," Au replied, agreeing to Po's earlier observation.

The bus inched its way past the towers of the Chatham Detention Camp and on to the end of the line at the Star Ferry. On the Hong Kong side Au and Po snuggled into the disembarking crowd going up the ramp. As they walked Po remembered where the path led and he longed to be back in the lane that included memories of Chen and work and happiness. He hurried.

Au watched the strong legs taking huge, positive steps. The cane that had reappeared once they left the familiar school grounds hung down, feeling without touching, as though it had eyes of its own. When the tunnel floor inclined to take them up to street level Po's stride accepted the change without slowing. This was no child. Almost equal in height with his father and matured beyond his age by his handicap, Po was unafraid, assured, prepared to accept the responsibility of someday leading his family back to the home of all Chinese–China. Au smiled confidently. It would happen. Po would take him home if, when his time came, he was too old to go alone. The family would continue through the nation's history in spite of this generation's blindness.

As though meant intentionally to undermine Au's confidence, Po's delight increased until it became childish in anticipation. As they walked out of the tunnel to cross Chater Road, the cane began tapping a frantic sidewise search.

"The wooden path is gone," Au said, answering the cane's question. "The new building was finished some months ago. There's a cement sidewalk and a door where you once stood."

Po sighed. Time had extracted its price. "Is the old newsman still here?" he asked in a voice loud enough to be overheard if Chen crouched over his newspapers nearby.

"I used this lane," Au remembered, "morning and night. A short while ago the old man was replaced by a younger man. Was the old one such a good friend?"

"Yes."

Chen was gone. Accepting the absence without regret was impossible. Many things had changed. The sound of water splashing and people walking came from where the foolish white government had once fenced in nothing. The cement sidewalk was too wide to work as he once did, and its hardness would disguise footsteps. Po flinched at the days he had wasted in school, days that should have been spent adjusting to these new obstacles.

Concentrating on where Au was leading, he put off reminiscing until the route recalled familiar sounds and landmarks. Past the bank and down Des Voeux, next Au would lead him up the ladder street. In the familiarity he resolved to return to the lane one day to talk to the younger newsman. Certainly old Chen would keep the business in the family. The younger man had to be a son or grandson. Perhaps the old man needed a visit from a friend just as Po had needed Chen's visit on first going to school. When the recognizable sounds of merchants chatting on the ladder street freed Po's mind, the finality of death crept in. The thought of Chen dying disturbed the memories. He quickly rejected them.

While sniffing the odors coming from the three-chaired barbershop, Po let his mind retreat to the days of happiness, the days before the tragedy. Thus, he was unprepared for Au's sudden question.

"Do you remember this place?"

Po stopped to give his senses time to catch up with his location. His shoulder pushed against a brick pillar, crowds milled all around, the smell of fresh yau tu came to mix in his nostrils with the smell of boiling grease. The goodness was enhanced by the emptiness of his stomach.

"No," he admitted, smiling at Au's puzzle. Memory

catalogued the hints. Lyndhurst! Au must have re-turned to living in the old flat. His route of youth returned—and brought back the dream that had made youth so exciting.

"Is this the tea shop?" he asked with a laugh.

"Yes," Au answered, happy it had not been forgotten.

"It can't be," Po objected. "I don't smell any dust!"

Au shoved an elbow into his tall son. "The shop has a new owner. Also a new cook. She's the daughter of the cook in the restaurant where I used to work. She's very good," he added, apologizing for her presence. He watched, pleased, as the smile on Po's face got wider. Po was too smart to be fooled. "Someone in the family . . . a good man . . . someone who can count . . . has to collect the customers' money from behind the counter."

Po let the good news linger until it prickled his skin. He extended his arms so his hands could find their way to the entrance. Someone bumped into him, but could not push him off course.

He dug his toe into the track that guided the metal shutters that closed at night and followed the channel to the corner where the glass counter stood. He squeezed his body through the narrow opening that excluded all except the man who worked there. Slowly, deliberately, he saw the small space with his hands and found the stool and the abacus.

With the abacus positioned, he next pulled out his braille board and punch along with a pad of paper. The shop, the family, the secret code, all were present and all belonged to him. More important, he belonged to them.

Po sat erect, facing the open shop with his head

tilted slightly downward to hide the sightless eyes from those who preferred not seeing them. He sucked air deep into his satisfied body and rested his waiting hands on his knees.

The new shop opened officially with the rustling sound of artificial flowers, the smell of soy sauce, the popping of firecrackers, the sweet odor of burning joss sticks, and the tears of Po.